BOTHER

To brother Benjamin,
In Christ &
for His glory!!

Richard Song

BOTHER

A Story Of Forgiveness

Richard L. Song

Copyright © 2013 by Richard L. Song.

Library of Congress Control Number:		2013917767
ISBN:	Hardcover	978-1-4931-0767-4
	Softcover	978-1-4931-0766-7
	Ebook	978-1-4931-0768-1

All rights reserved. No part of this book may be reproduced or transmitted in any form or by any means, electronic or mechanical, including photocopying, recording, or by any information storage and retrieval system, without permission in writing from the copyright owner.

This is a work of fiction. Names, characters, places and incidents either are the product of the author's imagination or are used fictitiously, and any resemblance to any actual persons, living or dead, events, or locales is entirely coincidental.

This book was printed in the United States of America.

Rev. date: 10/17/2013

To order additional copies of this book, contact:
Xlibris LLC
1-888-795-4274
www.Xlibris.com
Orders@Xlibris.com

140700

CONTENTS

Chapter 1	*March 1967*	*7*
Chapter 2	*1967—Judy*	*17*
Chapter 3	*1967—Life without Mom*	*21*
Chapter 4	*My Childhood Memories*	*27*
Chapter 5	*1966—Coming to Mee-Goog*	*34*
Chapter 6	*1967—Mother Buried*	*37*
Chapter 7	*Dad's Recollection of His Childhood*	*41*
Chapter 8	*Dad's Account of His "Box"*	*46*
Chapter 9	*1967—Life as a "Bother"*	*55*
Chapter 10	*1968—Joey*	*61*
Chapter 11	*Apes and Bullies*	*65*
Chapter 12	*The Chain*	*69*
Chapter 13	*1971—Graveyard Shift*	*73*
Chapter 14	*1972—Senior Prom*	*80*
Chapter 15	*1972—Uncle Phillip*	*86*
Chapter 16	*1972—Boot Camp*	*88*
Chapter 17	*1973—Aboard USS* Dixon	*92*
Chapter 18	*May 1976*	*103*
Chapter 19	*The Fight*	*107*
Chapter 20	*The Arraignment*	*110*
Chapter 21	*Summer of 1983*	*114*
Chapter 22	*1979—The Big Case*	*123*
Chapter 23	*1983—The "Fat Boys"*	*127*
Chapter 24	*1984—Toqui and Jamey*	*139*
Chapter 25	*1998—Oktoberfest*	*149*
Chapter 26	*Monie*	*163*
Chapter 27	*Summer 1999*	*175*
Chapter 28	*January 2012*	*188*

CHAPTER 1

March 1967

When you are thirteen years old, you think you know everything and fear nothing. The year since the big move to America went by in a blur. I was settling well into a new life in Denver, Colorado. In comparison to the fast-paced life of Seoul, the Mile High City had offered a much smaller population with a simpler and peaceful way of life.

War has a way of robbing the innocence from everyone. Whoever said "There are no unwounded soldiers in a war" had spoken in truth. A famous saying in Seoul was "Close your eyes and your nose will be stolen," which described its hostile environment, the aftermath of the civil war. The conflict came to an end in 1953, three years after it had started. The war had created vicious gangs made up of war orphans tired of being hungry. They took from wherever they could find whatever they needed.

I left all that behind and came to live in *Mee-Goog*, which in English means "beautiful nation," referring to the United States of America. I came to believe it meant more than the beauty of its land but more so in describing its people's heart. Everyone I met in Denver seemed kind and generous.

It was not unusual for folks to stop and push a vehicle out of snowbanks or ditches, frequent events during the snow seasons. I have come to enjoy the warm and fuzzy feeling that I get after helping someone in trouble as I emulated those good Samaritans.

In Seoul, no one stopped to help a stranded motorist, especially in lonely and dark places. There were too many stories of good folks stopping to help someone only to fall for the trap. It had made everyone cautious to help someone.

My peers in Denver had respect for the elders still, and crew cuts were yet to be replaced by long-haired hippies. The Vietnam War was very active and so were the antiwar demonstrations. According to the media, the economy in America was sound and well.

It was an exciting time for a music lover like me. It was a time of mourning and grieving for the folks back in my homeland. Many people were still in mourning, and upbeat music could've been deemed offensive in gesture. So coming to America with lively music created by the likes of Simon and Garfunkel, the Beatles, Jimi Hendrix, and the Rolling Stones was exciting, to say the least.

A generation that revolved around sex, drugs, and rock 'n' roll was upon America as it was about to go though some serious changes of attitude. It drastically changed the way the young and the women expressed themselves. Acculturation to the American way of life as its ethos shifted did not necessarily cause difficulty for a child full of curiosity. I thought it was far out when women began burning their bras and walking around without them.

I was looking forward to the Easter break. There was not a care in the world for me as I left JFK Junior High, where I was about to finish my eighth year. Life was good. All my family members seemed to be happy and healthy.

Even though I was struggling a little with my English class, I was doing pretty well in the others. I had in my schoolbag a recently aced algebra test, graded and returned to us today, and was looking forward to the kudos from my mom. Mother was never shy to share with anyone near or far that her three children would graduate from the Ivy League universities. It was a rather bold prediction if you'd asked me. The chance of someone getting into one of those colleges was pretty slim even for the kids who grew up in America. It was nice to know your mother believed in you and would do anything to support you.

The way Mom was helping Dad through his PhD program, she had shown how dedicated she was to her goals. Once, she did not sleep for two days, working on Dad's paper to meet the deadline. She learned how to operate English typewriters just so she could help Father with the typing. She had turned Dad's handwritten thesis into a beautifully typewritten product. She did not relax until Dad's paper was turned in.

BOTHER

The excitement in my heart had brought springs to my steps as I visualized the moment of giving Mother a small token of validation for her life's dream. As I turned the corner of my block, I noticed a black-and-white squad car parked in front of my house. As I walked by my neighbor's house, I saw Mrs. Parker pointing at me from her front door. *Mrs. Parker pointing her finger at me?*

Her husband was a national candy company representative to the grocery stores throughout the Denver metro area. On occasion, I would see him in King Soopers or a Safeway Grocery Store near our home. He would stop from stocking the shelves with his company products to talk with me. Each time he did, it made me feel very special. Mrs. Parker was just as friendly, always willing to lend a helping hand.

Their twin daughters, Karen and Nancy, attended the University of Colorado at Boulder. They always returned home during the weekends and holidays. These girls were gentle souls with hearts of gold. Both were aspiring teachers. Rain or shine, you could see them on Sunday mornings as they walked to the community church three blocks away.

Mrs. Parker would often stop by our house to chat with my mom, bringing samples from her husband's company along with her own baked goods. It was always delightful to see her.

It caught me by surprise that Mrs. Parker was pointing at me. Curiosity stopped me to look at her. Only then did I realize there was a police officer in uniform inside her living room, speaking with her. It was for that officer's benefit she was extending her index finger my way.

The officer seemed to show quite a bit of interest in me, which scared me a lot. Warning bells started to go off inside me. In South Korea, getting arrested by the police usually came with beatings.

I thought of running, but it was too late for that. Obviously, Mrs. Parker was already cooperating with the police. Besides, Mom would have been upset with me if she found out I tried to run from the police.

A mid-aged tall and slim officer called my name as he walked out of the Parker's residence. His long legs might have given me a run for my money, had I took off running. I faced him as if to give him my full attention, but my mind was racing frantically, trying to figure out why a policeman would want to talk to me.

His face was that of a caring individual and seemed gentle in demeanor, which disarmed me a bit. He had a small notepad in his left hand and a pen in his right. As he started to walk toward me, he put the pen and the notepad in his left shirt pocket.

He then took off his hat to wipe his forehead with a white handkerchief. It was an unusually warm day for early spring in Denver. Hard to believe it had snowed a foot only a week ago, delighting the skiers to head for the mountains. For a moment, I thought the policeman appeared to be just as nervous as I was. *Why would that be the case?*

"You James Lee?" he asked as he approached.

"Yes . . . ?" *So much for the no-English defense.*

"My name is Bernard, Sergeant Bernard from the Lakewood station. Can we step into your house so I can speak with you in private?" As he neared me, I could see his eyes were piercing blue.

"I don't think my parents are home."

"That's okay, son. It's you I want to speak with."

"Okay, I guess." *He wanted to speak with me. What the heck did I do?* I could not think of any reason for which I should be in trouble for.

As I took out my front-door key from the pocket, the first thing that came to my mind was the odor of kimchi. If you aren't familiar with the Korean condiment, you could be quite offended by the smell of the fermenting cabbage. It can be pretty bad at times.

As I opened the door, I took in a deep breath and was relieved to realize it wasn't noticeable at all. Dad was always telling Mom to be mindful of its odor, and she was on top of it.

The tall peace officer followed me in and, without asking, took a seat on the couch. He took a quick look around our meagerly furnished living room. He had failed to notice that I took off my shoes as I walked in. It bothered me at first that he had walked into our living room with his shoes on, but I decided to let it go. He removed his hat, revealing his salt-and-pepper hair, which was cropped neatly. He sat his hat down next to him, keeping his blue eyes on me the whole time.

"Your neighbor Mrs. Parker told me you are the oldest kid in your family. Is that true?" He didn't sound like someone ready to arrest me. He seemed more like a man trying to get information about me instead. I was getting suspicious.

"Yes," I said.

"I'm sorry I have to tell you this, but your parents were involved in a car accident earlier this morning. They were taken to the Denver General

Hospital. Mrs. Parker told me you don't have any relatives living here in Denver, is that true?"

"Yeah." *None in the USA for that matter.*

"Do you know when your brother and sister will be home? I need to take all three of you to the hospital."

"What happened to them?" I was feeling nervous. Some terrible images began to play in my mind.

"I can't say anything more than what I've told you already because I don't know all the details."

"Are they okay?" *Yeah, dummy. That's why they are in the hospital because they are okay. What a stupid question.*

"I don't have much of the details to share with you, I'm afraid. My job is to get you over there so you can see them. When will your siblings get home?"

"Siblings?" *I've heard the word before, but at the moment, I couldn't remember what it means.*

"Yeah, your brother and sister. Joseph and Judith, isn't it?"

Oh yeah, siblings. "They should be home soon. Sometimes they're home before me."

As if on cue, my ten-year-old brother, Joey, walked in through the front door. He was small for his age. To make up for his size, he was quick and very strong. I noticed the presence of the police officer had made him uncomfortable.

"You must be Joseph." The officer didn't wait for Joey to answer.

"My name is Sergeant Bernard, and I'm here to take you guys to the hospital where your parents are being treated. They were in a car accident this morning." Normally very quiet, Joey didn't have anything to say to the officer, but he looked at me questioningly. I remained calm to assure him everything was okay, even though I wasn't sure of it myself.

"Where's Judy, Joey?" They attended the same elementary school. Joey had the duty to safely escort Judy to and from school. On Fridays he had to carry Judy's cello home from school to practice over the weekend, only to return it back to school on Mondays. Today was Thursday.

"She's coming. She dragged herself all the way home, walking slowly," said Joey in Korean. I spoke back to him in English for the benefit of Sergeant Bernard.

"Tell her to hurry up. We have to go to the hospital now." I was anxious to go see our parents.

"Yes, son. Go get her so we can ride over to the hospital." Sergeant Bernard spoke very quietly, with a smile on his face. His blue eyes were twinkling. He reminded me of the actor Paul Newman who played in the movie *Cool Hand Luke*. It was the very first movie I saw in a theater since moving to America. I started to like Sergeant Bernard.

We exited, and I locked the front door. As we walked toward the squad car, Judy was approaching home, carrying her backpack, nearly dragging it on the ground. When Joey offered to take her backpack from her, she refused by moving it away from him. Judy, Miss Independent. At seven, she was as stubborn as a mule and would not ask for help if her life had depended on it.

Judy was already out-spelling her classmates only a year after coming to America. She chose to enter into the first grade when the principal and the first-grade teacher suggested she should begin at the kindergarten level. They believed it would help her ease into the new language. She was six then, old enough to be in the first grade, and by golly, that's where she was going to be. Our parents knew better than to try to talk her out of it. She had surprised everyone by studying hard to achieve beyond anyone's expectation. Now, she was the reigning champion speller of her class.

Everyone agrees there is something special about Judy. She would look right in the eyes of those who asked her what she would like to be when she grew up and say she would be a *wise* judge like King Solomon was. She was the delight of our mother. She was my delight as well.

I took the bag from Judy, against her will, and opened the passenger-side back door of the police car for her. She looked at me questioningly before getting in. Her bag weighed much heavier than my schoolbag. *What does she have in it?*

For a moment, I thought of taking it inside the house but didn't want to delay the trip to the hospital any further. I was anxious to get there. Joey got in from the other side, and with Judy in the middle, we all got into the backseat, with her bag on my lap.

"Where are we going?" asked Judy, the future prosecutor.

"I'm taking you kids to the Denver General Hospital to see your parents," said the blue-eyed man, looking at Judy through the rearview mirror.

"Why are they in the hospital?" the future counsel continued her examination with the lawman.

"They were in an accident and were taken there to be treated for injuries. They want to see you guys, so I'm here to take you there."

"Are they hurt badly?" Hers were much better questions than mine.

"Let me take you guys there, and you can ask them yourselves, okay?" Officer Bernard seemed to know more but would not share any more information about our parents.

"That means they're hurt really badly," Judy said, to no one in particular. I thought of how perceptive Judy was at such a young age, but I was hoping she was wrong nonetheless.

The ride took about ten minutes to the hospital, but seemed much longer. Officer Bernard took forever locking up the squad car once arriving at the hospital. When he had finally led us into the hospital, he spoke with the man at the information desk before walking toward the elevators.

When he reached the elevator, he stopped and turned to look at us. The three of us followed him like a herd traipsing toward the slaughterhouse. The elevator took us to the third floor.

We were greeted by familiar faces. Fellow parishioners of the Korean Christian Church had gathered at the visitor's lounge next to the elevators. The flock had gathered in concern for their shepherd and his helpmate. Dad had started a church for the Korean immigrants living in Denver when he first arrived here to find there wasn't a Korean-speaking church in Denver. The members of his congregation had come to see their injured pastor and his wife.

It seemed we were the last to find out, last to arrive. Immediately I was struck with fear as I saw all the women crying their eyes out. This can't be good. Too much tears for scratches and bruises. Perhaps Judy was right. My need to see my parents became quite urgent all of a sudden.

Bernard was standing in front of a room, waiting for us to finish with our greetings. He was very patient and noble. My heart was beating too fast and so strongly I couldn't concentrate on the greeters. I needed to see my mom and dad.

I separated from the adults hugging me, handed Judy's bag to Joey, and told him to stay with Judy and everyone at the lounge. I walked toward the room where Bernard was standing by. I saw Dad lying on his right side, with eyes closed.

He was the only one in the room. The only other bed in the room was empty. *Where's Mom? Maybe she's in another room.*

"Ah-buh-jee" (Father), I called out quietly, hoping to get his attention without waking him if he was asleep.

He stirred, indicating he had heard me. He was obviously in pain as he winced while trying to sit up on the bed and turn toward the entrance where Officer Bernard and I stood. I noticed his face was bruised and swollen. Bernard said something and walked away, but I didn't hear what he said. I approached Dad nervously.

"Jae-chul ah," he called out my Korean name. He had given us American names so it would be easier for us to blend in with our peers. Jae-min is now Joey, Jae-hyun has become Judy. I am now James. I liked my new name.

"Ye, ah-buh-jee." *Yes, Father.*

"Eh del un?" *What about the kids?*

"Baak eh it suh yo." *They are outside.*

Then my father did something I had never seen him do in my entire life. He broke out in uncontrollable sobs. He tried to say something, but I could not make out what he said. I was totally confused.

"Moo uh yo, ah-buh-gee?" *What did you say, Father?*

"Ni umma gah . . . jook ut dah goo." *Your mother . . . passed away.*

"Umma gah yo?" *Mother has?*

I refused to believe what I had just heard. Dad couldn't have meant what he said. Perhaps the medicine was making him delusional. But as it turned out, my mother did not survive the automobile accident that took place earlier while we were at school.

Someone had run a red light and plowed into the passenger side of our Plymouth station wagon as they were crossing the intersection. She had died in an ambulance on the way to the hospital. Now I understood why Bernard was so shy with the information. Judy's intuition had unfortunately proven correct.

Deacon Kim brought us home from the hospital. I was in a daze and woke out of it when Deacon Kim pulled into our driveway. Deacon Kim had a daughter my age named Sarah. They came to America many years before our family did. I thought Sarah was pretty and liked being around her. Deacon Kim offered to stay with us overnight, but I told him we would be fine. He argued and said he would run home and grab some hygiene stuff and return shortly.

The sun went down, and it was dark outside. I told Joey and Judy to get ready for school the next day. That's the way Mom would have wanted it. I wasn't sure how, but I was going to do everything in my power to fulfill Mom's dream of us accomplishing our goals in life. I had to be their mother now. I thought it was best that we go to school instead of staying home. I had a history exam and didn't want to miss it. It would only make matters worse for me later on.

Judy didn't even attempt to give me a hard time. She quietly went about her ritual before bedtime and went into her room, closing the door. Joey was already in his room with the door closed shut. I got the vacuum out from the hallway closet and vacuumed the living room where Sergeant Bernard had walked with his shoes on.

Someone was knocking hard on the front door. It was Deacon Kim. He had returned with his toothbrush and a change of clothes and a bucket of Colonel's chicken. I had forgotten about dinner. So did Joey and Judy. No one was hungry. I thanked him and took the chicken to the kitchen.

"Please use my room to sleep, Deacon Kim." I was touched by his kind heart and thought he should use my room instead of sleeping on the couch.

"If you have a blanket and a pillow, the couch will be fine. By the way, I want you kids to stay home tomorrow and don't worry about going to school."

"I thought about that too, Deacon Kim. But I think we should go to school instead of staying home, thinking about what happened to Mom and Dad."

"Well . . ."

"Besides, I have a test tomorrow and, I think, Joey does too."

"I'm sure your teachers will let you guys make up for it later."

"A makeup test will make it more complicated for me, so I'd rather get it out of the way."

"I can't keep you from going, but it is my suggestion that you kids stay home tomorrow. Then you can return on Monday if you wish. I was planning on staying with you tomorrow, but I guess I can go to work after all, if you insist. I better arrange for either myself or someone to meet you as you return home from school.

"I told the kids to get ready for school tomorrow, and they've already turned in for the night."

"I am so sorry for your mother passing away so suddenly like that. Everyone is so shocked and sad for your family. I always thought you are a fine young man, and it touches my heart to see you staying strong, caring for your brother and sister. Bless your heart, son."

"I put out a new towel for you in the hallway bathroom. Let me know if you need anything else. Good night, sir."

When I was alone in my room, I was unable to hold back the tears any longer. Deep sorrow that was only suppressed by the terror of life without Mom was finally being released. I silently cried until the sleep carried me away into deep rest.

CHAPTER 2

1967—Judy

Marcy Perkins didn't come to school for almost three weeks after her mom had died of cancer. She's my friend from my first-grade class last year but is in a different class now. Marcy told me she went to stay with her grandparents in Grand Junction, Colorado, after the funeral. She had always dressed prettily and wore bows and ribbons on her hair before her mother had passed away.

When Marcy returned from her grandparents', she no longer wore smiles or ribbons in her hair. At times, Marcy was wearing the same clothes two days in a row. Since that time, whenever I came across the word *unkempt*, I thought of Marcy. She rarely spoke to anyone anymore. Even when her friends tried to get her involved in games and activities, she was unwilling and kept to herself.

I decided not to be like Marcy even though my mom had also died. She made everyone around her feel sorry for her, and I did not want others to feel sorry for me.

Mom said if I believe in Jesus, I would go to heaven when I die. Mom believed in Jesus, and she was in heaven now. I believe in Jesus, so I will see her in heaven after I die. When I was a little kid, Mom used to read me stories from the Bible each night before I went to bed.

Many nights I fell asleep listening to her version of young King David as he fought off lions and bears while tending to his father's flock. She would read about young Joseph as he was sold as a slave to the traveling merchants by his own brothers. The story I enjoyed the most was about King Solomon, who was the wisest man ever. He was a wise judge who made decisions fairly and kindly for the people of his kingdom.

I had told Mother I wanted to be a judge when I grow up. She said I would be a good judge, and that made me feel good. She shared with me about her friend from college who was an attorney in Korea and was trying to become the first female judge in South Korea.

Mom's friend was very intelligent and spoke eloquently. Her success as a constitutional lawyer made her famous, but South Korea was not quite ready for a lady judge. Mom said it would be much easier for me to be a judge here in America, that I should be grateful to be living here. Mom said I had to study hard like her friend had.

Soon after coming to America, I found out about the annual spelling bee contest. Randy Fallon in sixth grade, who represented our school now for two years in a row, lost during the state finals and never made it to the regional or the national bee contest. I went on to become the champion representing the second grade. I daydreamed that I could go further than Randy Fallon had when I become the school champion bee.

Unlike Marcy, I had to go to school the next day after Mom had an accident. My big brother Jimmy said it was important that we don't fall behind in our schoolwork. He said it was important that I study hard to become a judge as I had promised Mom.

I told Jimmy I was no longer going to keep my promise to her now that she had died and gone away. She was no longer alive to care what I become. Jimmy told me I was wrong to think like that. I liked it when he spoke to me in Korean. I felt closer to him when he did.

"You know, Jae-hyun, just because we can't see her doesn't mean she can't see us."

"Do you know for sure if she can see us?" I spoke back to him in Korean. According to Mom, I was supposed to call Jae-chul *keun-oppa* (bigger older brother) and my other brother, Jae-min, *jagun-oppa* (littler older brother). I just call them *oppa* (big brother).

I'm glad that we live in America now, where I don't have to call everyone by these confusing polite terms. I think it's nice to call them by their names.

"It's even more important than when Mom was alive for you to keep your promise to her. If she were alive, you could undo your promise to her. Now, it's too late to change your promise."

"I don't think it is too late."

"Well, she's no longer around for you to tell her you've changed your mind. Besides, you would make a great judge, and you know it."

"If Mom can see us, then maybe she can hear us also. I want to tell her I can't become a judge without her help."

"Of course you can. Mom never helped you with your work. Heck, you wouldn't let anyone help you with schoolwork. You're the smartest kid I know. You can do anything you want to if you try."

"Mom said she was going to teach me how to play the piano if I finished learning the cello another year, but now she can't keep her promise to me. Why do I have to keep my promise to her?" I felt so sad I began to cry. Oppa pulled me into his arms and held me.

"I bet you she will make sure you will get that piano lesson, and I will also see to it as well."

"Will she . . . help me . . . to do well . . . in school?" I asked, sobbing.

"I'm not sure. I don't think she would help us with schoolwork and tests and stuff. That would be like cheating."

"Did she die because I stepped on the cracks on the sidewalk?"

"What?"

"That's what Marcy said. She said her mom died because she stepped on the cracks on the sidewalks. I didn't believe her when she told us, but now Mommy died too, and I stepped on the cracks a lot."

"You're silly. No one died because somebody stepped on some stupid cracks on the sidewalks. Mom died because some guy ran a red light and ran into our car. Nothing you did caused our mom to die, you know that, right?" Oppa wiped away the tears on my face, and in a cheerful voice, he said, "Why don't you wash up and get ready for bed. Did you do all your homework?"

"Yes, while I was waiting for you talking to Daddy at the hospital. When will Daddy come home from the hospital?"

"Deacon Kim said probably tomorrow or the day after. Are you hungry?"

"No. I don't feel like eating. I miss Mommy."

"Me too, Jae-hyun ah. Now, go wash up. Let me check on your homework."

"Okay. Oppa?"

"What?"

"Does Mommy have wings now?"

"I felt as if she had wings when she was alive. I felt so safe and comfortable in her embraces."

"I wish I could see her, oppa." *I wanted to die so I could be with her.*

"Maybe if you're really good, she might show up to tell you that she is proud of you. Now hurry up and get up there."

"I wish I didn't step on the cracks."

"I told you that's nonsense. Now get up there, hurry."

"Why did Marcy say it then?"

"I don't know why she said it, but it's not true. If that was true, all the moms would be dead now, wouldn't they? Everybody steps on the cracks one time or another. Don't you go and believe in something silly like that anymore, okay? Now go get your homework for me to check on, hurry."

"Okay, oppa."

I felt a little better. I will wear a pretty dress and a bow in my hair tomorrow. Oppa is right. I must study hard to make Mom really happy.

CHAPTER 3

1967—Life without Mom

Thirteen-year-old boys know nothing about maintaining a household. Overnight, I had taken on the responsibilities that had belonged to Mom all these years. Some, such as laundry and cleaning the oven, I had seen Mom doing enough to handle them. Others, I had no idea how to go about.

Keeping the odor of kimchi from making the whole house smell funky was one of the tasks I knew very little about. Once the batch of kimchi on hand was gone, however, that problem was solved.

Until now, cooking wasn't anything I had to think about. My mom was wonderfully talented with culinary skills and knew her way around the kitchen. My family had to be content with cereals and canned food for quite some time.

Eventually, I would discover the wonders of the oven and began broiling various meats and frozen dinners, which pleased everyone. I began spending more time shopping for groceries, searching for different stuff to add to my menu. Before long, I began to develop impressive culinary skills of my own.

Dad came home from the hospital on Saturday morning, two days after the accident. He hobbled in using a crutch. He refused the help from the ambulance attendant even though he was in pain and experienced stiffness. The details of Mother's funeral had prevented him from the rest he needed, as he spent time on the phone with various people.

When the doorbell rang, I opened the door to find a police detective who needed to speak with Dad regarding the accident. He was not as polite as Bernard had been. He took off his shoes, however, before entering our living room.

"Can I get you something to drink?" I asked the detective.
"Yes, a glass of water would be great," the detective answered.
"May I have some too, son?" Dad said, sounding like Mr. Cleaver.
The detective spent about half an hour with Dad, asking questions and taking notes. I could see Dad was visibly upset with the interview. On several occasions, the interview was put on hold so he could recompose himself after becoming emotionally disturbed. I was glad when the detective was finished and gone. Dad went upstairs, and after a few minutes had gone by, I heard the shower going in his bathroom.

Deacon Cho and his wife came by around noon, with bags full of Chinese food. The bag indicated it was from the Peking Palace Restaurant, which was owned by them. One of the earlier immigrants from Korea, they were experiencing great success with a Chinese restaurant on the corner of Colfax and Broadway, next to the state capitol building.

They catered to the downtown crowds, including the state senators and the capitol-building employees. My father had taken me to their restaurant on several occasions when their dishwasher or busboy had failed to show up. I didn't mind pinch-hitting for the absentee employees since I was paid in cash on the spot. The fringe benefit of all the good food I could eat while I worked was a bonus for me. I was also flattered that they thought I was a good hire.

Deacon Cho was a distinguished political science professor from Seoul University with great followings and recognitions during the Syng-Man Rhee administration. Many proponents of Rhee had fled from South Korea to avoid persecutions and death following the revolution led by General Jung-Hee Park on May 16, 1961. Many supporters of South Korea's first president, Rhee, who had remained in South Korea had indeed been silenced by imprisonment or death. My grandmother spoke about a relative who had to flee Park's army and moved to New Zealand.

I recall vaguely the military activities during the takeover by Park's army as I started elementary school in Seoul. When Rhee died, his body was brought back from Hawaii to be buried in South Korea. By then, Park had become the new president. As a child, I witnessed the nation mourn for Rhee as if a king had died.

People continued with the tradition of burying kings from the dynasty days that had ended less than a decade ago. To the majority of South Koreans, Rhee was equal to a king. My relatives who had moved away were not allowed to return to Korea for Rhee's funeral. The Park administration would not allow it in fear of any actions in defiance from the exiled dissidents returning for Rhee's funeral.

Most of the exiled had settled in Hawaii, where Rhee had lived after his self-imposed exile until his death in 1965. Professor Cho and his bride had made it all the way to Colorado, leaving behind a beautiful estate in Seoul. I recall him say it was the distinctive four seasons similar to Seoul that drew him and his bride to the Rockies as their pied-à-terre.

They invested well in several real estate properties and the restaurant, which had become very popular among the downtowners. They owned a mansion-like home in a newly developing suburb of Aurora, where many Korean families began to settle.

In his house is where the members of our church congregated after the Sunday worship to break bread and to fellowship with one another. Some folks who followed Buddhism and did not attend the church would join in on the gathering to hear the latest news from the homeland and to share some "Seoul food" with us. Their conversations usually went from heated political topics to the rather somber topics involving life as immigrants.

Deacon Cho's home was larger than the church building we worshipped in, with a huge backyard. He had a pool table and a tennis table inside his supersized family room. His house was a place of comfort, and people always felt welcome there.

Deacon and his wife were generous people, liberally sharing their wealth with anyone in need. Their tithe and offerings reflected the majority of the church's income. Deacon Cho made sure all the church expenses were met. He was soon to be ordained as the first elder of our church.

I liked Deacon Cho a lot. He neither condescended nor encroached upon others with his social and financial statuses. Years of quality-control duties at his restaurant had put some extra weight on him, but he wore it well.

A couple who works for him also attended our church. Their descriptions of the deacon would fit anyone's expectation of what an ideal boss would be. I had admired him from the time I first met him. I wanted to grow up to be a man of quiet strength and integrity like him.

Mrs. Cho was like our second mother. We needed her now more than ever. Perhaps since they did not have any of their own or due to the fact that we were the pastor's children, Mrs. Cho always treated us very well.

The rumor had it she was pursued by many suitors due to her extraordinary beauty. Her father, who was also a prominent political science professor and a mentor to the younger, was so impressed with Cho's refreshing attitude and his stance on the modern government that Cho had easily won out over the other suitors. Some, I am told, were quite wealthy and from very powerful and prominent families. Everyone would agree, however, that she had done well in marrying Cho.

Mrs. Cho was in her midforties, but her radiant beauty still stopped men on their tracks. While some may have felt sorry for her that she was wasting her beauty away working at a restaurant, she was obviously very happy with her life as Deacon Cho's wife. I suspected many of her male patrons had become regulars, as she was quite pleasant for their eyes.

I was more than willing to let Mrs. Cho commandeer the kitchen away from me. Judy welcomed the tender attributes of female companionship, shadowing Mrs. Cho, carrying a conversation with her. They were too far away from me to hear their conversation.

Something Judy said made Mrs. Cho stop what she was doing and kneel beside Judy to hug her. The length of that hug made my heart ache for Judy. Obviously, Judy was hurting too. Here I was, feeding my face with Peking duck while she sorrowed in pain.

I couldn't eat any more as my throat became constricted and my eyes welled up with tears. Joey did not notice any of this, simply too happy to continue on, sans competitor.

When I turned to see what Dad and Deacon Cho were doing, it gave me an opportunity to wipe away my tears. I saw Dad had fallen asleep on the couch. Deacon Cho had that kind of effect on people around him. Dad had felt relaxed enough to finally get some rest he needed. Deacon Cho had managed to find a blanket and was covering Dad with it.

It wasn't until near sundown before Deacon Cho was finished with the details of the funeral and the restoration of our Plymouth station wagon. He knew the ins and outs of taking care of business. He had the experiences and the contacts to make any job seem easy.

Mrs. Cho emerged from Judy's room to join her husband. Judy did not follow her out. Joey was watching a boxing match on television, munching on egg rolls.

"Jimmy," Deacon Cho called me in a quiet voice and motioned me to him.

"Yes?" I responded just as quietly.

"Your mother's funeral will be immediately following the Sunday worship. When we had gathered at the hospital on Thursday, we had an emergency meeting and decided to have your mother's funeral on Sunday. Everyone agreed combining them into a single day on Sunday was most ideal. Your father agreed as well, so we planned it for tomorrow. Do you and your brother have dark-color suits?"

"Yes. I'll make sure Joe and Judy will wear something dark tomorrow. Thanks for the food, Professor Cho." I preferred to call him professor rather than anything else. I thought it honored him the highest.

"You should call me if you need anything at all, do you hear me?"

"Yes, sir. Thank you."

"Make sure your dad gets plenty of rest tonight. There will be a limousine here to pick your family up at eight thirty tomorrow morning, since your dad can't drive yet. Make sure everyone is ready by then, okay?" said Deacon Cho in his commanding yet comforting voice. "My heart aches for you guys. You are a fine young man, Jimmy. You need to continue being strong for your family, okay?" he said matter-of-factly.

"Yes, sir." I meant it. I was going to stay strong for my family.

As the couple said good-bye and drove away, the overwhelming grief returned. It nearly took my breath away, and I had to gasp just to catch my breath. The sun was setting around the Rockies, casting darkness over the land. The inside of our house was very dark, yet no one had bothered to turn the lights on.

My spirit was just as dark. Mother was about to be buried. She was the source of my strength, the source of light that guided my path, all my life. Now my spirit was lifeless, sinking into the darkness that surrounded me.

It was a good thing the weather had turned warm, thawing out the ground that had been frozen by the snowstorm only a week earlier. Mom was easily chilled. She preferred warm weather. "Thin blooded," she would often say.

I went around the living room and the kitchen, turning on all the lights I could find. I needed to chase away the darkness that overwhelmed me.

"Joey, you want any more of this food?"

"No."

"You want to help me clean up?" He did not even respond to that. I thought of saying something but decided against it as I thought of Judy.

I put away the food and cleaned the kitchen. I needed to find Judy. She was upstairs in her room, with the door shut. I needed to know what she had said that made Mrs. Cho stop on her tracks to hold Judy so tightly in response.

I needed to let Judy know I was also available for her to share the pains with. She had to know she wasn't the only one with an aching heart. I needed to be there for her.

Judy didn't want to speak with me. I quietly opened her door, which could not be locked from the inside.

"Oppa, I told you I don't want to talk now," she spat at me in Korean. She had been crying. I responded in Korean.

"Jae-hyun ah, let me get the dress you need to wear tomorrow so I can iron it for you. Which black dress do you want to wear, the velvet one or the one with all the fancy white trimmings?"

"I don't want to see Mommy getting buried," she said, catching me off guard.

"You have to say good-bye to her," I said, choking down my emotions.

"I don't want to go. I won't say good-bye or see her being buried."

"Judy, we have to honor Mom, whether we want to or not. It will make her sad if you aren't there to say good-bye to her."

She started to cry, and I held her without another word. I let her cry in my arms. I held my words and tears, simply holding her. I realized I did not want to attend the funeral either.

She fell asleep in just a few minutes. I covered her with the blanket and left her room, carrying the dress with all the fancy trimmings.

I realized that Mother had ironed it before hanging, and it was ready to be worn. For some reason, it made me cry again. I returned Judy's dress back in her closet and quietly left, checking to confirm she was asleep.

I went up to see if Dad was doing okay. He too must have fallen asleep, because he did not respond to my knock. I was exhausted. As soon as my head hit the pillow, I was asleep. I was too tired to cry.

CHAPTER 4

My Childhood Memories

I came into this world exactly nine months after my parents' wedding. While the nation would be divided in the middle of the peninsula, one man from the most northern part of the nation would go on to marry a southern gal from Busan, unifying the peninsula through their marriage. At the tender age of twenty-two, Mother gave birth to me. Dad was twenty-six when I was born.

Dad was a South Korean army chaplain stationed in Busan when he met my mother. More accurately, it was my grandma he had met first. Of course, to my grandma, Dad was an ideal candidate to court either of her twins.

It was only fair and the natural progression for the older one to marry first, so it was Mom who was officially introduced to Dad by Grandma, and Dad had fallen in love at first sight. After all, she was a beautiful young woman with a degree in home economics. He tells everyone how lucky he was to have a bride like Mom. Everyone always agreed.

Dad's first post after his term with the military was in O-Jung, a small village about fifty kilometers south of Daejeon. O-Jung was populated mostly by physically handicapped individuals who had suffered injuries or became casualties during the war.

Even after the war, many civilians came across the hidden land mines placed there by the retreating Red Army soldiers. It was meant for the UN soldiers pursuing them, but years later, it ended up harming the children playing in the fields or a farmer plowing.

This village was oriented to meet the needs of those with challenges. Facilities were built from the ground up by the American missionaries who had physically challenged individuals in mind when they designed restrooms and ramps, which were so innovative they would not be available elsewhere in South Korea for years to come.

Some folks with children born with physical defects came to this village for the obvious reasons. People with disabilities could not have found a more comforting place than O-Jung.

In the end, they would benefit far more from the missionaries than the modern facilities. These selfless individuals from *Mee-Goog* came to this war-ravaged land to create a better life for the physically challenged. In addition to building housings and facilities for them, these folks from America provided counseling and support for the challenged as well as to their family members to overcome their needs.

Whether they were physical, emotional, or spiritual, the missionaries were ready and willing to help my village folks without asking anything in return.

It was amazing to see these amputees and individuals care for themselves. They ran chicken farms, maintained vineyards, and raised various crops, such as peanuts and yams. The Concord grapes produced from the area were the tastiest grapes around. There was even a catfish farm near the village, where the fish were raised for consumption.

Many village folks worked at the cannery that was built on top of the mesa, which was on the other side of the river where they canned peanuts and vegetables harvested locally. A tiny bridge that had only enough space to allow one vehicle at a time was used by the townsfolk to get to their work at the cannery. It carried them over the river and the railroad tracks.

As I was growing up in O-Jung, I would spend days watching these individuals with missing limbs in prosthetics, doing things that would be complex even with all the body parts. When they were not working, they played *ba-dook* (Go) and *jang-gi* (a Korean chess game) with metal hooks placing the game piece into a tiny spot on the game boards, without disturbing other pieces.

Double amputees with no legs were racing each other in sprints during the annual sporting events. With wooden prosthetic legs and crutches, they were able to move almost as rapidly as the nonamputees.

Men with missing limbs wrestled each other in Korean style (*ssi-rem*) and an ex-soldier with only one leg kicked *jae-gi* (Korean Hacky Sack) fifty consecutive times as he hopped on one leg, to which everyone counted along. He needed to rest his weary leg after that. Most of us needed to rest after watching his efforts and counting along.

Another ex-soldier did eleven pull-ups on a high bar with his right hand, as his left hand up to his elbow was gone. They did not dwell in what they are missing or unable to use but raised the bars to excel with what remained. With the help from the missionaries, they also found spiritual strength from deep within themselves.

Dad was assigned as the pastor of the only church in the village but ended up serving as their social worker as well at no additional pay. When the missionaries came, he was hired by them. It was a nonpaying position with the Americans as well, but he was happy to be a servant of God, meeting the needs of the village folks and the Americans who needed his translation.

Dad was able to use his contacts to obtain grants and scholarships for various individuals to pursue their education or learn trades. Many village folks had considered him a hero for having paved the ways for the various American organizations to help the villagers for years to follow.

Helping with the construction of the buildings was a way for the missionaries to share the Gospel with the South Koreans, who were predominantly Buddhists. After months had gone by, these missionaries had learned enough Korean to converse with us in *Han-Goog mal* (Korean language), needing my dad's help less as they continued on. The missionaries thought highly of Dad and eventually gave him an opportunity to study in America.

While everyone was very proud of Dad as he was receiving the recognitions, what made the impressions on me was the way these Americans cared for others totally strange to them. These strange breed of folks taught victims of war to forgive the enemy soldiers rather than to hold grudges.

One missionary from Grand Rapids, Michigan, provided a place for Dad to stay while attending a seminary in his hometown. It was the first time I recognized Christianity as something more than a thing taking place in church on Sundays. It was a way of life, as exemplified by the American missionaries. Even as a young child, I admired them, and the love they shared with the strangers made lasting impressions on me.

These unfortunate victims of war that even their own had forgotten would not be ignored by these strangers from the other side of the globe. Some South Korean soldiers who had lost their arms and or legs during the war had chosen to settle in this village as well, as either counselors or residents.

The village was a flat area of houses surrounded by farms and fields. Dense forest surrounded the village with a river running next to it. The river irrigated the farms and the orchards, making their products luscious and plentiful. It was an ideal playground for a young boy with wild imaginations.

I swam the river with the older boys missing various limbs of their bodies. I would hear their accounts of stepping on a land mine or being near a friend who did and received the injuries that led them to this village. Younger ones who were nonvictims living with injured siblings made the efforts to walk and talk as the big boys did, in admiration for their courage. I certainly looked up to them in awe.

An older boy who had lost both legs was able to dog-paddle faster than most of us who had legs. The same boy had taught me how to crawl under the orchards' barbed-wire fences to enjoy the grapes to our hearts' content. He had shown me how to wipe away the DDT (now banned toxic bug spray) that was sprayed on the fruits prior to popping them into the mouth.

I would get caught each time by Mom and Dad the moment I walked in the house. They knew I had been stealing grapes by the purple stains on my shirt where I had wiped the grapes to remove the toxic DDT. The forbidden fruit tasted the sweetest. Grapes became my favorite fruit henceforward, stolen or not.

Ravaged by the war, food became scarce and precious as I was growing up. I learned how to glean peanuts that were overlooked by the harvesters by watching the older ones in action. They would fill their socks or beanies with gathered peanuts. Some would use their hooks that replaced the missing limbs to rake the ground and then pick up their findings with metal hooks, as normal a person would, with ease.

They would also teach me how to roast the gathered peanuts in the fire they had built by the river, using their hooks to stir the peanuts cooking inside hubcaps or tin cans found on the road. During harvest seasons, there were plenty of locusts to catch and roast along with the nuts. Baked yams were my favorite. They tasted so good fresh out of the bed of the glowing embers. You peeled away the crusted skin to yield the most delectable treat inside.

Years later, I would realize that the most important lesson I learned from these older boys were not the survival skills but their willingness to forgive. Even the individuals responsible for making them limbless they forgave. I learned that during their support group meetings, the missionaries had suggested they pray for the Chinese and the North Korean Red Army soldiers, asking God to forgive them for injuring and maiming their bodies.

I was too young to understand the true meaning of forgiveness, but I understood what they did was something very difficult to do. I knew forgiving someone who had done you wrong was not something that came easily. Their examples would serve me greatly many years later.

With the contacts he had made with the Americans, my dad was able to travel to the United States of America for the first time in the summer of 1957, shortly after Joe's birth.

Even as a three-year-old boy, I felt abandoned, betrayed by him that he would leave us behind in war rubbles while he traveled to *Mee-Goog*. Mom, on the other hand, did not seem to mind it at all. She took over some of Dad's obligations as a coordinator for the village activities.

One of the fondest memories I had in O-Jung was on my fourth birthday. Mom had gathered all the children of the village, including the older boys, to have a birthday party for me. There was lots of food, including Korean pastries, for everyone's enjoyment. I was floating in the air with joy and pride. The big boys made me feel important as they came to celebrate my birthday. For a day, I was able to forget about Dad.

When Dad returned from America with his MA, he was given an assignment at Severance Hospital in Seoul as a social worker. We left O-Jung behind, the place where I had such fond childhood memories. Severance Hospital was part of Yonsei University's teaching hospital. They catered to the physically challenged, either due to the injuries from the war or those born with the musculoskeletal diseases.

An American psychiatrist, Dr. Stephen Davis, was in charge of the Severance clinic. He was a double amputee with no hands. I thought I had seen all there was to see with the fascinating things the amputees could do. That is, until I saw Dr. Davis type with his metal hooked fingers. He was amazingly quick and accurate with those hooks on that typewriter.

Dad dove right into work at his new post, while Mom and I tried to settle into the new life in Seoul. Jae-min was too young to know what was going on. We moved into a two-bedroom house in Mo-rei, a suburb of Seoul.

I enrolled in Chang-Chon Elementary School. My class alone had more children than the whole village of O-Jung. I was experiencing a cultural shock. I missed O-Jung dearly. I felt dizzy trying to stay on my toes and keeping my nose from being taken by these fast-talking city slickers.

Life in Seoul was nothing like the dreamy world of O-Jung—no trees to climb, no snakes to catch, and absolutely no skinny-dipping in the river. First thing I noticed was the lack of camaraderie among the people. Adults were competing against one another, trying to survive while keeping their nose intact. Children followed suit with heavy competitions of their own in school. It was a dog-eat-dog world.

High-rise buildings were going up everywhere, replacing the buildings that were destroyed during the war. Roads and streets were being carved and paved, replacing the old and the damaged. There was presence of both American and Korean soldiers everywhere, busily going about their business in various military vehicles. It was both ominous and festive to a young boy trying to fit into the new surroundings.

Dad's office was near my school. Every morning, Dad and I would get on the same bus to ride into Seoul. The thirty-minute ride each morning was the most treasured time of my day. I had Dad all to myself. Sometimes when there would be two empty seats for us to sit next to one another, he'd put his arms around me, which made me feel so secure. He would talk to me silly just to make me laugh. Other times, he would talk to me about the dangers that lurked in the streets of Seoul. He would describe some of the ways the fast-talkers and swindlers would con the unsuspecting victims. Listening to him talking to me so seriously made me feel grown-up. After getting off the bus, we had to travel on foot some distance before we parted to go our separate ways. During these times, our conversations resembled that of friends rather than between a parent and his child.

"Jae-chul ah, why do you swing your arms when you walk?"
"I don't know, Dad. Why do you swing yours?"
"So it looks good when others look at me."
"That's not why. You are silly, Dad."
"What about this? Why isn't our nose turned upside down so that the holes are facing up? So the water doesn't go in when it rains. How about, mmmm . . . what is the purpose of having a nose bridge?"
"I don't know."

"So the glasses won't slide down, see?" He'd show me where his eyeglasses were sitting on his nose to emphasize his point.

Those fond memories would help me through the difficult times ahead, when his love seemed no longer. It helped me to carry on my love for my dad, as our relationship turned south and never looked back.

CHAPTER 5

1966—Coming to Mee-Goog

In Korea, the school year begins in February. There are two breaks a year, each about six to eight weeks long between the semesters. Summer break starts in July to the end of August. The winter break begins with Christmas and throughout the month of January. The school week consisted of six days, but Saturdays were half day only. School rested on Sundays.

Mostly, August consisted of pouring rain. Using the descriptions "cats and dogs" or "by the bucket" does not even begin to describe the rain that poured during the monsoon season in Korea. Experiencing what Noah had in his ark would better describe it. It was unfair that the monsoon season was right in the middle of the summer breaks. It was one thing I would not miss about home.

In Korea, while I grew up there, only six years of public education were required by the government. Junior and senior high schools were public schools as well, but no longer free. In Korea, schools are ranked and rated as first, second, or third.

These rankings and rates were the result of a standard test given to all the schools. The schools with higher average scores would rank higher than those with lower average scores. Tuition amount increased with the higher-ranking schools.

The accumulated grade point average during the six years of elementary school determines which junior high school one should try out for. It required passing the strenuous written exams of various topics as well as a physical test to enter the school. The higher ranked among the first-rated schools were known to have the most difficult exams.

If you failed with the first effort, you would have to hurry and choose a school from among the second-rated schools to test for. If you fail again, you either go for the choice from third-rated schools, pretty much guaranteed to accept you, or sit out a year and study for the exam the following year, in hope of getting into a better school. Many of my friends ended up making the latter choice. The process starts all over again for the senior high school entry exams.

Many kids chose to settle for the minimum six-year education and enter into a vocational school instead of junior high school. It was matter of survival for some, to earn a living rather than go to school. While the first six years were free, the junior and senior high school tuitions were very costly. Many just couldn't afford to further their education as I was growing up.

The children whose parents were killed during the war or separated from them during the evacuations couldn't even attend elementary school. They became shoeshine boys or peddled gums and newspapers on the streets just to eke out a living.

It was not unusual to see ten-year-olds selling newspapers on the streets when they should have been in school. To them, even attending elementary school was not an option. In the event the orphans happened to be fathered by the American soldiers and abandoned, their chances of making it on the streets were even more difficult.

I benefited tremendously from growing up in O-Jung, where physical activities were a daily part of living. Physically, I fared well against the fast-talking city slickers whose legs weren't as quick as their mouths. As I entered second grade, Dad enrolled me into tae kwon do class, where I would learn discipline and self-defense.

It was an added bonus for me to spend time in a *do-jang* (a gym) near my dad's office, which allowed me to catch the same bus home with Dad after his work. He seemed genuinely proud of me as I walked into his office in my *do-bok* (uniform) after each lesson.

Under the nurturing care of Mom, I excelled in my classes. In each class, everyone was numbered accordingly, from the highest grade point average (being number one) to the lowest GPA student. Mom did not expect but demanded that I maintain being top three or better. While my peers may have felt the strain from such demand, I thrived in it. Kyung-Gi and Seoul Junior High were two of the most vied for schools among the top students from each elementary school in the nation. None other than those two schools would have satisfied my mom.

To my father, the only ranking he cared about was the result of the latest tae kwon do tournaments. He had left the matter of his children's education to his wife. It pleased me tremendously to make the best efforts in everything I did just to see the joyous expressions of my parents.

When Mom had discovered that some students who failed to pass the entry exams had committed suicide, she backed off from pressuring me too much to study. Deep down in my heart, I knew I would pass the entry exam and make her proud.

My parents were busy making their move to America just as I was beginning to feel the pressure in preparing for the entrance exam. First, Dad began his doctorate program in Denver Seminary in the middle of my fourth year in school.

Shortly after I began my fifth year in school, Mom joined Dad in America, leaving me, Jae-min, and our five-year-old sister, Jae-hyun, with our maternal grandmother. It was most ideal that her parsonage was a walking distance from our school.

Our grandmother was sensitive to our needs, loving, and nurturing. She tried to do her best to care for the three of us. Jae-min was in second grade in the same school I attended. I was three grades ahead of him. I was in charge of his safety and escorted him back and forth to school.

I began my sixth year at Chang-Chon Elementary, ranking number one in the class. I had narrowed it down to Kyung-Gi by then, the number-one-ranking junior high school in the nation. Shortly thereafter, my siblings and I moved to America, where our parents were waiting for us. I was old enough to enter the second semester of seventh grade, allowing me to finish high school in only ten and a half years of schooling.

I would never realize the goal I had pursued for the past five years in Korea. Embedded deep inside me was the question that stayed with me for years to come: Was I good enough to pass the Kyung-Gi entrance exam? I believed so. Was it a blessing or a misfortune in coming to America? The answer would change with the seasons.

CHAPTER 6

1967—Mother Buried

Sunday represents the resurrection of Jesus, his victory over death. I am told that is why Christians worshipped God on Sundays rather than on the Sabbath, which is Saturday. This victory of Jesus gives us the comfort in knowing we would see our mom again in heaven.

But when her coffin was underground, that knowledge was hardly enough to sustain me from being overwhelmed with the grief. She was taken from us at a tender age of thirty-five. My heart ached so badly I wanted to die. I wanted Mother to resurrect on that Sunday, the third day after her death. It was not to be so. She went on to join Jesus by his side, leaving us behind. She was in a place of no more pain and sorrow.

During our ride home from the funeral, in the limousine, Joey and Judy were preoccupied with all the neat stuff that makes limos so cool. I was unable to concentrate on anything other than the way Dad was behaving.

He didn't even open his eyes. He had already loosened his necktie and slumped against the seat. His face seemed so pale. He had aged a good ten years in the last three days.

Once we arrived at home, he went straight to his room, closing the door. There was something seriously wrong about the way he was acting. I was witnessing a side of him I had never seen before. This was the man who had taken on the cares of the whole village and enjoyed every moment of it.

Normally, he would have welcomed the opportunities to show his flock that no matter what the circumstances are, God was there for us. Today, he was letting the opportunity slip away from him as he was subdued by his grief.

Whenever he had experienced difficulties in the past, he had the luxury of having Mother on his side. He had drawn strength from her as we all had. Now she was the cause of his pain and sorrow. She was no longer there to speak quiet yet strong words of encouragement to him.

After the funeral, the ladies of the church took on the duties of the host back at our home. The well-wishers made up of Dad's classmates, professors, students, and parishioners from the church along with our neighbors had gathered at our home to console us.

I couldn't get out of my suit fast enough, as did Joey. When the crowd had dissipated, the ladies did all the cleaning and putting away of the food. It looked as if we wouldn't have to cook for the next several days. Soon, all the guests had left, and we were left alone.

Once again, darkness loomed over us. Joey and Judy were watching the television in the living room. When I asked them to get ready for bed as it was a school night, the usual disagreements and groans did not come. I should have been glad, yet it actually made me feel sad. I thought I was to expect some haggles and negotiations, and the way I was feeling, I would have welcomed a little sassy talk from Judy.

Dad did not eat for the following three days. For that matter, he didn't even come out of his room. When I knocked on his door with the food, he had simply told me to go away. I stopped knocking on his door. Dad's depression kept him mostly in his room. Officially, he was on emergency leave from the school and church duties. I didn't know if a parent could take a leave of absence from caring for their children.

When he had finally emerged from his room to eat and read the mail, Dad was nonresponsive to me and the children. He ate while reading the letters and cards from the well-wishers and returned to his darkened room, leaving behind the dirty dishes and the opened letters for me to tend to.

I had to learn how to write checks to pay the bills. I would fill out the check, leaving it for Dad's signature, which he would sign and place on the kitchen table. I would place it in the envelope and stamp it before mailing it. It wasn't so difficult.

I was willing to take on all of Mom's duties. I didn't think I was capable of taking on Dad's as well, but some things I could manage. I needed Dad so badly, but he was unable to take care of himself. I was forced to grow too fast too soon.

It was a couple of weeks after Mom's funeral that I received my first beating from my dad. It came out of nowhere. I'm uncertain of what had caused it. All I did was to tell him I needed some money for the groceries. He slapped me hard across the face and then started to imitate Cassius Clay doing one of his finishing acts on his opponents before putting them down for the count, except it was my dad doing the number on me.

I couldn't believe what was happening. The second-degree black belt in me said to counterattack. Instead, I began pleading with Dad to stop hurting me. It was scary as he did not seem to hear me. His eyes were glossy and unfocused, like a zombie. He was chasing me down the stairs, kicking me, in a blind rage. He didn't stop for nearly ten minutes.

I tried to avoid him after that beating. I was unable to go to school for the following three days due to the bruises on my face. I tried on Mother's foundation cream I found in the living room to cover the bruises, but it was simply too big of an area to try and cover.

Trying to avoid him was awkward as staying home from school meant he and I were spending the whole day in the same house without speaking to one another.

By the time the weekend came around, the black eye had turned yellow green. By Monday, it was nothing more than a slight discoloration around my left eye. No one had suspected that I had sustained injuries from my father.

Eventually, I would become quite good at masking injuries and bruises. I got pretty good at telling lies to excuse away the injuries. But some of my friends began to suspect I was being abused by my dad.

The thoughts of suicide began entering my mind. It was bad enough that Mom had died. Now, I had to shop for our groceries, vacuum and clean the house, do the laundry, and feed the family, while Dad was fighting with his depression.

In addition, I wanted to be a good student. If that wasn't enough pressure for me to deal with, I was getting beat up by my own father. If I had failed to perform any of my duties as a son or as a brother, it would have seemed less painful and I would have been less resentful.

I began thinking of how I should end my life. I thought of the older boys back in O-Jung, praying for the commie soldiers that had maimed them, asking God to forgive the soldiers for their acts.

I wondered whether I could forgive my father for what he had done to me. My desire to die became even more prominent as I thought of forgiving him. How is it that those older boys were able to forgive the enemy soldiers? Why is it that I could not even forgive my own father? There had to be something wrong with me, so I believed. My heart and spirit were disjointed. My love for Dad wasn't enough to forgive him for his attacks on me.

It was years later that I came to understand my father was not a bad person but a sick individual with a disease. Such a realization became instrumental in forgiving my father and asking God to forgive him.

For now, I realized I didn't know how to go about forgiving him. I was simply too young and in too much pain to try and understand the man who was hurting me. It was going to take some time, some healing, before I could forgive my dad from the bottom of my heart. For now, it was all I could do to keep myself from committing suicide.

CHAPTER 7

Dad's Recollection of His Childhood

When the presence of Kim Il-Sung's North Korean Army became increasingly hostile just prior to its attack on South Korea, my village evacuated and headed south. My father was a town mayor whose authority had long been taken from him. They had repeatedly arrested my father and forced him to spend many days in the wet clay-floored prison cells, which lead to his tuberculosis condition that caused him more than a little trouble during his remaining years.

Some village folks from this northernmost region of our nation had chosen to stay, but most of us had gathered what we could in knapsacks and headed south. We waited until the beginning of the year when the rivers froze so we could cross them on foot. A few months after we had left on Sunday morning of June 25, 1950, Kim's army attacked the unsuspecting south resting before their Sunday worships.

I had just turned twenty-one and was the oldest of three boys. My brother, who was nineteen at the time, was killed by an errand bullet meant for someone else, as our family was going through Pyongyang during the evacuation.

He was in the wrong place at the wrong time. A rebel was being chased by a Red Army soldier whose aim was much to be desired. Instead of the rebel, my brother got shot and killed. He was not only my brother but my best friend as well. We had a wonderful time together as we grew up.

We were unable to give him a proper burial. My parents and I and my baby brother, who is seven years younger than me, stood beside a shallow grave, silently praying we'd be granted an opportunity one day to return home and give him the proper burial.

As it turned out, that opportunity never came as the peninsula remains divided ever since.

It was not uncommon to experience such tragedy during this frantic period as many of my neighbors had buried their young ones in haste as well. Many had rebelled against the Red Army soldiers, sacrificing their lives.

My father gave us instructions that if we were to become separated during the evacuation, we'd meet at the Seoul central train station on his next birthday, a month away.

During our escape to the south, our family did split up. At times, it was too dangerous to be grouped together, when the commies were patrolling. Those caught were shot to death as they were deemed traitors running to be with the enemy Americans.

As instructed by my father, I rejoined my parents in Seoul, in front of the train station, on his birthday. I recognized my parents right away as they crossed the open plaza toward the building. My younger brother, who was thirteen at the time, did not join us that day. We waited until after five o'clock before we left the train station.

It was a bittersweet birthday for my father, unwilling to celebrate until he was reunited with his baby boy. He hugged me and held me for a long time before leading the way to a temporary housing he had secured for us. It was near our dinnertime, so we stopped on our way to have dinner at a restaurant famous for its North Korean—style *soon-dae goog* (sausage soup). It was jam-packed, and some of the people were recognizable from during the evacuation. My father was glad he had at least one son by his side. He was going to celebrate by having a fine meal.

It would be two years before my baby brother reappeared, a month after we had buried Mother after she had died of tuberculosis. Instructed by my father, I was sent to Seoul train station on each of his birthdays, hoping my baby brother would show up. I located my brother among the crowd. He had grown a lot in two years, but I was able to recognize his walk right away.

He had been shining shoes for the American GIs in Busan to survive, forgetting the instruction given to him by our father. Two of Father's birthdays had gone by before he had realized he needed to be in Seoul. He made his way and waited at the train station for two weeks until Father's third birthday since the evacuation. At fifteen, he was already taller than my father and me.

I turned twenty-two years old when the bickering between the two sides of the peninsula had turned into a full-blown war. As we settled south of the border, I was accepted by the army academy to become an officer. Two years later, I graduated from the academy as a clergyman.

The school program was accelerated and in many cases without the appropriate texts for the courses. However, everyone enrolled in the academy had considered it a blessing to study during the war. There were evacuations during the course of our studies, but everyone took it in stride.

I enjoyed my work as a chaplain even though I was far too young to understand all the implications of wearing a collar. While I did not face the actual battles against the Red Army, I did have plenty to battle against. Most of my challenges were against the predominant Buddhism that made up the general population of the soldiers.

I gladly gave my pay to my father, who was living with me and my baby brother in Busan. My brother continued with his high school education while making extra money working for a rice merchant, making deliveries on their bicycle after school.

I began making friends with the American chaplains and studied English hard to improve my vocabularies. Soon, I had gained many American friends. My English improved as days went by.

Shortly after becoming a chaplain and during the ministers' gathering in Busan, I met a dynamic lady pastor. I discovered that she had two beautiful unwed daughters who were well educated. I would fall in love with the elder of the twins, and she would accept my proposal a few months later. Less than a week after hearing the news that his son was about to be wed, my father passed away due to TB as well. My brother and I buried him next to our mother, joining them once again. My brother moved to Seoul to begin attending a business school on a scholarship.

My fiancée and I waited until the war was over before the matrimony took place. It was a simple wedding. Soon Jae-chul, our first child, was born in 1954. Three years later, my wife gave birth to our second son, Jae-min.

Shortly thereafter, my American friends had paved the way for me to study at the Calvin School of Theology in Grand Rapids, Michigan, to earn my masters in theology.

I returned home two years later to a beautiful family, with a wonderful future ahead of me. I was given a position in Seoul as a social worker for the physically challenged. I relocated my family to a suburb of Seoul. About a year later, Jae-hyun, our third child and first daughter, was born.

My wife and I could not have been happier. While she was happy with the two boys, I knew she had secretly wished for a girl. Even with the birth of a baby girl, my desire to return to America had never died out. In 1964, my dream came true when the School of Theology, a graduate school of Denver University, had accepted my application for their doctorate program.

I began a fall semester that same year, and shortly after, my lovely bride had joined me. Our three children were left behind with my mother-in-law in her parsonage. Their visas were yet to be approved. It would be another long year—a total of two years since I left Korea—before our children joined us in America. Life seemed complete and satisfying.

I stayed busy working on my thesis while ministering to about sixty members attending the Korean Christian Church I had founded. A handful of Korean women who had married American soldiers and moved to America had ended up in the area of the Lowry Air Force Base located on the east side of Denver. Their children wished to learn Korean, and the parents wished their children be bicultural as well as bilingual. I decided it was time for Denver to have a Korean-speaking Christian church.

What had been a three-year plan to earn my degree would turn out much longer than expected. It seemed much more challenging than I had anticipated, caring for the needs of my family as well as the congregation becoming a higher priority to my studies at times.

I could not have done it without my strong-willed wife standing by my side. She was the solid rock on which I stood while the world around me shook with challenges and difficulties. Often, it was she who had stayed up all night to have my paper ready on time.

On that fateful day, after our children had gone to school, my wife and I were returning home from Montgomery Ward after looking at some china sets. We had been entertaining lots of guests, and our plates seemed so inadequate for some of the occasions.

The traffic light had turned green for us, when a man who had been drinking all night ran a red light and hit our station wagon just as we started to cross the intersection.

My lovely bride died on the way to the hospital. I had sustained numerous physical injuries, but nothing as serious as the emotional trauma I had sustained from losing my wife. It shook and rattled my faith in God.

All the training I received as a social worker and experiences gained while serving as a pastor was unable to prepare me to deal with the pain I experienced. How do you prepare for such an event as this? I tried to muster up enough energy to be strong for my children.

I prayed and I called out to God. It seemed less than effective in helping me to regain my strength and maintain my mental health, let alone spiritual health. God was listening. Silently, God listened to every word uttered in moment of devastation.

Without the support of my wife, I did not think I could carry on with my life. I realized just how much I had come to depend on her during my difficulties. The rock was no longer there for me. I simply collapsed as a being. I ran to my box to hide.

CHAPTER 8

Dad's Account of His "Box"

It's been three decades since I had been inside that wooden box. It was a wooden crate, actually, that had served as my secure hiding place during my childhood. In 1933, when I was five years old, our neighbor who shared a dividing wall with us to the east had a celebration of the decade at his house. Mr. Lee (unrelated to us) had sent his only son to Tokyo University medical school to study medicine.

The younger Lee returned home four years later as a medical doctor, which was the cause for a bash so memorable that village folks talked about it with much fondness for many years.

It so happened that our young doctor had brought with him, through the ocean voyage from Japan, a wooden cube crate about three and a half feet in each length. In this box, he had with him valuable medical books and references along with some delicate equipment that would have been difficult to obtain near our village.

Once the contents were emptied, this well-crafted wooden box with a fitted lid was too precious to be discarded and found a home in their barn. This barn was nothing more than a large storage shed. As a preschool boy I would use the box for hide-and-seek games. It was nearly a perfect place to hide away from everyone. Not everyone had the liberty to go in and out of Lee's barn as I had. I found a piece of wood to serve as a prop against the lid, keeping it open as I climbed in and out.

Once I was inside the box, I lowered the lid with the stick, keeping it from slamming down and making a loud noise. The hinge made a creaking sound, which almost gave me away once, so I found some axle grease and silenced the noise that might give me away.

During my first year in school, I was forced to fight a bully a year older than me. Neither of us could edge out the other, and the fight had ended in a draw.

As I turned to walk away, this bully who was a bit taller had tackled me from the back, knocking us both to the ground, with me underneath him. When my forehead hit the ground, it bounced back upward toward the bully's face. His upper front teeth came in contact with the back of my head, leaving a nice gash on top of my head.

When we stood, his two upper teeth were bent inward and loose, barely hanging. He looked goofy, and I laughed, forgetting for a moment that I was in pain and bleeding badly. He would begin crying and stop me from further laughing when his teeth ended up between his fingers. It broke loose as he tried to push them forward to its original position. It became completely separated from the gum, leaving a wide-open gap in his mouth.

My mother was normally very calm, but when she saw the bloody shirt and then found a gash in my head, she went ballistic. She nearly dropped my baby brother she was nursing, and she took me to the druggist who used alcohol to sanitize the injured area before using a razor to shave the top of my head. I looked like a monk—bald on top with bush of hair all around the shiny center. He then put some medicine and ointment on my gash before placing gauze and tape over it.

Holding the items from the druggist in a paper bag, I followed Mother home. Realizing that I was not in danger of dying, her attention had returned to the baby boy she had left with the maid. She dearly wanted to arrive home before my father did. She was doing double-time steps, making it difficult for me to keep up with her.

My father was summoned to the constable's office that night. The constable had asked for me to come along as well. The parents of the bully had made a claim against my father for their son's dentist bill. They threatened to ruin my father's reputation as a politician and the town's real estate broker if he did not pay them in full. Once the eyewitnesses' accounts were gathered, it was a slam-dunk case against the bully. The bully had caused the fall and the injury and was thus responsible for my medical bills instead.

I was exonerated, and Father did not need to pay the bully's medical bill. His honor remained intact. No harm, no foul. Until I got home, that is. I received the first beating of my life.

The whole town must have heard the beating and my loud wailing that went on for quite some time. Everyone knew I was innocent, yet no one blamed my father for giving me that beating. No one, including my mother, came to the rescue of a boy with a gash on his head getting a beating of his life. Anyone who tried would have ended up in the receiving end of my father's ire.

There were other such beatings that took place in the village that no one made any fuss about. Mrs. Jun was beaten up by her husband on their honeymoon evening, and it continued for a decade before he eventually broke her ribs.

The town elders had to put a stop to his drinking-and-beating sprees after that incident. Mr. Jun was known to beat the mules that pulled his fish wagon. These mules would be fine on their way to the harbor, pulling an empty wagon. Their return trip would usually begin with some serious whipping as these lazy animals refused to budge with such a heavy load, now going up the hill. All that fish weighed down with salt and chunks of ice was plenty heavy.

His method of coaxing the animals was less than kind to everyone's view, but no one said anything to him. They were his stubborn mules, and he could do whatever he saw fit. You would think his wife would have thought longer about marrying a man with such bad a temper. Then again, every male in town did the same and got away with it as well.

The town's fish marketer finally learned to get along with his bride once he stopped drinking his profits away. Now, his wife could be seen at their market alongside her smiling husband as they served their customers. It was a nice ending to their story.

For the older boys in the village, broken bones were reasons for bragging and not for sympathy. The folks will tell you the first beating usually leaves the worst of scars and can be the most terrifying.

I agree. Until that moment, my father was my safe haven. In an instant, he became the terror of my life. Subsequent beatings were just as painful, just not as shocking. Father had unleashed the beast in him that we had not seen before.

The beatings came more frequently, and my injuries got more severe. I learned to brag about the broken nose, the fat lips, and the bruises as I believed it was part of growing up. It certainly was in our village anyway.

Several months after that fight incident, I broke the living room mirror. This mirror that my father used to check his appearance each time before leaving the house was shattered into pieces. Mother and the maid had gone to the market to gather ingredients for our dinner. Perhaps the dinner that would be my last one.

The maid, a young widow who was hired to help Mother with the cleaning and cooking since the birth of my baby brother, had used too much wax on our wooden living room floor that morning.

I discovered I could slide all the way across the large room on my socks if I gave a little running start. I started to slide across the room back and forth until I lost control and ran into the mirror that hung in the middle of our living room wall. Now it lay, spread across the floor in thousand pieces.

My life flashed by me, and I knew I was dead the moment Father came home. I had a two-hour window of opportunity before Father would be home from work, to pack up a bag and leave town. Then I remembered the box.

I dressed in warm clothing and went to the kitchen to look for food to eat while hiding in the box. A bamboo basket full of boiled sweet potatoes was on the counter next to the hard-boiled eggs. I knew better than to touch Father's favorite, so instead, I grabbed one tuber on each hand and went to the box. I climbed in and pulled the lid over me.

For the next six hours, I remained in that box inside the neighbor's barn, leaned up against its side. At first, I felt scared, but soon, my attention turned to just how uncomfortable being in the box could be. I thought of getting some candles and matches for future use.

I heard Mom and the maid call out for me, searching anxiously as the dinner was ready and I was nowhere to be found. Never have I ever been late for dinner before. Eventually, both of the ladies gave up searching and went inside. Father would not enjoy being kept from his dinner. We ate dinner at six o'clock every single day. No variations.

They went in to have their meal on schedule. I ate my first sweet potato and decided to save the other one for later. About three minutes later, I ate the second.

I stayed inside the box, trying not to make any noises that could give me away. The ladies must have finished with their supper and the cleaning, as they returned outside to resume searching for me. I could see Mother had strapped my baby brother on her back in blanket, as I peered out the thin space between two boards. I did nothing to help them find me. I remained motionless, breathing ever so quietly.

When Mother walked by the barn her third time, I almost called out for her, hoping to solicit her help to defend me against Father's beating. It had dawned on me that wasn't going to happen. Mother would never face Father in defiance. She had learned her lesson by now. I swallowed my breath as she walked away, calling out for me.

Her voice had become far more urgent, and her pace had quickened since her first search. I just remained silent, letting my mother terrorize her mind with all the terrible scenarios happening to her son.

She frantically searched for her evil son so she could present him before the royal throne for that royal whipping. It seemed less than wise to reveal myself to her. I did not think it was wise to give away my hiding spot either. So I remained quiet and wise in that box for the remainder of six hours. I planned to sneak out after the lamp snuffer had made the rounds, extinguishing village streetlamps.

When I tried to sneak into my room, I realized how loud my sliding door was. It made so much noise it stopped me stiff with fear of being caught. Everyone must have heard me.

Sure enough, I heard the stir from the parents' room across the living room. It was my baby brother who began crying. I braced myself for the inevitable punishment I had thus far been able to delay. I slid open the door and quickly got into my room and into the rolled-out mat, startling my six-year-old little brother, waking him out of his sleep.

Then I heard a door open and close. I placed my hand over his mouth, as he lay next to me. Someone was definitely walking across the wooden living room toward my room. I pulled the blanket over my head.

My door opened and closed. I just remained inside the blankets, motionless. Quiet steps approached and sat next to my backside, as I lay on my left side, motionless. It was Mother. She quietly pulled the blanket down and placed her hand on my cheek. It smelled like my baby brother. Then, she proceeded to pinch me really hard. It felt as if my face was torn off from me.

"Owwww. Mother, what are you doing? Ooowwwww," I protested quietly. The more I protested, the harder she pinched me.

"What? Owwww? You crazy son of mine, do you think you have the right to open your trap and make a peep after what you have put your terrified mother through? You are no good, that's what you are. Tsk, tsk, tsk." Mother was yelling, but I could tell she was relieved to see her child was safely home.

"You are hungry, aren't you, my good-for-nothing son? Your father will kill you tomorrow, and I must bury you then, but I suppose I could go and get your last morsel. My crazy-and-dead son is what you are, beaten to death and buried come tomorrow." As Mother stood, I heard my brother snickering, holding his nose with his fingers, trying hard not to break out in laughter.

"I don't feel like eating, Mother," I protested quietly. I feared all the fuss would encourage my father into activity of his own. He did not appreciate being disturbed during his bedtime. Rarely would he get out of bed unless it was an emergency.

She was gone by the time the words escaped my mouth. Minutes later, she returned with a tray. She had *shik-heh* in a medium-sized metal bowl and a wet towel.

The *shik-heh* was nicely chilled from the block of ice inside the large jar container where she kept it. *Shik-heh* was my favorite drink. It is made by sweetened fermenting rice consumed before it becomes alcohol. "Drink this. It's too late for you to eat a heavy meal," said Mother.

I gulped the bowl in one swig. My gulping noise had made my little brother sit up. I gave him the bowl. Realizing it was empty, he protested. *Who's laughing now, you little unsympathetic one?*

Mom used the wet towel to wipe away at my face, then my hands and feet, before quietly closing the door behind her and walking away. I heard no more from her until the crowing of roosters. I slept soundly.

As I came to, I sat up in terror the moment I remembered the broken mirror. Father was about to come into my room to reckon with me, rendering his judgment upon this fragile body. Woe is me.

My father had two methods of punishments. When he had the time to ponder on the crime I had committed, he could be rational and use his "concentration rod." It was a wooden dowel a meter long, with an average size of a man's thumb in diameter. He had grounded the ends smoothly as to not scratch me or poke my eye out while beating the crap out of me with it.

He also had a volatile and unpredictable side that when he lost control, he would kick and choke me until I passed out. Of course, I was more than willing to extend my hands side by side facing up so that my father could render his punishments upon them. It stung but was nothing compared to his choking and was certainly my preference among his corporal punishments.

Never had there been a greater sin committed by me than shattering Father's mirror. It was one of the few and cherished items from Father's childhood. But I figured he had plenty of time to calm down and thus will soon enter my room with his concentration-inducing rod.

The door will slowly open, as he is a methodical and deliberate man who did everything slowly. Then, in a like manner, he will start to whip me with his rod. Soon, my concentration will be restored as I repent for my sin and seek his forgiveness. I will once again be standing on a clean slate. We will all go back to our lives as if nothing had happened.

Father did not come to my room that morning. He was gone by the time I got ready for breakfast. The shattered glass pieces were gone, and the wooden part of the mirror was not there either. I looked at the bare wall where the full-length mirror used to be. It seemed so bare.

Before heading out to school, I noticed the bare wall glaring at me, blaming me for its nakedness. When I returned home from school, I saw Father's shoes at the entrance. He was home earlier than usual. He came home early to teach me a lesson I would never forget.

When I entered the living room, I saw the same mirror that I had shattered yesterday, hanging in the same place it had always been. So focused was my mind on the mirror as I approached it, I did not see or hear my father slowly approaching me while rolling up his sleeves.

In the mirror, I saw him just as his fist flew toward me. He proceeded to give me a whipping that no eight-year-old boy should have experienced receiving from his beloved father.

As I came out of unconsciousness the following day, Mother was sitting next to me, nursing my baby brother while murmuring about her rotten and abusive husband. I could not open my eyes. My face felt twice the normal size, completely numb. I was black and purple from head to toes.

My father said he would never forgive a son who runs and hides after his misdeeds. He said he had the duty to teach me to be responsible for my actions. That was the last thing I remembered before he knocked me out cold.

Most of the bruises came after I was knocked out. I felt betrayed by the man I had placed all my trust in. The man who should be protecting me from the dangers of the world had violated the sanctity of his son's trust.

In a few days, I was up and running again. I would anger Father again, or should I say, he would anger himself again because I never intended to anger him. Stubbornly, I would learn to resist more each time. Each time I thought he was planning to beat me, I ran to the box and stayed there until I felt safe to come out.

Since the mirror incident, I took an old blanket and some padding materials for the box. Later, I would find candle stubs and some matches to keep in the box. I stayed in the box all night long a few days later, when I felt Father was going to punish me. He was furious when he saw me the following day.

I ran away from him and stayed under the school building that Saturday night. School was empty, but I stayed in the crawl space under the building, fearing Father would have the constable looking for me in the buildings.

The following evening, I returned home but could not go in. I could not muster up enough nerve to do it. So instead, I went to the box and slept there. I had not eaten for two days and was cold but felt safe.

I slept peacefully until the crowing of the roosters. By the time my father had finally caught up with me in a few days, he had calmed enough to be more rational. I had banked on that. This went on for about a year.

Then one day, while I was hiding inside the box after getting into a fistfight with a classmate, I heard someone walking toward the box. The lid was lifted open. A lantern in his hand had revealed the face of my angry father who would beat me for the next hour.

He told me to get out of the box. He had been curious as to where his little weasel of a son was hiding each time he had disappeared and did some investigation of his own.

One day, after a rain, he had found my footsteps leading right to the Lees' barn. It didn't take long for him to figure out that I was inside this box. There, in the middle of our neighbor's barn, he gave me the most severe beating thus far. I cried out to him.

"Father, please stop." The voice sounded as if from an echo chamber, coming from elsewhere and not from me. When I opened my eyes, I was not in the barn getting beat up by the town's mayor, my father. I was in America, and my son Jimmy was on my bedroom floor, bleeding from his mouth and nose. He was looking up at me in bewilderment pleading, "Dad, please stop."

My God, what was going on? What just happened? Something that I had dreaded since becoming a Father seemed to have just happened. Having learned about the likelihood of a person being abused becoming an abuser in my counseling courses, I had it at the back of my head all these years.

I had feared I would one day become abusive to my children as my father had been to me. One moment, I was a child hiding in my box of safety; the next minute, I was the monster attacking my child.

As I had kept my anger and violence in check since the marriage, I had thought the disease had been eradicated and that it was managed. I truly believed that I was able to live normally. Now, I just became a validation of what the social scientists have claimed.

When I realized I had slapped my son, I should have stopped immediately. Yet I became even angrier. I was consumed with anger I felt as a child beaten by my father. I began hitting and kicking Jimmy as I chased him down the stairs, but I could not stop myself.

I should have been grateful to my son Jimmy, whom I had named after my favorite professor, Dr. James Hill. Jimmy took on the responsibility to care for my younger children when I was unable to as I was overwhelmed by the pain of losing my wife. He was more than I could have asked for as he took on the household chores as well as taking charge over his siblings.

I would never have forsaken the children had James not taken on the responsibilities to care for them as thoughtfully as he did. Unwittingly, he had enabled me to neglect my duties, and here I was attacking my biggest supporter, my number-one fan.

I knew Jimmy was trying very hard to fill the void I had created with my neglect. What I wanted to do was to hug him and tell him I loved him and that I appreciated all that he was doing. Instead, I was overwhelmed with anger and sadness at the same time.

My heart was aching with remorse, yet I was unable to apologize. It led to anguish in frustration. Now I was a coward as well. How many times have I said to myself that I would not be like my own father? Yet here I was doing exactly what I said I would not do.

I had become the monster I had despised so badly as I was growing up. Later, when I saw James with the bruises and walking with a limp, it broke my heart. An abused had indeed become an abuser.

Here I am; I could not even stop myself from hurting my own child. I believed I could help others and became a minister, but now I realized it was a mistake. My self-esteem was at its lowest point in my life.

CHAPTER 9

1967—Life as a "Bother"

At first, it wasn't so difficult being a "bother." A *bother* is a brother with motherly duties. "Bother" is what I have become to Joey and Judy since the death of our mother.

Checking to see if the kids had done their homework was easy enough. Both Joey and Judy were passionate about anything that had to do with school. Actually, I had to work hard just to keep up with their enthusiasm. Getting them to clean their rooms and take baths, however, was becoming more and more challenging each day.

At first, I tried diplomacy. When that didn't work, I tried the bribery, which didn't last long either. Eventually I had to implement martial law. After all, I grew up in South Korea where President Park ruled the country with his army after his successful coup d'état.

I've learned that martial law meant "you do what I say." President Park did not, however, have the likes of Judy as an opposition. It wasn't that she didn't enjoy having a clean room or taking a daily bath. She simply didn't care for anyone ordering her around. So I even tried to cheer them up whenever possible.

"Hey, guys, you know what I was thinking? Since you no longer have a mother and I have to fill in for her, now that makes me your 'bother,' get it? Brother and a mother combined to a *bo-ther*."

"You're a *bother* all right, oppa. I wish you would stop *bothering* me and go *bother* somebody else, tee-hee." It pleased me that Judy hadn't lost her sense of humor. It pleased me a lot.

One Saturday morning, I discovered that Joey's and Judy's rooms were in need of straightening. I told them they wouldn't get any food until their rooms were in order. Joey took about half an hour to finish cleaning his room. But Judy would go on all day without any food. She refused to give in.

The next day after church, we were at professor Cho's estate, following the Sunday worship service. I couldn't impose the "Lee house" economic sanctions on Judy while at Cho's, so she ate, chewing with extra motions while looking at me with a smirk on her face after each bite.

My maternal grandma became widowed at the age of twenty-six. She was about to commit suicide with my mother and her womb-mate. Ending her life with her two newborn infants seemed fitting to her. My maternal grandfather was the eldest son of a wealthy family. They were able to send him to Tokyo to study. He had died suddenly, leaving my grandma and her twin infants behind.

Just as my grandma, with her two children, was about to jump into the fast river from the bridge above, she had heard the voice of God prohibiting her from doing so. She had dedicated her life at that moment to become an evangelist to spread the Gospel and the love of God.

She was promptly disowned by her devout Buddhist father-in-law. She and her children were not allowed to return to their estate until she came to her senses. My grandmother never returned to her in-laws.

She raised her two daughters well on her own, sending both to a prominent college. During the war, not many young women had the luxury to attend a university. It was a rare and precious privilege, even for the wealthy. It was nearly an impossible feat for a single mother of twin girls to accomplish on her own.

Her spirit was both revered and feared. Many men had gone toe-to-toe with Grandma to discover they were no match for her. It was from Grandma that Judy got her stubbornness, her strong will.

Eventually, Mom and Aunt would attend Ee-Hwa, a top-notch women-only university. Mother majored in home economics. Aunt became a teacher, eventually serving as a principal at a prominent private school. It was considered a great catch to marry an Ee-Hwa graduate.

Grandma had instilled in them the importance of education. Her dedication to family was passed on to Mom and subsequently to us.

Caring for her family was a joy and pleasure for Mom. She enjoyed discussing with my aunt how to go about motivating us children to excel in our studies and take pleasure in doing so. I certainly enjoyed pleasing Mom who seemed to enjoy excellence in my efforts.

My mom knew how to run a tight ship. She supported my father as he was finishing his PhD on a meager salary from the church. We didn't have a whole lot, but we never experienced lack. Until now, that is.

We were disorganized. We couldn't find things, forcing us to go without. Most of all, we were doing without some good homemade food. Some soul food from Seoul could've lifted up our hungry spirits.

Without Mom, life was not the same. Judy lacked some female touch in her life. I needed a protector as Dad's beating became more frequent, more injurious. Dad needed to get his life back in order. We needed our mom back. She would have turned over in her grave if she knew what was happening to us.

It pained me at first as I believed it was my doing that caused Dad to lash out at me. I was a bother to him when I wanted to be a good son instead. I never asked Dad for money again. I found out there was money to be made by mowing lawns and shoveling snows.

During the summer of 1968, I started a lawn-care business. I mowed neighbors' yards and helped them plant flowers and provided care for their flower gardens.

During the fall, I helped rake their yards and clean out the gutters. When the snowstorms hit us, I was ecstatic, knowing there was money to be made shoveling tons of snow out of the way so my neighbors could get out of their garages.

Within a year, I had saved nearly two thousand dollars while spending some when there were needs, such as repairs to my lawn equipments and upgrading my bike to handle the paper route.

Considering the down payment for our home a couple of years ago was only three thousand dollars, it was a considerable amount of money, especially for a fourteen-year-old. I offered Dad all of it. I thought if it was the money situation that made him go off on me, I would help him get it. Soon, I discovered it had nothing to do with money.

The Maroni family lived across the street from us. One day, shortly after Mom had passed away, Mrs. Maroni brought us freshly baked lasagna along with her homemade sausages slowly cooked in the roaster.

When I begged her to teach me how to cook the stuff, she invited me over the next day to learn how to make marinara sauce and to prepare spaghetti the proper way.

What should have been a happy moment had turned into a nightmare for me. I had forgotten all about one simple instruction given to me by Dino's mom. "Dino Maroni Full of Baloney" was what everyone called my neighbor, who was a year behind me in school. He was a short and pudgy kid who was not well liked by the others.

I walked to the school bus stop two blocks away with him each morning during the weekdays. I thought he was a nice kid, but he was getting picked on a lot. I think his mom knew I was looking out for him at school. Maria Maroni knew how to cook Italian dishes, and she knew how to show her appreciation.

She said when you're cooking with tomato sauce, it required constant stirring, or else it would burn at the bottom of the pot. I found that out the hard way.

A week after learning the secret to Maroni's spaghetti sauce, I proudly prepared and served my family the best spaghetti they've ever had. Even the finicky Judy had asked for a second serving.

Once the dinner was over and during the washing, I discovered that at the bottom of the pot was a layer of blackened sauce. My effort to scrub it away had failed to meet the approval of my dad.

Just as I was headed for the shower to wash away the smell of burnt char and the sweat from all the scrubbing, I heard Dad yelling for me.

"Jimmy." Dad was obviously upset about something.

In horror, I answered, "Yes, Dad?"

"Come here," he summoned me into the kitchen. His voice sounded threatening, and I dreaded finding out what was bothering him. "You call this clean?" Dad shouted at me as I walked into the kitchen. He was pointing at the pot I had just finished scrubbing. He was going to put it away for me and discovered the bottom of the inside was still black.

"I scrubbed on it, and it just wouldn't come all the way out, Dad," I tried to explain to him in my best pleading voice. It didn't gain his sympathy. Instead, he slapped me across the face, knocking me down to the kitchen floor.

He started yelling at me that I should have done a better job of cleaning the pot and that I was a lazy, no-good kid. I mostly shut him out, trying to duck and avoid his punches and kicks. My efforts to minimize my injuries caused him to be upset even more. Eventually I would learn not to move around when he was beating me.

That was against my tae kwon do training and very difficult to do, but it made the ordeal end quicker. On that day, however, I blocked one of his punches by automatic reflex, which caused quite a bit of anger in him. His raging went on for at least ten minutes even after I stopped blocking him.

When he was tired of beating me, he made me kneel and sit still on the kitchen floor. I could not move no matter how uncomfortable or painful it was.

To me, he was behaving like a psycho. After slapping me around or beating me, he would then turn around and act as my best pal. He would yell at me for five minutes and then ask me in a calm voice if we should take the kids and go to the Yum Yum Tree Chinese restaurant for dinner. He was no longer someone I could confide in or rely on. I didn't know who he was.

I was sitting on my knees for nearly fifteen minutes. My dad came into the kitchen on several occasions, silently, to see if I had moved since he had checked last. I was onto him and did not move.

"Try cleaning it again, and this time, do it right," he said, in a gentle and calm voice. As I stood up, he yanked at my hair and forced me to sit on my knees again. "I said, try to clean it better this time, you hear me? Why won't you answer me? Are you being defiant?" he screamed at the top of his lungs, not the voice of Yoda just seconds ago.

"No, sir, I was anxious to get to the pot, that's all," I pleaded with him, only to be smacked on my face again.

"I will kill you before I allow you to get smart with me, you understand?"

"Yes, sir. I would never do that, Dad."

"Go and get it right this time," he said as he pushed me on my face, nearly knocking me down backward.

Ten minutes later, after a box of Ajax scrubbing pads were used up, I was pretty sure it was clean enough to satisfy him. All the black stains were gone, as I nearly put a hole on the bottom of the pot, scrubbing on the charred area.

"Dad, I'm finished with the pot," I spoke outside his bedroom door. He came out and passed by me and walked quickly to the kitchen. As he examined the pot, he seemed satisfied with my effort this time. I looked at him, trying to determine if that was the case. To him, however, my looking at him was deemed an act of rebellion. At least that's what he was saying as he continued to shout at me for the next few minutes.

I thought twice before cooking with tomato sauce again. I would learn to do magic as I discovered the Crock-Pot that did not stick. You put all the ingredients inside, turn it on, leave it alone, and go to school. When you come home, dinner is ready to be served.

What an invention. It solved my problem of sticky pots and pans. I wished all problems in life could be solved with Crock-Pots.

CHAPTER 10

1968—Joey

When you are a middle child, you could easily become invisible, as was the case for me. Especially with the exceptional siblings I have. When you look up in the dictionary *persona non grata*, you will see my name and photograph in the definition section.

The world is small to a little child. Mine was even smaller as what there was had been consumed by the extraordinary *keun-hyung* (big brother). When Jae-hyun was born, my world became even smaller, if that was possible. She was the most amazing girl, soaking up attention from everyone wherever she went.

When we moved to America, a lot had changed. There weren't many Asians living in Colorado at that time. That was good and bad. Good, that I was no longer invisible as Americans were curious about me. Bad, because everything I did became visible to everyone as well. I was making some silly, attention-getting mistakes at first. Some of the stupid things I did were not entirely my fault though.

For example, in America, when someone asks you a question and your answer is yes, you repeat yes over and over when the questions are repeated again and again. Not in Korea. When your answer is no for example, and they say, "No?" as in trying to confirm your answer, you will say yes to agree it is indeed correct. It is quite simple, yes?

No.

I was in Mrs. Taylor's class. It was the fourth-grade homeroom. Someone had brought a dead frog and placed it on the teacher's desk. When Mrs. Taylor walked into the classroom and discovered it, she asked who had done it. Someone said it was me. It was a terrible lie.

"Joseph Lee, did you put this frog on my desk?" she asked me.
"No," I answered.
"No?" she asked.
"Yes," I confirmed that she was correct.
"Did you say yes?" she asked again. *What is she, deaf all of a sudden?*
"No," I said, adamantly.
"No?" she asked again, much to my amazement.
"Yes," I confirmed once again that she has it correctly.
"Yes?" she asked.
"Noooooooo!" I said loudly. I was about to start crying. The whole class burst out laughing, and Mrs. Taylor finally backed off of me, trying to bring order to her class. She must have sensed that I was about to lose it.

It was quite some time after the episode I realized what had taken place on that day. Meantime, I was considered a troublemaker to Mrs. Taylor. And the whole class thought I was stupid or retarded.

When I was in Korea, I was the little brother of Jae-chul, the superstar of our school. He was good at all the sports, always making the school team. He was the top-ranking student of the school when we left Korea.

I was nobody, unless someone recognized that I walked home with the big man of the campus. Here in America, I was the big brother escorting Judy back and forth to school. I would never have to go to the same school Jimmy was attending at the same time.

When we moved after Mom's death, Jimmy transferred to Byers Junior High. When I'm ready to attend Byers, he'd move on to South High, not like JFK, where junior and senior high school were combined in one campus. The only problem was, now Judy was becoming recognized for her excellence in school, while I remained an average Joey.

Judy is a brilliant, perspicacious child with an ambition to be the best in everything she participated in. I decided to study as hard as I can, never to be outshined by a sibling again.

BOTHER

When my mom died, of course I was very sad. The only thing I had benefited from her passing was that I would no longer be sick to my stomach with jealousy when Mom doted on Jimmy and Judy while forgetting all about me. That sounds mean, and I would gladly let them have all the attention if it would bring Mom back.

Lots of things changed when Mom passed away. The mood around the house was dreary and gloomy, which was understandable. Jimmy seemed different—older and fastidious. He acted as if he was our parent, ordering me and Judy around. I was resentful of him and determined not to give in to his demands.

Something made me change my mind altogether. One day, while I was watching television with Judy in the living room, my father did something that was totally freaky. At first, I heard Dad yell something at Jimmy. Then, I heard loud noises and realized he was hitting Jimmy and kicking him down the stairs.

I was never so scared in my life. Judy began crying. I took her to my room and closed the door behind us, hoping Dad would not open it.
That evening, Judy and I went to sleep without our dinner or showers. We huddled together until Judy fell asleep in my bed. When I looked into Jimmy's room later, I saw him sobbing.
When I sat next to him, he turned and looked at me, with bruises all over his face. When I asked if he was okay, he told me he was fine. He was barely able to speak but told me and Judy to get ready for bed, as it was a school night.
I told him Judy was sleeping already. I got some ice from the freezer as he told me to and wrapped the plastic bag with a bath towel and started icing his wounds. Eventually he fell asleep. I sat by him all night long, watching him sleep, wondering what the heck was going on with our family.
I had a renewed respect and love for him from that day forward. He never spoke of it to me or Judy. When we asked him about it, he simply smiled and told us he had screwed up and got punished for it.
His desire to take care of me and Judy seemed to take away his personal motivations. He was no longer trying to be the best at everything. He was no longer motivated for his personal gains. He genuinely showed me his desire was for me and Judy to be the best we could be. He had grown up so much in a matter of just a few weeks.

I was proud to have a *hyung* like him and appreciated him more than ever before. One day he told me and Judy while laughing that we should call him "bother"—not quite our mother but no longer just a brother. I had gained a "bother."

I had lost a loving father and gained a mean and hateful monster. I wished Mom were still alive. Life no longer had any meaning for me.

CHAPTER 11

Apes and Bullies

Ron Stuckey had come to school one day with bruises on his face. When the teacher had discovered that his father had caused the bruises, police was alerted, and this resulted in the arrest of Mr. Stuckey.

Ron was taken to a foster home across the city while the court figured out the best place for him. He had to transfer to another school. I wasn't going to let that happen to my family. So when I received a beating, I didn't go to school. My injuries were too obvious to fool the teachers. I hadn't missed a day of school since coming to America. It was my first but wouldn't be the last. Of course, my GPA took a nosedive as well.

Shortly after that incident, our family moved near Washington Park. This community was totally different from the previous neighborhood. We left a newly developed urban area for the aging inner-city area, where the streets were narrow and heavily traveled. The neatly cared for huge yards were replaced with smaller turfs.

JFK Junior High consisted of predominantly Caucasian students and did not have many ethnics, while the new school had plenty. JFK was a new school with new buildings, while at Byers, the buildings were dilapidated and much smaller. So was our new home on Center Avenue. It was much closer to Dad's school and our church, but gone were the Parkers and the Maronis, as were the baked goods and all the pasta dishes. It was definitely a step backward, in my opinion.

On my first semester at Byers in ninth grade, I came home with four As and one B. My new best friend, Dwight West had three Bs and two As. His parents were so proud they bought him a Flying Dutchman ten-speed bicycle. His father was hoping Dwight would eventually go to a law school and join his law firm in the future.

For my effort, I got chewed out by my dad because I did not try harder to get all As as Joey and Judy had done. How proud he would have been, he said, had I done that. Instead, he was disappointed. So was I.

There was a school bully named Harold Addison. Everyone called him Addison the Ape behind his back. He was a head taller than most of us at school but clearly missing some fries upstairs to be a complete happy meal. He was flat-footed and not too graceful in movements, but had the reputation of packing a mean punch while able to take all the punches thrown at him. He was as strong as an ox and resembled an ape.

One day, during my lunch period, Dwight and I were sitting in the corner of our school cafeteria, eating and having a chat. Dwight could appear to be goofy with his long wavy auburn hair and freckles and carrying about ten pounds more than he should.

He was a gentle kid who was always polite to everyone. He didn't have a mean streak in him. I couldn't have asked for a better person to be my friend. He was loyal to a fault and backed me up no matter what. For some reason though, Addison the Ape never cared for my buddy, Dwight.

Addison and his buddies were sitting a couple of tables away from us. Over the chattering noises of the cafeteria, the Ape yelled out "Hey, carrottop" in his deep and loud voice, to which everyone started to laugh. Everyone but Dwight and I thought it was funny.

Since Dwight did not seem to have a problem with it, I was going to ignore Harold Addison as he kept on calling Dwight all kinds of names. But when the seventh graders joined in, I decided to put a stop to it.

It was before Bruce Lee (unrelated to me) or David Carradine (the actor) had brought popularity to the ancient art of kung fu through the movies and television series. Tae kwon do was not yet popular in America. Until that day, no one had seen anything like flying spin kicks or jumping side kicks.

This bully made a big mistake when he stood to face me as I approached him. It took only three kicks to send him to the nurse's office with cracked ribs. My spin kick had given him a set of fat bloody lips as well. His parents were summoned to take him to the hospital.

I was taken to the principal's office to be held until the police came to take me to the juvenile hall. It was protocol, the principal said, in a situation when a student was injured, to notify the police.

I felt exhilarated as I released my frustrations and bitter anger that was building up inside me on Addison the Ape. Dwight was waiting by the police car as I was handcuffed and led into the backseat. He had skipped his favorite class in order to see what would happen to me. The concerned look on his face was comforting for me to know I had a true friend. I winked at him to let him know everything was cool.

I stayed overnight at the juvenile hall. The next morning, I was both grateful and embarrassed to find Mr. West had come to appear before the court as my attorney. Dwight had told his father what had happened at school, and Mr. West appeared pro bono on my behalf. I would learn much later just how helpful it was to my case, as Mr. West was one of the most prominent criminal attorneys in the Denver area.

I spent an hour or so with the district attorney in his office, going over the charges and the settlement to be placed on probation. Any other defendants would've had this conversation in an interview room by an ADA rather than the DA himself in his office. Having Mr. West by my side had benefitted me tremendously.

Then, I was taken to stand before the judge. My father was ordered to stand next to Mr. West and me. The judge threatened to send me away for a long period if I did not get my act straight immediately. The misdemeanor charge of public disorder was to be expunged if I successfully completed probation.

As recommended by the prosecutor, I was given six-month probation. Returning from the court with Dad, I felt there was another beating on its way. My old man did not disappoint my intuition.

I ached everywhere from the beating, but I rode my bike for forty minutes to Littleton, where Mom was buried. I sat there not knowing why I even came to see her, but it felt comfortable just sitting there next to Mom. I fell asleep in peace.

Everyone at the school talked about the incident with Addison the Ape for quite some time. There would be more fights since that day, as I had learned to enjoy the release I experienced. At times, I looked for a good fight and got one most of the time when I went looking for it.

Addison the Ape never messed with Dwight or anyone else in my school. His parents took him out of our school and enrolled him in a Catholic school. But there were plenty of other apes around to replace Addison. I took out all the frustrations and bitterness toward my father on the bullies and the apes that picked on the little ones. It wasn't about justice, as many had falsely given me the credit for. It was about venting my frustrations.

CHAPTER 12

The Chain

At the beginning of my sophomore year, my dad finished his PhD in theology. Denver University gave him a teaching position. Dad was a beneficiary of the affirmative action. He taught ethics to the future attorneys and pastors at Denver University.

Imagine that. The man who stood in front of future lawyers and ministers, teaching ethics during the week and preaching the love of God on Sundays, was the same man beating me whenever he was upset.

He taught others the love of God and to love one another as God has loved us. But the whole time, he was unable to do what he was preaching others to do. It was a time of confusion and discernment for me.

My relationship with Dad became awkward and distant. I still loved him and wanted to honor him. In public, Dad put on the air of a caring father doing his best even after his wife had passed away. I did nothing to taint that image. When he felt threatened that he would be exposed as an abuser because of my bruises, he simply removed me from the scene.

In many of the social functions which Joey and Judy would attend, I was not asked to come along because of my scars or injuries. I did not mind. It was the time of relaxation away from Dad and the pressure that came with him.

Meantime, Joey and Judy had done well in school. Judy never got a single B, always As. Joey began taking judo lessons after school two days a week, in addition to tae kwon do lessons on the other three weekdays. He had started to grow, and he was almost as tall as I was.

Joey started at Byers as I began my first year at South High School. Judy would go on to represent her third-and fourth-grade classes as their champion speller. She was in her fifth year now.

During my junior year, I took an Intro to Psychology class. I didn't care for it, but it was a prerequisite.

Near the end of the semester, the class went through the topic of domestic violence and its devastating consequences. There I came face-to-face with the fact that would jolt me and then haunt me for years to come. Chapter 11: "An Abused Becoming an Abuser: The Chain."

The chain, said the text, which passes on the pain and suffering to the generations thereafter, was a disease that had found its cure. I was anxious to know more. I wanted to know how to stop the disease from being passed on to my kids, if I ever had my own someday. It had come far enough.

The statistics, according to the text, indicated that the majority of the prison population, junkies, and the prostitutes were the products of abusive childhoods. These victims, in turn, became the next generation of abusers.

Social scientists had learned the devastating consequences that domestic violence had on our society. They began implementing many ways to help the abused and abusers alike, in hopes to break the chain of violence.

I felt grateful there were programs out there to help people like me and Dad. I would do anything so that my children and their children would not deal with the consequences of this terrible disease in their lives. I had to know more about this cure.

Less than a mile away from our home on University Boulevard was a large church with over a thousand people attending each week. Their acres of parking spaces were full each Sunday, three times over. There was a huge promotion about a lady who was giving her testimony of having survived the sexual abuse from her father. It was scheduled at this church on Memorial Day weekend. Its theme was "Love Overcomes the Chain of Hate."

There was that word again. *Chain!* I was so intrigued I asked Judy if she would be interested in going to hear the lady. For three nights, we sat near the front of hundreds of folks who came to hear her testimony. The church praise team played their instruments and sang before each of her testimonies.

This young woman, who had been sexually abused by her biological father and his sex-cult friends from the age of seven until she turned eleven, stood before us and said that she forgave her father and those who had perpetrated against her.

She shared about how she lived in pain and hatred for over a decade, consumed with anger against her father. It was destroying her life and causing problems for the loved ones around her.

During her desire to get help, she came across a nun who specialized in inner healings. The nun invited her to stay at the convent while the inner healing took place. A couple of years later, she emerged as a brand-new soul and went to see her father in prison to tell him he was forgiven.

I was able to identify myself in her story. I had healed from the injuries my dad had inflicted on me a few days after each time he had assaulted me. It was the hidden wounds within that were destroying me from inside out.

I knew about the power of forgiveness, the impact it has on the individual's life, and how it promotes a positive attitude and a healthy lifestyle. I saw it with my own eyes while growing up in O-Jung.

It wasn't the pain that was caused by her father's abuse that was killing her. The poison from the anger within was the cause of the unbearable pain. In forgiving her father, she found closure.

After a decade of life without focus, she finally had a purpose in life. She decided to share her ordeal with the world in hope that it would encourage some other people to forgive their abusers. This lady pointed to the scriptures that said that vengeance belongs to God the Father. Instead of focusing on getting even, God tells us to leave that to him and move on. Focus on doing well with the life given to us while learning to forgive those who wronged us.

She walked from one end of the podium to the other, speaking of how God sent his own son to demonstrate the degree of humility God was willing to take in order to forgive those who trespassed against God.

The following evening, she said nothing in life is a coincidence. She said by facing the challenges while relying on God, we are certain to have victory. This victory gives us the confidence to trust in God during the subsequent ordeals. The trusting becomes easier and easier, gaining confidence with each step we take. This confidence is called faith.

Through the ordeal, we realize God is faithful to his promise. We become equipped with this knowledge and become his instruments to share the message with those who are suffering around us. Hopefully so they may turn to God for help as she did. It gives purpose to the lives of those who had suffered through tragedies, turning their disadvantages into profitable tools for God's kingdom and his purpose.

The last evening of her testimony, she spoke of forgiving others before we ask God to forgive us. The prayer Jesus had taught us tells us that asking God to forgive our sins requires that we forgive one another. Just as the daily bread is important to our lives, so is the forgiving of one another. In the same breath we ask God for our daily sustenance, we are to seek forgiveness from God as we forgive others.

Without forgiving her perpetrators, the disease that consumed her father, and nearly her, could strike at any moment as it awaits the next opportunity to strike.

It was the most worthwhile investment of three evenings in my life. It was interesting how, in a span of a couple of months, the word *chain* had become such a significant one to me, making itself known to me in its most profound ways. Now, I was not only aware of the monster but was motivated to confront and slay it.

CHAPTER 13

1971—Graveyard Shift

As I started my senior year in high school, I got a job at a Safeway Grocery store as a courtesy clerk. It was a fancy name for a bag boy. My dad seemed to be pleased with my employment, and I got to stay away from him during the night. When I got home, he was on his way to work, and he never bothered me while I was asleep. Our contacts with each other became very little.

I enjoyed the working environment. It did not seem like work to me but more like a fun school project while getting paid really well. I liked having money. I no longer had to wear clothes purchased from the Salvation Army stores, as Dad was accustomed to do so for me and Joey. For Judy, it was always purchased from the department stores.

Soon, I got a promotion and became a full-time midnight stocker two weeks before my eighteenth birthday in January of 1972. One day, an elderly lady shopper who was having a severe incontinence problem ended up making a terrible mess in one of the aisles. The manager called on me to do the cleanup job. It was the most unpleasant task I had ever performed, but I did it without a word of complaint. It impressed the management enough to give me the promotion.

Most of the men working the graveyard shift with me were married and with children. Knowing that at my age I was earning enough to support a family had given me a tremendous confidence as a person. I was well liked by the crew of a dozen men, but more importantly, the big boss appreciated my hardworking attitude.

At first, my job was to cut the top of the boxes with a razor so the crew could get to the items inside the box to be placed on the shelves. Then, I had to break the box down when they were through so they could be stacked out in the back for the truck to come pick them up. Soon, the crew leader began allowing me to fill in for the guys who were off or sick. Eventually, they gave me the rotation shift, becoming one of the most efficient relief man they ever worked with.

Everyone was off on rotation basis, and each time someone was off that night, I filled in the spot. Each time I was assigned to a new spot, I began looking for ways to improve and make each task easier to perform.

The big boss wasn't aware that each night during our lunch break, the younger crew members were ambitiously studying tae kwon do from me. When the crew saw me breaking the wooden crates with my fist before throwing into the incinerator, they freaked out and thought it was the most far-out stuff they ever saw.

I went on to demonstrate some of the techniques of self-defense, tossing big guys around like rag dolls and actually hurting the biggest of them all with a thumb hold that brought the 220-pound man to his knee, begging to be freed. He cried actually. Seeing that, a handful of guys begged me for days before I gave in. They offered to pay me, to which I declined.

They were getting pretty good at it. Most of them had purchased a *do-bok* (uniform) and changed into it during the lessons when I changed into mine. For some reason, our productivity improved even with shortened work hours from overrun practices.

A few months following my promotion, my uncle and his family moved to America in the summer of 1972. Once Dad had received his tenure at Denver University, he initiated the paperwork to invite his baby brother's family to come live in America. The process took hardly any time at all. My uncle couldn't sell his house fast enough to move to America.

Dad gave Uncle and Aunt each an English name—Phillip and Cindy. Uncle Phillip had worked for a mega company in Korea as an upper executive and initially balked at the idea of moving to America. Aunt Cindy, however, thought it would be a great opportunity for their two daughters to receive the highest education available.

Uncle Phillip was much larger than Dad, both height—and weight-wise, yet his temperament was as gentle and loving as a teddy bear.

Aunt Cindy was a musician, who gave up her career as a concert pianist to raise their two daughters. She was the most loving person you would ever meet. She was a wonderful match to my uncle.

When she sat to play the piano, her appearance magically transformed into an angelic being, her torso would sway to the melody, and her eyes would slightly close to concentrate on the beat. I thought only an angel could create such heavenly noises, and my aunt must have been one.

She was an only daughter of a Christian minister who also had three sons as well but cherished his only daughter as his treasure. He was a senior pastor at a large congregation in Daejeon, near O-Jung, where I grew up. She grew up with strong ethical values, and I had never seen her doing anything she thought wrong or illegal, not even jaywalking or littering.

The two girls chose their own names: Lisa and Sharon, older and younger, respectively. The older was turning thirteen, a year older than Judy, but entered the same grade as Judy. Sharon, the younger at eleven, was the smarter one, always outdoing her older sister. She entered a grade below her sister. Sharon thought it was just fantastic she was no longer two years of school behind her sister.

The girls were taking after their mom, extremely artistic. While they were known for their outgoing personalities, their lack of confidence in English seemed to have tamed their persona somewhat. It was refreshing to have these bright and cheerful folks in my life, and I welcomed their presence.

Judy was being a good sport, allowing a double bunk to be added into her room to accommodate our cousins. She was quite the tutor and translator for them in school. Judy never said a negative word to express her discomfort in sharing her room with the girls. Judy was happy with the presence of her cousins to share her thoughts and trade female secrets with. She no longer had to live with three guys alone. I vacated my room for Uncle and Aunt, moving my bed across the room from Joey's bed. Since I slept while Joey was in school during the day, moving in with him had worked out pretty good. We had to purchase some extra beds and dressers for the new members of the family. It was a fun and exciting time.

I asked Dad to take all of us to Mom's grave the next day after their arrival. He was preparing for his lecture and could not get away but allowed me to take his station wagon. Joey did not care to join us, citing too much homework to do.

The six of us crammed into the Plymouth and headed for Mom. Uncle and Sharon joined me in the front, with Sharon in the middle. She was a fun person to be around. She was always cheerful and never complained about anything.

Aunt Cindy was very kind to shed tears for Mom, her sister-in-law, whom she did not know very well. She paid respect in a way I was pleased with. She always behaved as a loving and caring individual. Her feminine touch around the house was welcoming sight to all of us. As Aunt Cindy took over the household duties, my life had suddenly become liberated.

Aunt Cindy took over the church pianist duty as well. We bought a used piano for our home so Judy could finally begin taking piano lessons. Aunt Cindy proved to be a very good instructor as well. The addition to the family had brought melodies back into our lives.

I had gotten a driver's license when I was sixteen, and by the time I was working, I had purchased a blue 1968 Chevy half-ton truck. It was four years old and slightly dinged up, but it ran like a champ. I had met the graduation requirement during my first semester of the senior year and thus did not need to take any classes during the second semester.

Against the advisement of my counselor to take at least a couple of classes to make the transition to college easier, I chose not to. I had decided not to apply to college, even if it was against Mom's wish. I was going to make lots of money instead. I was left with plenty of free time to work on my truck and sleep during the day.

Life seemed to have a meaning for the first time since Mother had died. I was going to be a hardworking man, to save lots of money and do good deeds in life. I wanted to make plenty of money to open shelters for abused women and children.

I found out that a shelter was unable to care for the children of the women running from their abusive spouses. A father would wait around the school and would follow his kids home, right to the shelter where their mother was hiding.

For that reason, children were taken to a child-care agency ran by social services with school programs, separating them from their mother.

I envisioned a shelter that provided in-house teachers for the children so they could be with their mother during the ordeal. I thought it would be great that mothers would be taught trades to give them careers, such as being a hairstylist or an x-ray technician. They could live with the income generated from their trades and eventually find their own place to live and start anew.

For that purpose, from each and every paycheck, I paid tithes to God, and another tenth went into my savings toward my dream to build shelters.

Safeway hired Uncle Phillip to replace one of the crew members who was retiring after thirty years of service. His English skills, or lack thereof, was not a factor since Uncle would not come in contact with the customers. We worked after the store was closed for the day.

He worked harder than everyone, being grateful for the opportunity to earn good income so soon after coming to the United States. I asked our boss if we could have the same off days, which were Thursdays and Fridays. We would ride to and from work together in my truck, enjoying the conversations with each other. One day Uncle Phillip opened up to me during our ride to work.

"You know, Jae-chul, I can't believe I gave up a cushy executive position in a mega company making top-notch annual income to come to a strange land where I'm considered incompetent and lesser of a man, working for hourly wages. I can't understand what people say. I can't communicate my thoughts to them, and people consider me uneducated and incapable of handling even trivial matters. Even your aunt thinks less of me now."

"That's not true at all, Uncle Phillip. No one considers you lesser of a man. You understand what people say just fine, what are you saying?" I looked at him.

He didn't say anything, so I continued, "You are a good husband, a good father, a strong brother, a wonderful uncle to us, and even though we're working on hourly wages now, no one said we had to work for hourly wages all our lives. We could even start our own grocery store or a restaurant someday. Besides, we're making pretty good money even if it is hourly wage, isn't that right, Uncle? Come on, cheer up."

Korea was a haven for male chauvinists. It wasn't that long ago that a Korean wife had to follow her husband a few steps behind. The modern woman would not tolerate such behavior, and Aunt Cindy was more than happy to come to America where such behavior was not condoned. She stood her ground against Uncle Phillip, and obviously it was bothering him.

"I miss home, Jae-chul ah," Uncle Phillip sighed in Korean.
"Then, why did you come to America?" I returned in Korean.
"I thought it would be better for your cousins. They're better off with an education from America."

"You could have stayed in Seoul and sent them here to study if you didn't want to come."

"Your aunt wouldn't think of it. Besides, she was worried that I was drinking too much and thought I needed to get away from my drinking buddies."

Now the truth finally emerges. It wasn't just him who was drinking a lot. Most South Korean businessmen were accustomed to conducting business around cocktails, usually long after the regular business hours were over. Ulcers and cirrhosis were accepted as professional hazards for South Korean businessmen.

I had heard of Uncle's drinking problem when I was still living in Seoul. Coming to America may have been a good thing for him as he was unable to drink around my father, which slowed his drinking to hardly any at all. I thought it was good thing that Uncle Phillip didn't drink much as I was concerned for his health.

Uncle Phillip and I enjoyed working with each other. He was well liked by the crew leader, and his English was improving rather quickly. His English pronunciations drew snickers from the crew, but Uncle Phillip seemed to enjoy being the cause of their laughter.

He had a sense of humor and quickly picked up the jokes among the men. During the tae kwon do practices, he would sit reclined on a chair, drinking coffee, and watch. He seemed pleased with my teaching skills and proud to be my uncle.

He became an avid football fan almost immediately. He would get caught up in the Orange Crush mania of the Denver Broncos. Our coworkers were more than happy to help Uncle understand the game. They were more than eager to teach him the rules and the strategies as they stocked the shelves next to him. It made our work time enjoyable.

His love for the game made it easier for the men to accept him as one of us, sharing the love for the Broncos. As a season opener, Denver was hosting the Houston Oilers at the Mile High Stadium.

My uncle purchased two tickets, along with everyone at work, and told my dad he was taking me to the game. I admired my uncle that he had the guts to stand up to Dad, even though I didn't think Dad was going to allow us to miss church to attend a football game.

"You can't miss a Sunday worship to attend a football game. It isn't a good example for the kids," protested Dad when Uncle told him of his plan.

"Jae-chul and I work hard all week, and it's good for us to have some fun every now and then, especially with the fellows from work. All work and no fun isn't good for a man. It's a season-opening day. Everyone at work will be there, and we should be there as well."

"You are acting like a childish kid. It's not what I would call setting a good example for the children."

"I bought the tickets already, *hyung-nim*. It's a sold-out game, and I hope you will allow us to go watch the game." I could see Dad was angry, but he did not stop our plans to attend the Mile High Stadium on that Sunday. I felt liberated, free.

I never loved football as much as I did on that day. It was the most fun I had in many years. Broncos won easily, 30-17. Nice way to start the season.

I felt like a winner, just like the Broncos, for the first time in ages. Uncle and I joined the crew that night at work, celebrating the great opening for the Broncos. Uncle joined the crew at Mile High Stadium for each and every home game the Broncos played. I was less bold and did not push my luck with Dad beyond that first game.

The Broncos would go on to lose nine of the next eleven games. Uncle teased me that since I stopped joining him to root for the Broncos, the teams had performed poorly. As a fan, Uncle was heartbroken during each loss and lamented for a day or two before being able to talk about the Broncos again.

The following year, he bought two season tickets, regardless of all the heartaches he had endured during his first season as a fan. He was loyal to a fault. Broncos had a fan for life.

CHAPTER 14

1972—Senior Prom

The commute between work and home became a time of sharing between my uncle and me. He talked about his past experiences, but at times, we would simply talk shop. Often, I would ask him about Dad's childhood.

I was horrified to learn that Grandfather had beaten Dad on numerous occasions and at times to the point where Dad was thought to be dead. Uncle Phillip's descriptions of some of those events were rather gruesome. At times, I thought I began to understand where Dad's ire was coming from.

Even when Uncle bought a car, he continued to ride to and from work with me in my truck. He said he was leaving the car for Aunt Cindy in case of emergencies, but I knew he was protecting his new vehicle. After the duo had passed the written test at DMV, Dad began teaching Aunt Cindy how to drive. Uncle Phillip drove in Korea, so he knew how to handle a vehicle well. As yet to be licensed, Uncle Phillip was legally unable to teach Aunt Cindy.

Uncle and Aunt Cindy became licensed drivers and celebrated it by buying a brand-new 1972 Ford LTD. The family went to Peking Palace Chinese restaurant to celebrate the purchase of their first car. Judy rode in Uncle's new car with the girls, while Joey and I rode with Dad in the backseat silently, without speaking a single word all the way to and from the restaurant.

About five weeks prior to the prom, I asked Sarah Kim to the dance after Sunday worship at the church parking lot. She said, "What took you so long?" I wasn't sure if that meant yes. Obviously, she saw my confusion and offered, "I said yes, in case you were wondering." Sarah looked at me and then said, "Oh my goodness, you're turning red. How cute." Sarah was having fun at my expense. Instead of renting a tux, I went downtown and bought me a top-of-the-line suit.

Uncle Phillip had offered me the use of his brand-new LTD for the event. Sarah was the only Korean girl my age in Denver that I knew of. But that wasn't the reason I asked her to the prom. I thought she was very pretty.

The fact she was a straight-A student had impressed me as well. She was rather slim and tall. She didn't speak Korean very well as she was six years old when she came to America but tried to speak whenever possible. When I would see her at school, she was usually by herself. But she was very friendly to everyone.

She loved playing tennis for the school team and was offered a scholarship by several universities, including UCLA. She was nearly as tall as I was, and that was rather intimidating for me. She was always dressed well and braided her long hair in single strand down the middle. Each time I saw her in the hallway or at church on Sundays, my heart would beat a little faster than normal. I really liked her.

She was easy to talk to as we dined at a fancy steak restaurant called The Library. I was surprised to learn that she had always liked me as well, ever since I had first come to the United States. She had hidden the fact well for the past four years. It was so flattering I could hardly hide my big smile. After dinner, we headed to our school where the dance was taking place.

"How come you never told me you liked me?" I asked her as we were in my uncle's LTD, feeling giddy with joy.

"You mean like, I would walk up to you and say, 'Hey, I like you' and make a fool of myself if you didn't like me back? You don't expect me to do something goofy like that, do you?"

"I guess not. Have you had many boyfriends?"

"That's kind of personal, don't you think? But since you so rudely asked, the answer is yes and no." Feeling the need to elaborate, she went on.

"I really liked this guy back in my sophomore year, but you know my dad, so strict and all, wouldn't let me date."

"I like your dad even more now. So you didn't date much?"

"I went to the homecoming dance with Spencer Peters last year, and he took me to a movie once, and that's about it. I didn't even get a kiss out of the deal, since Spencer is scared of his own shadow and thinks I may bite or something."

"I'm glad you were saving yourself for me."

"Ha, don't flatter yourself. What about you?"

"No, I didn't kiss Spencer Peters either. Actually, I've been saving myself for you all these years." I liked the way Sarah laughed with an occasional snort. I could tell Sarah was having a good time as well. She said, "You are basically telling me I'm your first date?" Before I had the chance to answer, someone honked behind me, as I didn't see the light turning green. I drove without saying anything for a while, to change the subject.

It was funny how our common experiences as immigrants made it so easy for us to understand each other. I felt as if we had known each other forever. She began sharing some stories of her life.

"Anyway, my dad pulls into a gas station, one of those new self-serve places, because he was almost out of gas. We sat and sat for a while before he decided to honk for the attendant to come and serve him. Eventually this guy came out and told my dad, 'You need to pump your own gas, sir.'"

"So what did he do?" I asked her, trying to figure out what was the point of this story.

"He started to pump on the accelerator because he thought the mechanic was talking about pumping the gas pedal and not the pump. I finally told him what the gas station guy had meant, and Dad was so embarrassed he just drove away." I laughed, envisioning Deacon Kim in such an awkward situation.

"I slapped a guy right in his face on my very first gym class in America," I began, trying to top her story with mine. "In Korea, the only wrestling I ever saw was the professional wrestling you see on television, and Greco-Roman style wrestling was yet to be introduced to me. During the first day of my school in gym, we were paired up to wrestle each other, and as I started to wrestle this kid, I decided to use some of the stuff I saw on the television back in Korea. When I went up to give him a handshake, he was about to charge at me and ended up getting slapped in his face. I figured since I had already angered him, might as well charge. I had his neck in a scissor lock between my legs as I was yanking backward at his head. Talk about a surprised kid running to the PE teacher to tell him what I had done."

"So what happened?" Sarah asked, snickering and snorting, as if she really wanted to know.

"The coach asked my father to my school next day and made sure I understood not to be suited up for the remainder of the wrestling season." Sarah could not stop laughing, and I realized how much I enjoyed making her laugh.

We had arrived at the school and entered the gym to find a live band blaring away. The band was called the Donkeys, and they were very good. Sarah and I danced all evening and enjoyed ourselves as everyone else at the dance had.

I was sorry to hear the announcement for the last song. Sarah must have felt the same way. We held each other to the Spaniels' "Goodnight, Sweetheart, Goodnight" swaying to the music, and before I realized, we were kissing each other, holding each other very closely. I realized I was in love, hoping she was feeling the same way.

We left the school gym, heading toward the parking lot, with Sarah holding on to my arm like two lovers. As she was about to enter the car, she pulled me closer to give me yet another passionate kiss. I don't recall how I made it to her house with my head in the clouds.

I didn't want the evening to end. However, I did not want to break the curfew that was set for us by Deacon Kim, Sarah's father. He was waiting up for us when we arrived at their home. He seemed pleased that we were on time long before the curfew and invited me in.

I declined reluctantly, as it was the custom for the Koreans not to be imposing so late at night. He asked if everyone of my family was doing well before wishing me good-night.

Sarah got her last enthusiastic wave of good-bye behind her father as I was about to turn and just before the door closed. I liked Sarah very much. I think I was beginning to know what love is like.

I am not sure what had caused him to be so angry, but when I got home, my dad was waiting up for me, fuming. Even before I had the chance to remove my rented tuxedo, he swung at me.

As I was being beaten, I promised myself this would be the last time I was going to allow him to hit me. I was on a coma-like sleep for the next two days, recovering from the injuries. I had to pay five dollars extra for returning the tux a day later than scheduled.

Sarah found out what had happened to me and actually called my dad to ask him if she had done anything that caused me to receive a beating. My dad told Sarah that he did not need to discuss matters of how he disciplines his son with her.

Sarah stopped attending our church from that day on, saying she could no longer rely on my father as her pastor. It did cause tremendous problems between Sarah and her father, Deacon Kim, for quite some time.

Two days after the prom, I went searching for an apartment. At seventeen, I was too young to live on my own. I could not even sign a lease agreement to rent an apartment. I had to lie in order to get an apartment.

When I was asked for my identification, I told the apartment manager I was a new student moving from Michigan to begin at Denver University, who got robbed in Kansas City by a couple of guys, leaving me all black and blue, with no wallet with identifications.

In the end, the manager was all too happy to let me have the apartment. There were surpluses of housings in Denver, and he considered it fortunate to have a tenant.

James Watts, US secretary of the interior, who needed thick cola-bottle glasses to help with his myopia, had given the Texas oil companies the right to strip-mine the Rockies. A brilliant idea if you wanted to turn the Rocky Mountain into piles of useless dirt, causing landslides and floods during each rain.

Long before the mining actually started, the oil companies came to Denver and built high-rise office buildings in anticipation to meet their future needs. In the mountains where the work was to take place, they built condos and apartment buildings that sat there for years, empty, waiting for the mining to start.

The mining idea was discovered by the EPA and groups supporting it, initiating the protests that eventually halted it. That created such surpluses of housing in the Denver market, it took decades to recover from it. It was good fortune to have surplus of housing in Denver to ease my situation.

Shortly before I packed to move out of the house, Uncle Phillip told me to forgive Dad and pray for him that Dad would find peace. I was not ready to forgive my father for his crimes against me just yet, I told him.

Even while I was saying it, my heart was being convicted for saying such thing. My mind had a flashback, taking me back to O-Jung, how those boys were praying to God for the forgiveness of the Red Army soldiers. In an instant, I felt guilty and remorseful for my unforgiving heart.

I realized I could not live with my dad any longer. Dad's anger was getting out of control. No one was able to confront him. He was as stubborn as the next guy his age, which just wouldn't show their emotions. My life was filled with doubts and confusions, but one thing I knew was certain—that I was not going to allow this madness to continue any further.

While I should have been planning for college and a career, I was too consumed with anger and bitterness to concentrate on anything that was constructive.

The next day, I walked into the navy-recruiting office and enlisted to join the navy as soon as I got my diploma. Just after the July 4 weekend, I was to become a sailor of the greatest navy in the world. I needed to get right. University wasn't for me. I needed to be far away from my dad. I drove to go see Mom. I needed to think.

I had to get out of the situation I was in. I needed to find the innocent boy from O-Jung that once wanted to become an *am-heng-uh-sah*, a secret police serving the king to maintain justice within the kingdom. Until then, I could not be a complete person. Not a proper son, brother, or "bother" for that matter and certainly not a father. I could not be a good husband either.

CHAPTER 15

1972—Uncle Phillip

Coming to America was both a blessing and a trial for me. I gave up a great career and all my friends, my comfort zone, for the sake of my girls' future. With my brother's help, my family was settling into the life in America with relative ease.

My nephew Jimmy helped me gain employment at the store he was working at. He was a hard worker, had earned the respect from the bosses, and his recommendation was all it took to get a job that paid well, with good benefits.

It was nice to see that the loss of my sister-in-law did not cause the children to spiral down academically. Their emotional and mental health was to be desired. I could not believe my brother was beating Jae-chul. He is a good kid with admirable ambition to do well, yet he was the target of my brother's angry attacks.

At first, I feared my brother and stayed out of his way. Soon, I was convicted of doing nothing for my nephew. He is the son I never had. He had given me more than just a job but dignity as well. He seemed to understand my feelings and thoughts, giving me the opportunity to release and vent to him.

One day, I could not take it any more as my brother was assaulting Jimmy. I thought Jimmy would fight back as he was capable of handling much bigger opponents during the tournaments.

That would have been the most difficult situation for me as I would have stopped him from doing what was dishonorable to his father, even though my brother's action was not honorable either.

However, Jimmy would not even raise his face in defiance against his father. He was like a lamb. I was wondering what was going to happen once all that anger and frustration he was suppressing had reached its boiling point.

I feared for Jimmy's mental health more than my brother's. As I spoke up against my brother, he told me if I didn't stay out of his way, I would have to move out. By then I had saved enough money to do so.

Jimmy told me he was moving out instead. He thought it would devastate Joey and Judy if my wife was no longer around to care for them. Jimmy made me promise him that we would stay until Judy was old enough to care for herself.

We stayed while Jimmy packed and left. I feared for that kid. He was only seventeen. I saw the light that once shone so brightly within him slowly being extinguished.

How could my brother not see what a wonderful son he had? My wife and I decided to stay and care for Judy and Joseph, making sure they would never be at the receiving end of my brother's angry attacks, a vow I was unable to keep.

CHAPTER 16

1972—Boot Camp

I spent as much time as I could with Sarah before I had to leave for boot camp the Monday after the July 4 weekend. Sarah had wanted to be a veterinarian ever since she was a little girl, and Colorado State University in Fort Collins was second to none in the nation in the veterinary medicine program.

She was offered a full academic scholarship to attend CSU. Numerous schools had also offered her tennis scholarships, but her heart was set on becoming an animal doctor. After she finishes her BS in biology at CSU, she hoped to continue with their veterinarian program.

She was enrolled in two classes during the summer. She wanted to get a head start on her curriculum. I would sit next to her in Bio 101 and English 101 classes as if I was a part of nearly a hundred students in the classes. Sarah was sad that I would be leaving in less than a week and wanted to spend the remainder of our time together just as much as I did.

The night before I left, I asked Sarah if she would marry me after I completed my tour. I knew it was asking a lot after we had only been dating a few months, but to my delight, she nodded and kissed me.

I went to visit Mom in the middle of the night. I had a flashlight, but I could find her with my eyes closed. I sat next to her, telling her Sarah had agreed to marry me. I said so long to Mom and headed to my apartment for the last time.

My flight was scheduled to leave Denver at noon. I drove my truck to the storage rental where I had rented a space for my truck while I was gone. I took a taxi from there to the Stapleton airport.

I had asked Dad if I could store my stuff and truck at his garage while I was in boot camp, but he said there wasn't any room, so no. I told him I was hoping to say good-bye as I brought my stuff and spend the night at home, but Dad didn't have time for all that and said good luck before hanging up.
Uncle Phillip brought the gang, minus Dad, to the Stapleton airport to see me off. Judy said her good-bye with teary eyes, and Joey actually seemed sad to see me go. Aunt Cindy and the girls didn't have much to say other than to wish me safety and health during the next nine weeks of boot camp.
Uncle Phillip pulled out a folded card from the crew I had worked with, their signatures and notes written on a Hallmark card. They could have given it to me last Friday when they threw a party for me. I took my time reading it, but when I was done, I gave it back to him.
I told him about the instruction given to us by the recruiter to limit our personal belongings, since they would need to be mailed back home as soon as we arrived at the camp. The United Airlines announced that our plane was ready for boarding.

I flew to San Diego along with a dozen other recruits to begin our boot camp at the naval training center. Two marine recruits sat among us as well. I didn't know at the time that I was running away from Dad more than toward my future. I was living a life of regret, knowing I had let Mom down by failing to enroll in a college, let alone an Ivy League one. I felt as if I was running out on Joey and Judy as well.

I sat next to a guy from Greeley, Colorado. Listening to him, I recognized he was running away from something as well. He shared with me in a slow and barely audible voice how his fiancée had broken up with him a couple of months ago. He quit his lumberyard job and joined the navy. In his rationale, he joined the navy to see the world.
I knew the truth was he didn't want to be in Greeley anymore. Had his fiancée stuck with him, the last thing he would want to do is travel the seven seas, riding in tin cans. I simply nodded and told him I joined up to see the world as well. He bought two miniature bottles of whiskey.
I told him I wasn't old enough to drink but thanked him anyway. After the second round, the attendant stopped selling my new friend any more drinks.

Had I known how hot the July sun in San Diego would get, I would have started the training toward the end of the year. My long hair was gone, and my neck was no longer protected from the sun. Within a week, there were sixty red necks marching together as Company 185, under the hot July sun. Other than the three days I had to spend at the hospital with German measles, nine weeks of training was uneventful and went by in a blink.

Just prior to the graduation from basic training, I was called to the headquarter office to speak with a commander of the base. I had enlisted to become an aviation mechanic. Mr. Bozzi, our neighbor, made a good living working as an airplane mechanic for Martin Marietta. I liked his lifestyle. I thought I would give it a try. As soon as the basic training was over, I was to fly to Oklahoma to begin learning how to repair navy fighter planes.

The commander didn't even bother to tell me to sit or offer a shake and went right to the point as I stood before his desk at a parade rest. I have yet to become a citizen of the United States of America. Therefore, I was unable to attend the highly classified training.

He was more than happy to offer a military police training program to me. As he was aware of my martial arts skill, he believed I could serve as their physical-training instructor, if I wanted to. If not, I would go through the training to be a military policeman serving and protecting the naval community.

The school was located in San Diego next to NTC and not in the middle of mosquito-infested Oklahoma, the commander stated. In addition, since the error was on the recruiters, I would be offered an opportunity to skip two pay-grade statuses as soon as I finish the training school, which was twenty-four weeks long.

"Sign me up," I said. I had already given up my locks and gotten used to being a "red neck," and becoming a cop sounded very interesting to me.

I went through the NTC graduation march in front of four people who beamed with proud smiles. My uncle flew to San Diego with Joey and Judy two nights before the graduation and went to the San Diego Zoo the following day.

Sarah flew in to San Diego early morning of my graduation. I was able to spot them on the stand as we stood as a company before all the brass and the guests.

We listened to the congratulatory speech from the NTC commander before we marched as a unit around the stadium behind the marching band that played the "Anchors Aweigh." The song that was composed by Charles Zimmerman six decades ago became a theme song for the US Navy since.

After the ceremony, the company was dismissed and allowed to mingle with family. There was a midnight curfew for the grads. I was anxious to leave the base with the family and start the celebration.

We found a steak house and had a wonderful meal. In front of the eye-rolling Judy and blushing Joey, I kissed Sarah after ordering the meal. Uncle just chuckled.

Uncle Phillip commented on the fact that I had gained some body mass. I had gained about fifteen pounds of muscles. I didn't like it as it had slowed me down quite a bit when kicking and punching.

They dropped me off in front of the NTC front gate just before midnight. It was hard to see them off, especially Sarah, whose kiss lingered on my lips all the way to my barrack.

Sarah stayed with Judy in her hotel room, talking all night as they looked down from their hotel room window at the beautiful San Diego Harbor in front of them. Everyone flew back to Denver the following day without me.

I finished the military police training as a top student and was given an E-4 ranking. I was now senior to all the classmates with whom I had graduated with from boot camp. I was given an order to travel to Norfolk, Virginia, to be aboard an aircraft carrier. I didn't think my Chevy truck could make it across the country. When I shared my concern with the master chief who was in charge of the military police training, he had pulled some strings to reassign me to a ship in San Diego. I found out it is not what you know but who you know.

I flew home for Easter. Sarah was home for the break as well. Sarah and I went shopping for our wedding rings and found a set that was pleasing to both of us—simple white-gold bands for the wedding rings, with a matching diamond-crowned engagement ring for Sarah.

We gathered both of our families at Cho's restaurant to announce our engagement. Everyone was very happy for us. Even Dad seemed to be pleased that I had chosen to marry a Korean. Mr. Cho picked up the tab, in a congratulatory gesture. I was very grateful as I had spent so much money on Sarah's diamond ring.

CHAPTER 17

1973—Aboard USS Dixon

I had an official order from the secretary of the navy to check in with the chief military police officer aboard the USS *Dixon*. *Dixon* was a submarine tender with about four hundred sailors aboard.

Three days before I was to report to *Dixon*, I left Denver in my Chevy truck with all my belongings, which were a duffel bag full of clothes, three boxes of knickknacks, and an old acoustic guitar. The next day, after twenty hours of continuous driving, I arrived at San Diego. I was excited and anxious to check in aboard the *Dixon*.

Docked at the Point Loma substation were two submarine tenders, USS *Sperry* (AS-12) and my ship, USS *Dixon* (AS-37). These two ships together took care of about thirty submarines, both diesel and nuclear subs, as mothers tending to their suckling babies.

During the wartime, the tenders served as floating cities near the battle zone, allowing the subs to refuel and restock their ammos and supplies without having to return to the distant mainland. Even the most major engine overhaul can be done by the tender haul technicians while the submarine floated in the middle of an ocean.

There were barbershops, laundry facilities and dry-cleaning stores, convenience stores, and even movie theaters for the submarine sailors to take care of their grooming and R&R while stocking up on their personal items, such as the recent edition of girlie magazines and shaving creams.

BOTHER

I had taken typing classes during my sophomore year in high school. I found out there were forty girls and zero boys in typing classes when I was looking for one more class to sign up to meet the requirement. Not only did I get friendly benefits from the girls, but I actually learned how to type fast and accurately.

I was about to reap from that training. As it happened, no one in the ship's police office was a decent typist when tons of typing was necessary for the daily reports. When they found out I was one, the cushiest position in the department simply fell onto my lap.

I was allowed to carry my military-issued .45 Magnum pistol. Not once would I need to pull it out of its holster during my three years of service aboard the *Dixon*, serving the military station at the base of Point Loma substation. As I enlisted, I hoped to become an aviation engineer. Instead, I became a lawman who used a typewriter instead of his gun.

Six months after coming aboard *Dixon*, our sister ship USS *Ajax* that was docked in Pearl Harbor, Hawaii, became damaged during the storm and required extensive repair. USS *Dixon* crossed the pacific to replace her duty for the six months *Ajax* was out of commission.

On our return voyage, I came across seven five-gallon cans full of top-grade Hawaiian marijuana during my inspection of the cargo room prior to pulling into our home port in Point Loma, San Diego.

The routine discovery had made me look very impressive to the superior officer, who had failed to discover the same during his inspection a day earlier. I would go on to make the E-5 pay grade due to his recommendation. I was sure there were some angry people missing eighty-four pounds of primo buds, but no one stepped up to claim the stuff.

I was assigned to the inspection duties ever since, in addition to being the office manager of the police station. A dog named Zion, a year-old male German shepherd, was assigned to me. He stayed in the kennel of our base while off duty. There were a total of four dogs assigned to our base. Zion and I got along well, and he was good at his job. Together, we would go on to discover contrabands one after another with his keen ability.

Zion was born without vocal cords and thus could not bark or make any other sounds, such as whining or growling. He was trained so that when he came across the contraband he was trained to detect, he would sit on his two hind legs, sitting up, facing the contraband, to indicate the location of his discovery.

I became quite fond of him and made it my regular routine to walk him around the tiny peninsula, which is the entirety of base, each day before we started our shift. At times, I would receive permission from the supervisor to take Zion to the Mission Bay Dog Beach after we were off duty, much to his delight. He just loved running freely on the beach with other dogs. I forget he is only a year-old boy, as he goes about his duties at work in such a serious manner.

Sarah flew to San Diego on several occasions and had the opportunity to meet Zion. Even when she returned home, Sarah and I often talked about Zion on the phone, and how she hoped she could be able to help him someday. Sarah had discovered later it was not possible to transplant vocal cords in animals yet, even though some successful operations were conducted on humans.

Taking care of Zion and being responsible for his well-being seemed to have given me the stability I needed, which helped my mental health. Perhaps I enjoyed my job more since I worked with Zion. I truly believed Zion enjoyed working with me as well.

I had a tremendous amount of respect for the submarine sailors whom I dealt with day in and day out. They were special breeds. Once deployed, they would spend months out in the ocean in confinements of what is nothing more than glorified tuna cans. For that, these sailors were treated well. Steaks and, on rare occasions, even lobsters were part of their regular menus.

When returned to the mainland, they were not searched for contrabands as other sailors aboard a ship would be, with sniffing dogs walking by everyone's locker, looking for contrabands and drugs.

At least that was the case until the discovery of paint cans full of marijuana aboard the *Dixon*. The security had tightened considerably around the base. Now, each arriving submarine had to be cleared with an officer and his dog before anyone was allowed to leave their submarines.

There would be lots of surprised sailors unaware of the change in policy and who may have decided to bring some contraband home.

My buddy Kino's submarine had just docked, and I was looking forward to seeing him. It's been three months since he was last home. He was a Pinoy from Manila, Philippines. Kino was a ship's serviceman, first class, aboard a sub that was ready for my inspection. His given name was Terrence Ricasa, but he told me to call him Kino.

Kino became my best friend while stationed at Point Loma. We met during the orientation as I came aboard the *Dixon*. He was being transferred to USS *Hawkbill* submarine from another sub he had served for the past three years. We arrived at about the same time. All new sailors stationed at Point Loma base were required to attend an orientation class where we happened to sit next to each other.

We hit it off well and befriended each other. As soon as Kino's sub, SSN-666 *Hawkbill*, came in for their repairs and supply-reloading trips, he was given long leaves to catch up on all the weekends he had lost out stuck inside a submarine. His sub was nicknamed the Devil Boat or Devilfish due to its number.

He was my running partner for the duration of his leave. He was fun to be with. He seemed to know where all the fun places in town were located. He knew everyone who was somebody and everything about San Diego. What I appreciated about Kino was that he was a dedicated family man and a loyal friend.

His word was as good as gold. He had the heart of gold and could not pass by someone in need of help without lending his hand. He lived with his mother, whom I called Mama Tessi, in a three-bedroom house in Chula Vista, south of San Diego.

He came to America by enlisting in the US Navy, which allowed him to bring his mother from Manila to live in America. Mama Tessi gets down in the kitchen and prepares dishes that were way out.

Kino loved to barbecue, and each weekend he was home and as weather permitted, he had me over for his baby back ribs. Many weekends, I slept in his spare room, which meant I was eating some good grub.

There were plenty of enlisted men joining the navy, especially during the Vietnam War. Everyone wanted to be the radarman or the gunner behind the canons. They wanted to serve the country, but no one wanted to be the laundryman or the barber.

No one thought of joining the US Navy to swab decks or become the person doing the manual labors, loading supplies into the ship when they arrived at the pier and removing the trash from the ship each day.

So the US Navy came up with a solution. They offered the positions of ship servicemen in the US Navy to the Filipinos living in the Philippine Islands to fill that specific void in navy recruitment.

Thousands of Filipinos jumped at the chance to come to America and joined the US Navy, enabling them to bring their family to America as well. Kino was one of the men.

Mama Tessi was a fragile woman who needed to be looked after. She became so lonely during Kino's long deployments, so I made it my regular duty to stop by and look in on her or at least call and check on her daily.

Kino truly appreciated having a cop friend who stopped by and checked on his mother, who lived alone while he was deployed.

Kino talked about how he didn't know where he would be if it wasn't for the US Navy. He was working on finishing his thirty years of service and to collect his pensions. That kind of security for his future would not have come so easily back home in the Philippines.

Unbeknownst to me, Kino had been working hard for a year to plan and smuggle some gold from his homeland. He was looking forward to quadrupling his investment with the pure-gold bars he had purchased from his homeland.

Unaware of the change in the security procedures at their home port of Point Loma, Kino and two other individuals were smuggling nearly $50,000 worth of pure gold that they paid only $9,000 for.

As soon as I came aboard *Hawkbill,* Kino came to me. He pulled me over and whispered that he had some contraband in his locker and that he had no idea the procedure had changed. He would never take advantage of my friendship; therefore, he was surrendering himself to me before I found it on my own.

I asked Kino which was his locker and searched the rest of the sub with Zion. I found no other contrabands and cleared the ship, and everyone aboard the sub was off, running to be with their family and friends waiting for them on the pier.

Only the handful of unlucky individuals whose watch duty had fallen on the day remained aboard the sub. I asked the cook on duty if there was some meat I could treat Zion with for his job well done.

He may be a mute dog, but Zion could make plenty of noises while eating a chunk of steak. The cook seemed to enjoy an appreciating customer, as he found more stuff to feed him. While the chef was occupied with Zion, I talked with Kino regarding what we were going to do with the situation.

Two of his shipmates appeared from nowhere as I was about to begin speaking to Kino. One was the disbursing officer, and the other, the chief petty officer in charge of the culinary. The cook named Paco, from New Orleans, did all the talking while the ensign just stood there next to him.

Paco was ready to take the fall in place of Kino, and the disbursing officer was ready to vouch for Paco's testimony of confession in order to clear Kino.

They knew Kino would be sent back to Manila along with his mother once he was arrested and found guilty by the captain's mast, but not before serving his prison sentence. Nearly fourteen years he had served in the navy would amount to nothing, and he would lose everything he had worked for.

Paco told me there was no friend like Kino, and he was willing to get kicked out of the navy and do some time at the brigs if that would keep Kino and his mother from being deported. He had transferred from the same sub Kino was serving a few months prior to Kino. They had been close buddies for some time.

I was touched by Paco's gesture. He was willing to lose everything, when he had gotten away with it and was free to leave the ship. He volunteered to come forward and harm himself in place of his buddy.

I looked at the pure-gold bars—two one-thousand-gram bars made of twenty-four-carat gold. I told them to remain aboard the sub until further notice from me, and I put the gold inside a bag. I took it with me. I walked off the sub and went to the parking lot to place the bag in my truck cab before returning Zion back to his housing area.

I went to the office and typed the report, clearing the USS *Hawkbill* of any contraband aboard. It was the most nerve-racking thing I've ever done in my life. I was so afraid someone would discover me and I would be the one to get in trouble. I walked back inside the sub to talk to Kino and his buddies. I told the three they were permitted to go ashore and be with their family and friends for now, but that there may be arrests to be followed. I told them to meet me at Kino's house that evening at 8:00 p.m. sharp to give them my decision. They had ten hours to eat their hearts out.

When I arrived at Kino's place ten to eight, all three were huddled together in the kitchen table. I could see they had been drinking for some time, judging by the amount of cigarette butts in the ashtrays and the empty beer bottles.

Mama Tessi was visiting overnight a sick friend, who was from her hometown but now lived in Escondido, thirty minutes north of San Diego. I was wondering about the absence of aroma coming from her kitchen as I walked in the house. You could almost count on Mama Tessi to have a pork or chicken *adobo*, marinated in garlic, soy sauce, and vinegar, or beef *afritada*, meat stewed all day with green peppers, onions, tomatoes, and potatoes. Instead, I was met with stinky bachelor odors and ashtrays.

They were sweating bullets about losing their careers, their reputations, and the change their family would have to face. Not only would I devastate the careers of otherwise fine men who got greedy, but their families would suffer.

I've seen it all before. When the sailors arrived at various Asian ports, there were strong demands for American items, such as watches and radios. It becomes very tempting to make some extra quick bucks. They could easily be used in bartering for everything from gold or diamonds to illegal drugs. Many sailors would load up on ten-dollar Timex watches to be used for their bartering.

Some of the torpedoes were missing warheads to make space for various illegal items. I was often reminded of how thankful the war was coming to an end with very little naval activities. Otherwise, we may have shot at enemy sailors with nonexplosive contraband-filled torpedoes.

Once these sailors reached their home port, their desires were to sell these items quickly for some profit, to recoup the cash for the next trip. Most of the time, they were without the connections to dump their commodities, such as gold, diamonds, or illegal drugs. Trying to recoup their investment before their sub leaves the port, these sailors try desperately to dump their stuff, and that's when they make their mistakes.

Trying so hard to get rid of the stuff, they often get busted by the local police or the MPs. Each year, there would be a handful of sailors in prison for smuggling charges. Kino was well aware of it. He spoke up first.

"*Pare*," he called me friend in Tagalog, his native language, but continued in English. "I'm not going to lie to you. I am scared about what is going to happen to my mother. If I am being deported, she goes with me, and to be honest, I'm not prepared to care for her back in Manila as I'd be in America. Once back home, I can go back to working all day as a cook or a laborer. What about Mother? What happens to all her medical and social security benefits? Oh my God, what did I do?" He started freaking out, pacing back and forth.

"Calm down, *pare*. There you go, doing that loco Pinoy stuff again, going all crazy and excited about nothing. I filed the report clearing your sub free of contrabands. There is no way I could live with myself if I sent Mama Tessi back to Manila. To protect her, I cannot arrest you." I looked at his two buddies.

"And of course, it will be unfair to your two friends if I arrest them and not you. You've put me in a very difficult situation here, Kino. I must deal with it the best I could." I needed a drink but continued.

"I thought about this with my heart, and I am going to grant you gentlemen a one-and-only pass from me, you hear me, *pare*? What I could use is a drink of your whiskey, if you got it."

As Kino went to the cupboard to retrieve a bottle of Crown Royal and some glasses, his buddy from Sioux Falls, South Dakota, spoke up in his tenor voice. He had graduated from the academy two years ago as a CPA and drew *Hawkbill* as the assignment and had been aboard her ever since, serving as their disbursing officer.

With Kino as a ship serviceman in charge and a chief culinary officer to team up with their disbursing officer aboard, all the comings and the goings of supplies aboard the ship were covered by these three. Kino wasn't stupid at all. In fact, he was quite the businessman, knowing which man was necessary to partner up with for his purpose.

The chef and the ensign hooked up with him, each coming up with the initial three grand each to get the ball rolling. The ensign from Sioux Falls pointed out that it could easily be split four ways, if I was interested. All I had to do was simply return the confiscated items in order to become the fourth partner.

I responded to him in a firm voice, "I can't and won't be part of anything illegal. I am willing to return your gold this time. From now on, I will be watching you three even closer, you can count on that. I will bust your asses as quickly as I find any more illegal stuff on your possession. Here is your gold. As soon as my whiskey wears off, I am going to walk away from here and all of this mess. The next time you see me, you better have your noses clean."

During the three years I served aboard *Dixon* as a military police officer, the amount of submarine sailors trying to bring contraband into our base was reduced significantly due to the presence of Zion and his reputation.

The ship commanding officer had contributed it to the tight ship our department ran. My supervisor was more than happy to take the credit for that.

Sarah was preparing to finish her undergrad and begin her studies as a veterinary student. She would keep in close contact with Judy as her surrogate "bother" on my behalf, becoming very close to Judy. On occasions, she would break my heart, sharing the news that my father was beating Joey. Now that I was gone, my dad was beating my brother.

I tried to forget about it by focusing on my job and learned the ins and outs of police work. It was exciting when there was actual crime to be solved. I was taught by a lieutenant named Dysart, who had the reputation of having solved every crime assigned to him.

That included a murder case while he served in the Thirty-Second Base in San Diego. That was a record that couldn't be topped. He was a lifer ready to serve out the remainder of his thirty years' active duty. He was a true crime solver rather than a crime stopper.

I had found favor in his eyes, and he would often ask me to tag along in his investigations, asking for my observations and take on things. He asked questions that made sense only to him. I enjoyed him rather fondly and cherished the times when he had asked me to come along with him on his crime solving. He was my own Lieutenant Frank Columbo, the far-out detective on television.

Life could be quite harsh at times, as it took my mom from me at such a tender age. On occasion, it could be mighty kind as well. This Lieutenant Dysart, my supervisor, had a brother six years older than him, a captain in the Denver Police Department. His brother had gone up the rank from a patrolman to a captain since being discharged from the Marine Corps twenty-three years ago.

By the time I was about to be discharged, my supervisor aboard the USS *Dixon* had a job in the Denver Police Department waiting for me. He had grown fond of me as I had faithfully and diligently served him. He had made a recommendation to his older brother to give me a try.

His brother, second only to the police chief of this tightly run police department, was looking to act upon the recently increased budget to hire more officers to serve the growing population of the Denver metro area.

To older Dysart, the recommendation his younger brother had made was regarded with much respect, as he loved and respected his younger brother's honest and straightforward style. I was going home with a job that came with benefits and retirements. Life could be quite generous.

I drove to Tijuana for some shopping. I bought a wooden chess set and other items that would serve as presents to my family and friends back home. I finished my shopping with a bowl of menudo, cow tripe soup cooked with hominy, and ate it under a tent. Then I drove back across the border toward Kino's place, where my going-away party was waiting for me.

When I got to his house, all my favorite people were packing the house. The ensign, who had become a lieutenant since, walked up to me and gave me a salute, then a hardy handshake. Then he handed me two small black bankbooks. I opened to find each book with $711,610 in balance. I asked him what it was, and he told me it was a going-away present.

"Let's just call it a very small token of appreciation for being our true friend especially to Mama Tessi and Kino. I won't go into details, but let's just say we found a better and legal way to get gold here and turned some mighty handsome profits each trip." I must have looked stunned.

Lieutenant continued, "All of us are walking away with over twice your portion, so don't think we were that generous. Your original cut was one of those books, but Kino matched it, saying he was doubly grateful for Mama Tessi's sake, which is the second book. I can't be that generous, you understand," said the smiling lieutenant.

Still dazed, I put the bankbooks into my breast pocket. The lieutenant told me books are only for the record. I could have the money transferred to anywhere in the world, with a simple phone call.

The party ended, and I looked for Kino and Mama Tessi to thank them for such a wonderful time. I asked Kino if we could talk about the bankbooks, but he said there was no need to discuss any further. He said he got the better end of the deal, and he ought to be able to show his gratitude without me putting up too much of a fight. I accepted his gratitude with my own.

The next morning, I made the long-distance call to Cayman Islands and had $11,610 transferred to my account with the Navy Credit Union from both accounts. I left an even $700,000 on each of the accounts but changed the names and passwords of both accounts.

The day before leaving San Diego, I went to my credit union and closed the account, leaving the bank with almost thirty-five thousand dollars. I had saved about twelve thousand dollars for the dream of building safe houses for the past five years. Twenty-three thousand was added to it overnight.

I was not sure when, but I was going to surprise Joey and Judy with their bankbooks when the time was right. I packed up my trusty Chevy truck with all my belongings. I was going home to the Rockies where my bride-to-be was waiting. It had been a year since I'd been home.

It was really hard for me to say good-bye to Zion. He was oblivious it was our last good-bye, just glad to see his buddy after hours. I gave him the treat I had brought him and walked away as he started to enjoy his steak.

CHAPTER 18

May 1976

I came home just in time for successive celebrations. First, it was the sweet sixteenth for my sister, Judy, followed by Sarah's graduation ceremony. She was accepted into their veterinary program at CSU, her alma mater.

Only a week after her graduation, our wedding ceremony took place before a church full of well-wishers. Everyone teased Sarah that she was so anxious to become a bride it only took her a week after her graduation to do so.

Joey, who at nineteen had experienced growth spurts and stood over me at six-one, did the honor of being my best man. Sarah's younger brother, Ken, stood next to Joey. My baby sister, Judy, was a baby no longer. At sixteen, she had become an unwitting competitor to my bride, Sarah, as she stood next to Esther, Sarah's matron of honor, along with my two cousins, Lisa and Sharon.

Originally, I had asked Dwight to be my best man, but he told me he was in the middle of law review while completing his BA from Columbia, desperately trying to get into Harvard Law School. He wasn't able to confirm at that time. He had even declined our invitation for a day or two in Honolulu after the wedding as it was just not possible.

I had also asked Kino to be my groomsman at the wedding. His sub was scheduled to be deployed just prior to my wedding, and he said it seemed impossible.

As I stood at the altar, Dwight walked out of the door next to the church podium where I was waiting for my bride to walk down the aisle with her father, surprising me with delight. He came to hug me as I stood dumbfounded, then asked me if he was allowed to stand next to me. Joey gladly made the space for Dwight, making Ken move over slightly farther.

Dwight had to fly back to New York immediately after the wedding but not before the reception and some photo ops with me and Sarah. He had final exams to tend to back in Columbia on Monday, two days after my wedding day.

Just as the preacher was about to start speaking, Kino came out of the side door and came to give me a bear hug. He went over and stood next to Ken as my fourth best man. He was decked out in his Cracker Jack—blue sailor's uniform. When their sub had pulled into Okinawa, Japan, Kino and the petty officer flew to the United States for my wedding after getting a special leave from the commanding officer of the *Hawkbill*.

He hadn't slept a wink as he and Paco travelled all night to catch the connector in Los Angeles. When they missed their flight, they had to wait six hours for the next plane to Denver. He was so glad to be a part of my wedding.

Lieutenant, Mama Tessi, Kino, and Paco flew back to San Diego together. The two submariners spent four days of R&R before flying to Busan, Korea, to rejoin their submarine.

Sarah would be Mrs. Lee as she began her veterinary schooling in September. The campus was located in Fort Collins, Colorado, an hour north of Denver. It was a teaching hospital university. The program was designed to allow the students to get their hands dirty by actually treating the animals in need and assisting during surgeries.

I made an offer to buy a house seven blocks away from Sarah's campus. It was on the market for just below thirty-two thousand dollars. Two months after the wedding, we moved into a two-bedroom home with an acre of yard. It was a humble beginning for Mr. and Mrs. James Lee. Sarah purchased a used bike at a yard sale and used it to commute to her classes.

Our marriage seemed to have started on the right path, and I found renewed strength within, as Sarah proved to be a wonderful helpmate. She was confident and secure as an individual, and I benefited tremendously from her presence. She made me look good in all areas of my life. I was truly a blessed man.

Our honeymoon in Hawaii was a major bash. It included the party of twelve. No one was aware of my savings and became suspicious when the spending became beyond what a sailor could have saved up for his wedding. I told them about the good investment tips I had and some success with it while stationed in San Diego.

My bride and I were joined by my father and Sarah's parents and Sarah's younger brother, Ken. He had shown quite an interest in my baby sister, Judy, and rightfully was being admonished by Deacon Kim. Of course, Joey and Judy came with us, as well as Uncle Phillip, Aunt Cindy, and the two cousins, Lisa and Sharon, to make an even dozen. We had a reservation for a honeymoon suite along with three additional suites for the family at Waikiki Marriott hotel.

We had booked the best of rooms available, many tours and shows, right down to luaus and hula shows. Even Dad got into the tourist spirit and, in his celebration, indulged in a little wine with his meals. Not used to alcohol consumption, he quickly became inebriated and transformed into a quite enjoyable fellow.

On the sixth and final day of our trip, I sent the five young ones free. I asked Joey to escort Ken and Judy along with our cousins on their own to do some shopping and sightseeing. I gave Joey five hundred dollars to spend liberally on our sister and two cousins.

The elder five members had joined Sarah and me on a helicopter ride to see a volcano crater before our lunch at the top of the mountain. For our dinner, we were aboard a cruise ship that sailed around the island while serving some exquisite menus. All of us had enjoyed a wonderful meal and entertainment aboard. Next day, we sadly had to pack up and return home.

A dozen well-tanned and rested folks in Hawaiian shirts, walking down the Stapleton airport corridors, must have been a grand sight. As we exited the airport building, we discovered that the temperature was nearly thirty degrees below the temperature in the Honolulu airport. There were storms on its way with strong winds. Everyone ran to their respective cars, trying to keep from being blown away by the gale.

The next morning, Sarah got a call from Judy that Dad and Joey had gotten into a fistfight, and Joey was arrested for assaulting and injuring Dad severely. A week in paradise, and less than a day after the return home, these two had a reason to fight each other. I could not believe what I was hearing.

I had to go see Dad and visit Joey. Before leaving the house, I called to speak with my new boss. Even before he was able to congratulate me on my wedding, I was asking him for help with Joey's matter. At times, a case can be dismissed during the preliminary hearing.

Having a friend in the DA's office could be a big help, and I was hoping the captain would be just the man to have such a connection. I wanted the case to go away entirely. I was hoping Joey would join the force and serve with me after he graduated from college.

He had accepted a scholarship from the University of Colorado last year. Only a few weeks into his summer vacation, he was locked up in jail. A felony record would eliminate any chance of Joey becoming a peace officer.

"It's your father, Jimmy. He has filed a complaint against your brother, which kind of ties our hands, if you know what I mean. A police department cannot disregard your father's complaint and make the case disappear. Let me look into it and see what's up before we get all bent out of shape, okay, Jimmy?" said my future superior.

"Sir, I cannot ask for more than that. Meantime, I'll go visit Dad and see if he had a change of heart. Thanks for your help, Captain. I'll report for training a week from Monday as ordered."

"Don't worry about your brother, Jimmy. It will all work out okay, as it always does."

"Yes, sir, thank you so much for looking into this matter. Good-bye, sir."

"Welcome aboard, son." Captain Dysart was a marine after all these years, with his military crew cut and the buttoned-down uniform down to the spit shined shoes. I was very comfortable with the captain's no-nonsense attitude, much similar to his brother. I was looking forward to serving him as I had served his brother.

I left Sarah to take care of the thank-you cards while I drove over to see Dad in the hospital.

Nine years ago, the day my mother had passed away, I had visited him at the same hospital on the same floor, a couple of rooms away from where I found him this time.

Before the beatings had started and my life still evolved around him, his injuries would have devastated me. Yet here I was, angry at my father instead. How can a man, after having abused his sons, have his own son arrested for fighting back?

When I saw the broken nose on my father's face, my anger had quickly shifted from him to Joey. What did Joey do? My dad was suffering in pain and looked like a mummy wrapped up tightly.

CHAPTER 19

The Fight

My dad had found Joey's stash of *pakalolo* (Hawaiian marijuana). When Joey had learned Dad had flushed it down the toilet, he approached Dad with great anger, as he had spent two hundred dollars on the stuff.

Dad had a choke hold, which he used on his victims. I had fainted more than once during his choking. When Dad grabbed Joey by the neck to begin choking him, Joey had kneed Dad in the lower stomach and freed himself from Dad. And in a blind rage, he head butted Dad on the nose and broke it.

Eventually, Dad would change his mind and drop the charge against Joey. By then, it was too late as the district attorney's office had used the discretion ascribed by the law to continue with the case even when the complaint had been dropped by the victims.

Mr. West was retained by me to represent Joey. I was extremely happy Dwight's father was willing to work on Saturday morning. The pro bono service he had provided for me back when I was in junior high school had yielded lucratively, as I gave him ten thousand dollars to retain him.

It was agreed that an additional ten thousand was to be paid if Joey's case needed to go to a trial. I was hoping it would disappear after the arraignment. If not, at least by the preliminary hearing.

I liked the aggressive style of defense West was known for. He did not care to plea-bargain. He talked tough and had the reputation to back it up in the courtrooms with his ability to litigate. He knew his stuff. He and I went to visit Joey after he had made me sign the contract outlining his fee schedules.

Joey was brought to us, escorted by an officer. Joey's hands remained cuffed together behind his back during the entire visit. It was not a regular but a special attorney visit, which allowed attorneys to speak in private, alone in a room with their clients.

Joey cautiously sat on a plastic chair bolted down to the floor, leaning forward. Mr. West looked into Joey's eyes. Without even a hello or introduction, he spoke with a voice that resonated much like John Wayne, the Duke.

"Listen, Joseph, you're lucky DA's office didn't follow up on their threat to file an elder abuse charge against you in addition to the assault charge. You're extremely lucky because that's a difficult charge to fight off. Had they done that, your fee would have been doubled, and your bail would be much higher when the judge sets it in a couple of weeks from now. He has to wait now until the probation interview and to see if you are eligible for probation, and then the psych evaluation to see if you are in sane or not, which is all brought on due to the additional charge.

"Meantime, you keep your mouth shut, talk to nobody about nothing, you got that? By the way, Jimmy, the more people showing up to support your brother in the courtroom, the better it looks. So gather as many people as possible, and show up on time, dressed nicely, can you handle that?"

"Yes, of course."

"And bring a change of clothes for Joe too. A dark suit with a white shirt and red tie would be nice. If you don't have any questions, I will see you both on Monday." He stood and shook my hand and nodded at Joey before exiting the visiting room. The guard did not come to take away Joey and gave me a chance to speak with him.

"Look, Joey, I want to talk about what happened, but if you don't want to, I understand."

"What the hell do you want me to say, Jimmy? It's not like you don't know. He's been beating you since Mom died. Do you know he beat me up the day you left for the boot camp? He got really pissed off at Uncle Phillip for taking me and Judy to the airport to say good-bye to you when Dad told him not to. Instead of taking it out on Uncle, Dad took it out on me that night. He left bruises on my face that lasted for days."

"I had no idea." I didn't know what else to say.

"And then, it felt like every day he was on my case for one thing or another. Just picking on me for everything I did or didn't do."

"..."

"What I can't figure out is how you took all that crap from Dad without ever going off on him or going completely bonkers?"

"O-Jung."

"O what?"

"O-Jung. You were too small to remember the time we lived in a village called O-Jung before moving to Seoul."

"What's that got to do with what I was saying?"

"I'll tell you about it when you get home. It's a long story, and we don't have too much time before the visiting hour is over." Sure enough, the PA system, with crackling speakers, told us the visit was terminated and for Joey to stand by the gate.

I wanted to share with my brother that I had been terrified since learning that it is the abused that becomes the abuser. I wanted to talk to him about the chain that needed to be broken and how I had found a counselor in the navy who had helped me undo what the abuse had done to me. He worked with me for two years, with weekly sessions helping me to cope with the abuse from the father that had caused deep scars on my emotions.

I wanted to tell Joey about all the stories that Uncle Phillip had shared with me, about how our grandfather had beaten our father on so many occasions until people thought our father was dead.

I wanted Joey to understand the importance of breaking the chain and that he and I would work together to not only cut the chain but heal from the injuries caused by it. It would have to wait for another time, as he was being escorted back to his cell.

CHAPTER 20

The Arraignment

It pleased me to see that everyone showed up on time, dressed appropriately as I had instructed them. Joey's friends, church members, Sarah, and I, along with my uncle and aunt, sat in a group occupying most of the pews.

Dad insisted he attend the arraignment, but Mr. West finally convinced Dad that his appearance would not only benefit the prosecution but hurt Joey, sitting there as a victim with bandages on his face. Dad reluctantly waited in the courthouse cafeteria while Joey's arraignment was taking place.

When Mr. West found out that the district attorney himself would be prosecuting the case, he realized something was up. Captain Dysart had friends in the DA's office, but Mr. DA himself was not one of them. Carlson did not have many friends.

"Charles Carlson present for the people, Your Honor."
"William West for the defense on behalf of Joseph Lee, who is in custody and present in the courthouse, and we are ready to proceed, Your Honor."
"Before we proceed with the plea, Your Honor, the people of the county of Arapahoe wishes to amend the charges against the defendant, Jae-min 'Joseph' Lee. In addition to count one of the aggravated assault, count two, a crime against the elders, is to be added. The injuries sustained by his father, the victim in this case, are most horrific and gruesome. We are also asking the court to grant the petition that a restraining order against the defendant

be placed to prevent him from any physical contact with his victim. We are ready to proceed with the plea, Your Honor."

"Your Honor, this is a prime example of how low a politician is willing to go to further his political career. Mr. Carlson and I are on the same side on the issue of safety for the elders. However, this case is not anywhere in the scope of being a crime against elders. In fact, it shall soon be evidenced in the courtroom, the victim of this case actually began the whole thing by choking the defendant, requiring the defendant to defend himself." Mr. West continued, "The restraining order, if I may address the court, is filed by the DA's office and not the victim. I am filing the motion to dismiss the request for the restraining order requested by the DA's office in this case, Your Honor." Mr. West stood quietly as he spoke, and he sat down when he had finished.

"Your Honor, we should let the jury decide whether such crime took place or not."

"I agree with the prosecution," said the presiding judge. "Let the record reflect the amended charges as it is entered into the docket. Let us proceed with the plea." It looked as if Mr. West was about to double his fee with the additional charge.

Joey was instructed by Mr. West to plead "not guilty" to both charges. The bail hearing was postponed for two weeks until the psych evaluation and an interview with the probation department to determine Joey's mental state during the time of his alleged crime.

He would remain locked up until the hearing that was scheduled in fourteen days. Two deputies escorted Joey out of the courtroom. Joey looked back at me, and I could see he was disappointed with the way things had gone during the arraignment. I drove to Mom's grave before heading home. I needed to think.

I had a whole week before starting my new job and was able to visit Joey each afternoon. On my third visit, he was escorted to the visiting room, dressed in an all-white jumpsuit instead of dark blue.

It had *Ad-Seg* printed on the back. Administrative-segregation, meaning he was in the *hole*.

Before the visit, I was told by the guard, who knew I was a cop, that Joey was being disciplined for an altercation he was involved with other inmates. The guard went on to volunteer information that three inmates that Joey had beaten up had been released as the jail administrator had feared being sued by them. Joey seemed to be in a bind, and I didn't know how to help him.

In the 1970s there was an influx of boat people from Vietnam. The American government decided to help the Vietnamese refugees by granting them access to low-income housing in various cities. In Denver, it had created heated rivalries between the incoming Vietnamese and the Hispanics being forced out to make room for these invading refugees. Joey was mistaken for a Vietnamese by the Hispanics. He was confronted by three hombres from the West Side. All three would regret they messed with Joey.

Joey had tried patiently to explain there were a thousand miles between Korea and Vietnam and that even though we looked similar, we spoke different languages and had distinctive cultures and civilizations. They had failed to see that Joey was not their enemy and went and flexed their *guete* (muscle). They had overestimated their odds against Joey as all three went on to receive serious injuries from him. Joey held nothing back and went off on the vatos until they were all out cold, to the cheers of all non-Hispanic observers in the dayroom.

Joey liked the single-man cells in the ad-seg, with meals brought to you three times a day—no hassles from other inmates. Not a bad way to do time for a loner.

"I taught those guys a lesson they will never forget, *hyung*," Joey huffed.

"And yet, you are the one who is in the ad-seg while they were cut loose early this morning. Who is learning the lesson here?"

"What? How in heck did they get out? Anyway, you know, Jimmy, some things can't be avoided," Joey said as he looked right into my eyes. "They wanted to teach me a lesson, they said. I had to show them I am not scared. I can't go down like that in here. Otherwise, they would have been all over me like hyenas on a meaty carcass or treating me like a woman. You know what I'm saying, right?"

"You got to remember something, Joey. You see, there are times in life when you will face challenges. Some, however, are not worth getting all hot and bothered over, while others will help us to learn and to grow as we face them. The trick is to know which is which."

"I remember you went to juvenile hall, so don't go preaching to me."

"Look, I was standing up for my best friend, Dwight, against a humongous bully a foot taller than me. I think it's a little different than kicking down some skinny punks for no reason. Forget that for a moment. You got to remember there are dog poops on our path at times. We go around it not because we are scared of it. We don't step on it just to prove we are not scared of it either. No, Joey, we walk around it because it is dirty.

"When we step into it, we have to clean up the mess. Why deal with the mess when it could have been avoided completely? No one will call you a coward because you walk around dog poop. But they may think you are stupid for stepping into it. Some people are no better than those piles of poops. Don't bother with them, ignore and walk around them. If you step on it, as you did with those guys, you will end up with felony charges against you like this time. Next thing you know, you are going down for being a habitual criminal, doing a life."

". . ."

"Your behavior while you are in here can either help or hurt you in the courtroom, and you know that. Thus far, you are your worst enemy. Be focused from this point on.

"Your attorney told you to keep to yourself and not speak to anyone. If you followed that instruction, you wouldn't be in this situation. You have to help yourself with this case and not hinder it any further, you got that?"

"I feel so stupid, Jimmy. I keep digging a deeper hole to bury myself in."

"Let's just hope they won't file additional charges against you for beating up those three guys."

"Okay, Jimmy. Tell everyone hello for me."

I walked away from the visiting room with a pain deep down in my heart. I was willing to accept the fact Joey did not get accepted by the Ivy League schools. God knows he tried. At least he was accepted by the University of Colorado.

I have failed Mom when I chose to join the navy rather than going to college. With Joey, I felt as if I had failed him as a "bother" as well. While I tried so hard to help him do what is best for him, Joey resented anyone offering tips or instructions.

I drove to Mom's grave with a heavy heart.

CHAPTER 21

Summer of 1983

Since her graduation from CSU Veterinary School in 1979, Sarah became popular among the denizens of Fort Collins, who had the good fortune to meet her during the four years since becoming a vet.

President Reagan began his first term by declaring a war against drugs and also revealing his Star Wars plan. He went on to declare Martin Luther King's day a national holiday. He became the first American president to address Japan's legislators. John Hinkley had attempted to assassinate Reagan but was found not guilty by reason of insanity.

OPEC cut oil prices for the first time in twenty-some years, and the United States invaded Grenada and easily won. You could not go anywhere without hearing David Bowie's "Let's Dance" or "Thriller" by Michael Jackson. Reverend Jesse Jackson launched his first campaign for presidency.

The NFL was playing in London, and the Oakland Raiders moved to Los Angeles. NFL players began their 1983 season with a strike. The LA Dodgers played twenty-two innings before finally beating the Cubs 2 to 1 in Wrigley Field. Wayne Gretzky became the first to score two hundred hockey goals, and Steve Garvey played in his one thousandth consecutive game, going zero for four. Pete Rose hit 3,772 to pass Aaron into second place. He would go on to make 13,941 plate appearances at the end of the season.

Reverend Sun-Myung Moon of the Unification Church married six thousand randomly paired couples in Seoul, Korea. Marie Osmond broke lots of guys' hearts when she married Steve Craig. Later in the year, Reverend Moon began serving his eighteen months' sentence for tax evasion.

Honda became the first Japanese automobile company to produce cars in the United States by opening a plant in Marysville, Ohio.

The Supreme Court ruled that the president cannot be sued for actions in office. Cyanide-laced Tylenol killed seven people in Chicago.

Russia increased their underground nuclear tests. The United States retaliated by doing nuclear tests of our own in the Nevada Desert. Russians shot down Korean Air flight 007, killing everyone aboard. The world seemed chaotic and frantic.

Life in the township of Fort Collins was much quieter and simpler. At the beginning of the year, I was offered a senior detective position by the Fort Collins Police Department. They hoped to recruit me away from DPD, where I became a sergeant in 1981. As Sarah and I became involved with the community activities in Fort Collins, they became aware I was a lawman in the state capital city and married to the town's famous animal doctor.

The new job would mean I didn't have to commute forty-five minutes each way to and from Denver five days per week. Sarah felt it was a much safer place for me to work. She was quick to add the increase in salary the new position was offering would be nice as we try to raise a family. It was an offer I could not refuse.

I had two detectives under my command. Together, they had three years of experiences as detectives. When the senior detective had a heart attack, he decided to retire and created an open spot unexpectedly. I enjoyed my new position. I had weekends off, including paid holidays. No more weekend duties or third watch for me.

Four years ago, shortly after becoming a veterinarian, Sarah had made an offer to her aging mentor, who was looking forward to his retirement. Sarah was assigned to Dr. Bill Simms's animal hospital during her final year of school to do her internship.

During that year, Sarah had come to respect the kind and gentle method the good doctor had used to treat his patients. He was an animal doctor with a heart. For the first time, Sarah had a vet she could look up to and emulate.

Sarah had come to learn that the good doctor was looking to retire within a decade or so, when he turned seventy. Sarah came to me with an idea that if Dr. Simms would make her an equal partner, she would add onto the existing building a state-of-the-art facility that could accommodate the medical needs for larger farm animals as well as the household pets.

Sarah had excitedly explained the new equipments and technology of today allowing doctors to use less-invasive, less-painful methods in treating the animals. To accommodate those equipments, she had to build from the ground up, with much stronger electric circuits.

It also required thicker walls lined with lead around the x-ray room. For the past nineteen years, Bill had sent his patients to another clinic for his x-ray needs. The idea he would have his own x-ray machine tickled the good doctor pink.

The current building Dr. Bill was operating from was nothing more than a three-bedroom house converted to a clinic. His property included three empty lots used as parking spaces, when a single lot could have been more than sufficient for the purpose.

It was Sarah's genius to see an annex built onto this charming clinic in two of the three lots, with a paved parking lot on the last lot. The plan included so that the clinic could receive ambulances that bring animals for care right into their OR. Their clinic would gain the prestigious status as a complete service hospital, setting them apart from the ordinary animal clinics.

Bill was so excited he was finally going to have a paved parking lot for his customers. Rainy days would not turn their parking lot and his waiting room into a mud factory anymore.

The bank was more than willing to lend us the money to build onto the clinic. They were impressed with the well-thought-out plans Sarah had presented to them but asked if we would put up the house for collateral. I was more than willing. Bill accepted Sarah's offer after the bank's decision. In a matter of months, as the construction and the inspection had been completed, they became equal partners of the property and the existing medical practice.

It was a wonderful opportunity for a neophyte veterinarian. It would go on to benefit her partner even greater. His share of the income was triple of what he had earned before it became a hospital. Likewise, their property value had increased in many folds from its humble beginning just months ago.

Three years later, our construction loan was paid in full. Sarah was ahead of schedule by two years. Bill began working half-time and enjoyed more time with his grandchildren. Without the bank payments, the hospital was able to buy the empty lot that was across their parking lot. Sarah had been talking to Bill regarding a better facility for their clients to recover from their surgeries and procedures. Their current recovery room was nothing more than a glorified storage room turned into a shelter.

Their plan was to build one story down and two stories up, a total of three floors on the newly purchased lot. The plan had an underground tunnel beneath the parking lot to connect the two buildings. There would be two large elevators and wide ramps to ease the transfer from one floor to the next, to accommodate even a large horse. The patients never came in contact with outside elements to go from one building to the next once arriving at the clinic.
The plan required no additional parking, according to the building department. The building was about to become a state-of-the-art animal facility with minimal cost, as the design was simple and efficient.
The surplus of space was to accommodate the animals as a hotel for them when their owners were traveling or unable to care for them, for modest fees. During their stay, animals could receive the best of medical and dental care from the friendly staff at discounted rates. Soon, many customers looking to stay at their facility were turned away due to the lack of space. Sarah was a true innovator.

The hospital became successful in providing the most modern treatments for the animals. Folks brought their animals from as far as Denver to Cheyenne, Wyoming. When other animal hospitals were unable to treat the conditions, they were referred to Fort Collins Animal Medical Center.
With the success of her practice, Sarah had the time to begin focusing on her other ambitions. She began noticing the noise her biological clock was making. Sarah and I both agreed to start a family as soon as possible, but not before we were ready.
I asked her if she would be willing to seek counseling with me, to prepare us for parenthood. Two years had gone by since. We had been seeing a counselor individually and as a couple since then. We were ready to become parents.
I hoped and dreamed of having a son or a daughter to love and teach all the beautiful things life had to offer. I wanted to nurture and to cherish a little soul into a loving and caring individual.

For some reason, Sarah and I were unsuccessful. We went to see a specialist to see why. That was when the doctors discovered she had endometriosis, which made it dangerous for her to bear a child. It was recommended she terminate her efforts to become pregnant. She was devastated at first, quite obviously. A true champ, Sarah was able to shake it off and get back to focusing on her patients.

For me, it was a time of both sadness and relief. It pained me to see Sarah dealing with the news. After all the planning we had gone through for the past two years, she was clearly devastated by the news.

I felt it was God's way of breaking the chain of abuse I was a part of. If that was the case, then I was willing to accept it. We could always adopt a handful of children later on in life.

Meantime, Sarah and I went on to adopt several animals, some requiring extensive medical care. We built eight-feet-high chain-link fences around our acreage so we could let our animals run free. Mostly, these animals lacked a limb or two. We adopted a blind cat as well.

Our home was slowly turning into an ambulatory clinic for the unwanted animals with needy medical conditions. It helped Sarah and me to forget about her medical problems by focusing on these animals.

Judy graduated in 1978 from South High School, my alma mater, with the highest GPA in her class and a perfect SAT score. There were only a handful of perfect scores each year, and my little sister was one of them.

Her college application would have impressed any university she was applying to. She applied to eight universities and received acceptance letters from each of the Ivy League schools. With the exception of Cornell, each school offered Judy a full scholarship for four years. Judy said she felt resentful toward Cornell.

Judy had made copies of her eight acceptance letters and rolled them up and tied it with a purple ribbon around the letters with a bow. She placed it in front of Mother's headstone, sat there for quite some time, crying, as I waited in the car as instructed by her.

She cried as if Mom had passed away yesterday, yet it had been eleven years since she was taken from us. Judy was a good daughter to honor our mom's wish even after all the years had passed since her death.

In the end, Judy's choices had narrowed down to Penn and Yale. She was quite intrigued with the University of Pennsylvania that was founded by Benjamin Franklin. Both Sarah and Judy had agreed with me that Philadelphia was an exciting and romantic city, as we visited the campus. She had opted to become an Eli in the end.

Judy had become quite active with the Young Republicans as she tagged along with me and Sarah in our involvement with the Republican Party campaigns. She came face-to-face with George Bush Sr. during his campaign in Denver as Ronald Reagan's running mate.

Mr. Bush had actually talked Judy into becoming his alum, with his charming personality that made her feel like he was her longtime friend. Yale was founded by Elihu Yale, the benefactor, whose nickname of Eli has become a recognized term identifying the students or graduates of Yale University.

She went through four years of Yale with a 4.0 GPA while serving as a legal aid apprentice during the last two. She enjoyed working with the group of attorneys helping the poor in need of legal aid. She began to learn the ins and outs of the court system during those two years.
Life in New Haven, Connecticut, was quite different than it was in Denver. She realized how important it was to obtain and maintain culture, thus, finally allowing her to take time off from her studying and participate in the social gatherings she was often invited to.

Last year, Judy had applied to Harvard, Princeton, and Cornell law schools. She was happy to decline Princeton and Cornell by announcing she had decided to attend Harvard law. Judy would share with me that the only reason she had applied at Cornell was to send them a letter to decline their offer. My little sister surely knew how to hold her grudges.

During her first year in Cambridge in 1982, she would run into my pal Dwight who had graduated from Harvard law in 1980. He was working on his PhD while serving as a teaching assistant when Judy ran into him.
I teased my friend of being a cradle robber when they started dating each other. In actuality, I was most relieved that she had someone as dependable as Dwight to look after her. He would go on to prove me correct when Judy became overwhelmed with her study load in her second semester. Dwight would cook for her and care for her when she truly needed someone in her life.

Dad was happy with his teaching position and was good at what he was doing. He had since turned the senior pastor position over to a younger minister.

Uncle Phillip and Aunt Cindy bought the Peking Palace from Mrs. Cho in 1981, when the professor was mysteriously shot and killed on New Year's Eve, in his restaurant parking lot. In his possession were over a thousand dollars in proceeds from the evening's business that was not taken.

I was not assigned to the case, but it had put a strain on the homicide guys for being unable to solve that murder. The Peking Palace restaurant became too much for Mrs. Cho to handle by herself. It was my idea that she allow my aunt and uncle to purchase the restaurant from her.

Uncle Phillip and Aunt Cindy offered Mrs. Cho eighty thousand dollars in cash for the restaurant. It was their entire savings that remained after buying the new LTD with cash. Mrs. Cho was happy to accept the offer, which was a good deal for both of the parties. She stayed on for two months to make certain Uncle Phillip and Aunt Cindy were able to manage the business without her.

All the full-time employees were given medical insurance shortly after Uncle took over the business. The business increased as the fresh energy had rejuvenated it. Soon, Uncle had opened his second location in Boulder, near the University of Colorado campus. The second location likewise experienced great success, even outearning the Colfax location. It seemed Uncle Phillip and Aunt Cindy had the Midas touch.

Cousin Lisa, who had graduated from the University of Colorado, Denver, became a CPA in 1982. She had developed a methodology that could prepare fresh ingredients in massive amounts for several locations from a single giant kitchen. With her concept, Uncle and her family would go on to open more locations in the Denver metro area.

Eventually, her marketing idea would expand to the frozen-food market. Thousands of packages were shipped each week from their kitchen to major grocery markets throughout the Midwest. No one could say any longer that her younger sibling was the smart one in the family.

My cousin Sharon went on to become a police dispatcher after graduating from high school. She went back to South Korea for a year after the graduation and, when she returned, did not have the drive to go to a university. By then, Uncle Phillip was about to buy the restaurant, and she chose to help her father with the business. After a year of waiting tables, she realized she needed to do more with her life.

It was when the Denver Police Department dispatchers went on a strike in 1982, demanding better benefits and pay. Sharon was hired to fill in, with just a minimum amount of training. When the strike had lingered into its third month, Sharon had proven to the department that she was capable to fill in while the veterans were on strike.

When the strike had ended, she was immediately hired to become a relief dispatcher, working the weekends, evenings, and holidays. Her genuine friendliness had dispelled the animosity that clearly existed at the onset of her position at the department. After all, she was a scab during their strike. Often, it was Sharon who had dispatched my partner and me on calls responding to emergencies. She began her criminal justice degree program during the day while working the third-watch shift.

Joey had found favor in the eyes of God and the presiding judge, as attorney West was able to take his case to trial and win with a not-guilty verdict. Sarah and I ended up paying Mr. West a total of twenty thousand dollars for his service.

It turned out to be a bargain, as West had to battle against a tough opponent. Apparently, the lesson he learned from the ordeal with Dad did not teach Joey well enough. Three years later, shortly after graduating from Boulder with a BA in physical education, Joey was arrested at a trendy Boulder nightclub for assault with great bodily injury.

Joey had kicked a man in the nose, who had flirted with his date, causing some serious damage to the man's face. Joey went on to serve two years of a four-year sentence in Canon City prison. He was given 50 percent off for good behavior, since it was his first offense.

When he was paroled in 1981 with two-year parole, he was deeply connected with a militia group involved in arms trade. His cell mate was one of the top-notch guys of this heavily armed and dangerous group of people dealing with automatic weapons and explosives. One thing led to another, and Joey was neck-deep in this illegal operation as their sales representative, so to speak.

He travelled with sample materials to potential customers, sealing the deals. Halfway into his parole, he was arrested with automatic-rifle clips and boxes of ammo. He violated his parole with additional charges of weapons possession by an ex-felon.

He was transferred from Boulder County Jail to Buena Vista men's prison, awaiting trial while serving one year for violating his parole. He was also wanted by federal prosecutors for interstate arms trafficking. When he finished his one-year term in a couple of months, he would be picked up by the feds for their trial.

Mr. West had jokingly made the comment that Joey was about to help him retire early. He was only half joking as in his hand was a check for twenty-five thousand dollars that Sarah had handed to him during our last appointment in his office. She had been saving to open her second hospital in Boulder.

I was so touched she was willing to spend it on Joey's defense even before I had asked her to. With my salary, it would have been difficult to come up with that kind of money. I didn't want to dip into the savings for the purpose of Joey's defense. It is good to have a doctor wife with extra cash even for my brother.

By then, Uncle Phillip was working on his second million. He was ready to handle any cost the defense was required to spend. He was a true example of what family means to you when it counted the most. He was the exact opposite of his brother, my dad. Dad never made the trip to the visiting room.

Sarah and I stopped by the grocery store and bought some sandwiches and soup from their deli. We went to Mom's grave and had a picnic. She knew just what her man needed. She came up with the idea for the picnic. I loved her dearly.

CHAPTER 22

1979—The Big Case

My first assignment after the completion of twelve-week training with the Denver Police Department in 1976 was to patrol the southwest side of the city in the heart of the Latino gang activities. I was assigned to ride with a partner who was a large Samoan American one year senior to me with the DPD.

While the east side of the city was active with the Bloods and the Crips going at each other, the west side had the story of its own. Chicanos, the Hispanics born in the state, were in war with the Paisanos, the children of the migrating workers born in the South American nations. What they shared in heritage, it was a different story when it came to sharing the turf.

I was becoming familiar with the major players in the area, arresting them repeatedly for the same crime over and over. These kids alone were job securities for all the peace officers in the area. My partner, Pat Lalua, who was on his fourth year with the department, had graduated a class ahead of me in 1975.

One day during our routine round, we came across a pusher that we had arrested just three days earlier. There he was, made the bail and was out doing the same thing he was arrested for three days ago. When my partner ran the pusher through for warrants at the station house, the sheet came back clean. There were no charges pending against him either.

The crime that my partner and I had arrested him for only three days ago did not appear in his printout as the case had been dismissed. His name did not come up during the search for his court date either. It was as if the previous arrest did not happen at all.

My partner was more than disturbed by what he was discovering. He wanted to know what is going on with this kid that his case disappeared into thin air. My partner personally supervised the booking process and escorted him to the county jail to be held until his arraignment.

Officer Lalua personally logged in the evidence with the clerk, who took the evidence into a secured room where they were kept until needed for laboratories for testing or for the courtroom during the trial.

You would think the kid was smart enough to pick a new area to peddle his dope after being arrested twice within four days from the same location by the same cops, but it was not to be. There he was, only a day after the second arrest, out and about in the same spot he had been arrested the day before.

It had caused my partner to finally lose his Samoan cool, and all seventy-five inches and 240 pounds of him expressed indignation. It was rather comical as his nostrils flared and his eyes became as big and round as a full moon in August, breathing deep and fast through his flared nostrils noisily. But I dared not laugh at him, though it took some efforts not to.

When I radioed in to run the kid for a warrant and bail status, again he came back clean, with no record of bail or court date for the second arrest either. My partner pulled the squad car he was driving ahead of the dope dealer, who was ready to walk away from the scene in a hurry.

The kid, whose name was Espinosa, had seven packages of heroin and five bundles of quarter-gram cocaine in his front pocket, much like the ones he had during his last arrest.

When he was cuffed, my partner did not drive to the station house. Instead, he drove to an abandoned building that was once a Kinney's shoe store before it became too dilapidated and abandoned as the store moved into a newly built mall less than a mile away. The back door was unlocked as he pushed it open and took Espinosa into the building with no lights.

Officer Lalua can be intimidating to anyone. Imagine Dick Butkus, the star linebacker for the Bears, who was the exact size of my partner at six-three and two-forty at his prime, standing before you in his war paint telling you he was about to kick your rear end from here till kingdom come.

Now multiply that by ten, and you have Pat in his imposing Denver Police Department uniform, with a face that needs no explanation that he is angry.

By the time Pat had stuffed the kid's mouth with a handkerchief and put the duct tape over it, this kid had wet his pants. Pat had used the tape-over-the-mouth trick before, which could put a fear of God into you real quick. He would tell his victims that it was to keep the noise from being too loud while Pat beat the information out of them.

It was all for effect and not to harm or injure the punk. In a matter of minutes, we had the information that he was one of the members of a team that had traveled north from Las Vegas with their boss man.

According to the kid, who stank of urine, this major dealer had made a deal with the DA to get his players released whenever one of the members was arrested. If that was true, the dealer was a major player with serious money. It had to be someone high up in the DA's office for that kind of deal to go down. We took the kid to the station house to be booked in for the third time in five days.

When we spoke with the captain, he decided to launch an immediate formal investigation. Chances were, Espinosa tipped off his boss and the DA's office connection that there may be possible police investigation. So we had to act quickly.

The FBI was brought in to conduct the investigation that led through the states of Nevada and Colorado. This major player turned out to be a Columbian cartel working out of Las Vegas.

The dealer had a major squeeze on Charles Carlson, the district attorney. Carlson was being blackmailed by the Columbian to release his dealers whenever they got arrested.

There is an old Korean adage that says, "If your tail's too long, you will get caught." No matter how careful you may be, it was only a matter of time before someone finds out what you are up to. It turns out that Charles Carlson led a double life. Eventually, his tail would be stepped on as it got too long.

While serving as the district attorney for the City of Denver, he was a respectful and professional man who had dotted all his i's and crossed all his t's.

While on vacations, however, he would be joined by a younger gentleman friend who had been Carlson's lover for the past decade. This younger man,

Carlson's lover, liked to do lots of cocaine while in Vegas. He became a regular customer of the very Columbian.

The younger man would brag about his boyfriend, the big shot from Denver, while copping some fine cocaine from the Columbian. Now, the South American used the information to blackmail Carlson for his drug-trafficking operation.

The deal was, whenever the dealers working for the Columbian would get arrested, Carlson would remove the evidence, then cite the lack of evidence and dismiss the case before being presented for the arraignment. No one was wise to it. A great system, had it not been for the stupid kid whose tail got way too long.

I had inadvertently revenged Carlson for frivolously prosecuting Joey two years ago. Even though Joey had won, Carlson had caused lots of problems for Joey by filing the charge for crime against elders.

Now, he was going down for his crime. It was enough to bring Carlson down after three terms and a dozen years of dynasty. The feds had arrested him, and he was taken to the prison in Leavenworth, Kansas, to be held before the trial. That was the last we had heard of Carlson around Denver.

The Columbian closed shop and disappeared before anyone was able to arrest him. He was not seen in Las Vegas area either. He simply disappeared from the face of the earth.

My partner Pat and I were promoted to sergeants, and Pat was given an assignment to head a newly formed gang task force for the Denver downtown precinct, which to him was a dream job. I earned a detective shield and began working on major felonies. It was good to get out of the uniforms.

I was in the right place at the right time. Being involved in one big case was enough to propel my career to the next level. I was just riding shotgun as Pat went about his thing. The good fortune simply fell into my lap. Life can be very kind at times.

CHAPTER 23

1983—The "Fat Boys"

It was Uncle Phillip's idea to get a couple of motorcycles for our semimonthly ride to Buena Vista. In his effort to quench his second childhood urge, Uncle Phillip purchased two brand-new Harley-Davidson Glider Fat Boys. A black one for him and a maroon-colored one for me. They came with all the bells and whistles, with AM/FM cassette stereo and communication system to speak with each other via microphones and earpieces.

I would ditch my truck once I arrived at his mansion in Boulder and hop on the bike every other Friday afternoons to go see Joey in Buena Vista. It was a most pleasant two hours of ride a man could ask for. Too bad Joey was locked up and we were on our way to see him in his prison garb.

Just like its name, Buena Vista is a beautiful part of the Rockies, just over the peak from the Aspen resorts. We would get on the I-70 West near Boulder for an hour and shoot down toward Leadville on State 24 South to arrive at this beautiful mountain village, where its main commerce is the state prison and its visitors.

We stayed overnight at an inn and then visited Joey on Saturday mornings. It was Joey's request that we would visit him every other week so his girlfriend could come see him during the week that Uncle and I would not be visiting him.

Visitors had to go through two electronically operated gates while walking on a pavement. On both sides of the paved walk were twelve-feet-high chain-link fences, with corrugated sheet metals on the top. You walked through this tunnellike sidewalk before entering the building. There, you had to empty all your belongings and place it in a locker assigned to you.

You are only allowed to carry twenty dollars in quarters maximum per person; no bills were allowed. Too many inmates were smuggling in currencies to purchase drugs and alcohol inside the prison, which was available to anyone with the cash. Quarters were harder to sneak past the metal detectors the inmates had to go through. It was our routine to stop at a bank and get rolls of quarters for each trip.

A visitor tried to smuggle some drugs inside a roll of quarters, so now we have to break the rolls up into a plastic bowl they give you in front of a guard.

There were vendors who would sell items such as burritos and Philly steak sandwiches, which were premade, during lunchtime. There were vending machines with various sandwiches and chicken wings to be heated in the microwave oven as well.

To Joey, visiting time was his feast time. He always complained that the jail did not give him enough food. There were eight wings in a package. Once, Joey went through five packages of wings by himself during a visit. I ran out of quarters.

"Hey, Uncle Phillip, *hyung*, it's so good to see you guys," Joey said, as he was walking over to us. He was rubbing on his wrists where the handcuffs had been irritating him while being escorted from the hole to the visiting room.

When Joey arrived at Buena Vista prison, there were certain *shot callers* who wanted Joey to submit to their rules and regulations. Joey told them to get lost. Seeing the potential danger of violent activity ready to jump off, a staff sergeant had placed Joey in segregated housing until things calmed down. The hole is where all the troublemakers serve their punishments for various prison rules and infractions violated.

"Hey, Joey, are you still growing? You seem taller since I saw you last." To uncle, we were his sons. He was so fond of Joey, and it broke his heart to see Joey locked up. Uncle would never show his disappointment to Joey. He was always the cheerleader who supported us no matter what Joey or I did.

"Heck, with the slops they feed us here, I'm lucky to be alive. Because I lost so much weight, it makes me skinny and I look taller, is all." Joey did seem taller to me as well. In medical books, it says a man could potentially grow until the age of twenty-six. He had another year to grow. He did not look skinny at all. In fact, he had definitely gotten bigger than ever before.

"You want some wings, Joey?" I asked. It was only nine in the morning, but it was never too early for Joey to start on his wings. I walked toward the vending machines without waiting for his answer.

I got two packages of wings from the machine and placed them in the microwave oven. I purchased from a lady vendor a breakfast burrito and a steak sandwich. I bought two bottles of water for me and Uncle and a cola for Joey from the machine.

Story has it, a fight broke out between inmates in the visiting room last year. Some injuries came about during the fiasco from the cans and glass bottles out of the vending machines. Since then, only the plastic-bottled beverages are sold in the visiting room.

It was sad to see Joey going crazy over something as basic as a cola or chicken wings. It pleased me as well that he was being satisfied for the moment at least. I felt guilty about the twelve-ounce rib eye steak I had for dinner last evening, chasing it with aged tequila.

I broke the breakfast burrito and gave half to Uncle before taking a bite of my half. "You are getting pretty buffed there, bro. You've been hitting the iron pile?" I asked.

"Man, I get one hour a day out of my cell for a quick shower and some phone calls. I don't even get TV or radio, *hyung*. Hey, don't you have some kind of pull with these guys or connection or something? Man, can you get me a stinking radio at least?"

"I wish. I'd have done it a long time ago to hook you up with a hi-fi entertainment system, a wet bar, and weekly conjugal visits. The fact is, they couldn't do such favors even if we were connected or something. So what do you do all day, doing push-ups and crunches, eating potato chips from the canteen?"

"Pretty much. I get to order up to three books at a time from the library, and this clerk rolls his cart over once a week and brings my literary pleasures. I'm currently reading *War and Peace*, the concordance of the Bible, and the *Webster's English Dictionary*." Joey looked at me and then continued, "You know I've read the novel by Leo Tolstoy and did a paper on it once, but there are only so many books that are available to us." Joey took a quick bite of his steak sandwich, and then he continued, "I order books that have enough weights so when I'm not reading them, I can place it in a pillowcase to be used as barbells for workouts, you know, to supplement push-ups and sit-ups. I work out inside the cell all day because I'm stuck inside. It helps me to work off my steam."

"No wonder you are hungry all the time. I can see you are getting better cuts and definitions to your arms and neck from what I can see. You must be getting some nice cuts to your pectorals too?"

"That's hard to do without bench-pressing, but I get by doing incline and decline push-ups." Then Joey turned to Uncle, taking a bite from his sandwich. While chewing Joey said, "I hear you are opening another location inside the Cinderella City shopping center south of Denver, Uncle." Joey took another bite.

"It's working out well for us. Now that Cindy's two brothers and their family are here from Korea, we are never in shortage of good workers. If her baby brother decides to move to America, as I think he will soon, we can keep everyone working by opening more restaurants. I love America. It's heaven here."

"Unless you are me and have a father like mine. Then it's hell no matter where you are." Joey had stopped eating and got emotional all of a sudden. I noticed his voice got a little louder, and it drew attentions from the visitors sitting near us. Uncle spoke slowly and quietly.

"Hell is what you make of it, Joey." It isn't often my uncle talked so philosophically. He was usually more jovial and never so serious.

"What do you mean hell is what you make of it?" Joey looked up from his food with a smirk in his face, before taking a big bite of his sandwich. Uncle Phillip continued, "There was a samurai who had come home to find all of his family killed by a group of bandits that terrorized the area. He set out to find whoever was responsible for the death of his parents and his younger sister."

Uncle took a breather then continued, "You see, they had died senselessly. When he had found the gang of thieves responsible for the death of his family, he slaughtered each and every one of them."

Uncle stopped to take a sip from the water bottle before he continued, "The problem was, he was not content even after he had killed everyone who had taken part in the death of his family. He was still angry and bitter, which caused him overwhelming misery. He was about to commit seppuku or hara-kiri, ritual suicide, when he realized he didn't know anything about heaven or hell, his next destination. He decided to go to the nearest temple and try to find answers there."

Uncle repositioned the chair and sat up straight before he continued, "When he had arrived at the temple after a day's walk, he saw a monk by the well. The samurai approached and asked the monk for a drink of water. After a deep drink, the samurai turned and asked the monk if he knew the meaning of heaven and hell. The monk responded, 'The answer must be found by the seeker, and therefore, I could not tell you the answer, my good guest.'

"The samurai drew his sword and slew the monk on the spot. Killing had become easy for him since the revenge began. His temper got the best of him where his samurai training would have made him think twice before killing a monk. In a blind rage, the samurai had beheaded the monk who had bestowed kindness upon him.

"He then sought out another monk and asked the same question. To which the second monk answered, 'The answer is within you. It must not come from me.' Again, the samurai killed the second monk as well in his rage. Then the samurai saw a third monk sitting inside the temple, praying." Uncle grabbed a wing and took a bite of it. He continued on, using his half-eaten wing as a pointer illustrating his point.

"So the samurai approached him quietly, and when the monk noticed him, the samurai asked the same question he had asked the previous two monks." Uncle stopped his story to finish eating the wing he was holding.

"What happened, Uncle?" Joey was impatient. I was beginning to understand that Uncle was baiting Joey along, getting to the punch line.

"The third monk said to the samurai, 'Did your mother dress you like that this morning, or were you able to dress like a slob on your own?' The samurai did not hesitate to draw his sword and raised it high above, saying, 'How dare you insult me?' The monk looked up and said, 'That, my friend, is hell.'

"The samurai understood, at that moment, that this monk had taken chance with his life to teach something. He realized how he had become so hateful while fighting for the justice of his family. He realized it was his anger that controlled him and not the other way around as a trained samurai should. His family would have never wanted him to go on killing, but to forgive and find peace within, to live a life of his destiny and not a hateful life of vengeance. He began weeping in repentance.

"The monk stood up and walked over to put his hand on the shoulder of samurai who was sobbing. Wiping away the tears that were on the warrior's cheek, the monk said, 'That, my friend, is heaven.' Said the monk, before walking away, leaving the enlightened man alone in his wake."

Joey also straightened himself on the chair. "That's so touching it makes me want to throw up all the good wings I've been eating." Joey made the motion to stick his finger into his mouth, making a gagging sound. Uncle Phillip simply chuckled and picked up his burrito and started to eat. I decided to use the opportunity to share with Joey what I had been hoping to do for some time.

"All I know is that I used to ask God to take my life because it was just too painful to go on when Dad was beating me. I wanted the beatings and emotional abuses to stop so badly I was asking God to take my life. I'm glad God was slow to answer that prayer. One thing is for sure. When I finally came to forgive Dad, I was able to live with peace and find joy in things I had not before. Do you know, when I told Dad that I forgive him for all that he had done to me, Dad looked right into my eyes and said, 'I am not looking for your forgiveness. I don't know what I need to be forgiven for.' I tell you guys, it was like he was beating me all over again. I could not believe what I was hearing.

"I spoke with my counselor during my next meeting with him, to realize that even though I may be ready and willing to forgive someone or, in repentance, ask for someone's forgiveness, the other party may not be ready to reciprocate.

"I have learned to not be bothered by what others do or don't. I have no control over that. I don't take it personally, but I'm willing to wait until he or she is ready to deal with it. You know what, Joey? I have learned it does no good to force things or demand my way, because in the end, both parties must come to their terms when they feel comfortable to do so."

"Are you trying to tell me you forgive Dad for all that he has done to you, Jimmy?" I noticed Joey stopped calling me *hyung*. It was a telltale sign of him being upset.

"Yes. Not just Dad but anyone who wrongs me. I try to find a way to forgive them. You see, Joey, I've learned that the suffering I may receive from someone else's action against me is nothing compared to the destruction caused by the poison that stems from the inability to forgive them. It prevents me from moving on with life."

"Even when Dad refused to apologize, you still forgave him anyway? I don't get that." Joey had stopped eating altogether, showing obvious signs of being upset and agitated.

"I didn't want to give Dad the power to control my emotions any longer. I wanted to give goodness a chance over the evil. Each time I let myself get angry, I considered it as giving Dad the power to control me. Don't get me wrong. It didn't come easy nor did it come by on its own. I sought counseling and therapy sessions for years to help me understand what I do now.

"I used to think it was good fortune for me to come face-to-face with facts regarding the chain of abuse that takes place in so many lives. You see, Joey, I found out that it is the abused ones like you and me that become abusers down the line. It's a known disease that can be treated and cured.

"The disease that remained dormant in Dad until Mom passed away, that disease was passed on to him by his father—our grandfather—when Dad was a child growing up in North Korea. No one knows for sure, but something had triggered the dormant disease in Dad, and you know what happened after that." I took a drink from my bottle before I continued.

"But it wasn't that I was lucky or fortunate at all. All along, it was God who had heard my prayers during those moments of anguish. He had placed all these tips along the way for me to find and benefit from. I believe now they were part of the training I was receiving from God. It was the providence of God that helped me find the cure from the disease, not any luck or even the counselors that I entrusted to help me. God had everything planned to get me on the right track. Only then could I know how to help others suffering from the same disease.

"Look at Dad, who was abused, and Uncle, who wasn't. See the difference in how they behave? Their outlooks in life are different. It isn't just between these brothers you can see the impact that abuse has in life. Between you and me, there are obvious differences because I have gone through the treatments and you have yet to be helped by all these professionals ready and willing to help you as I had been helped. I blame that same darn disease for you being here today." Joey acted as if he had something to say, so I stopped.

"You are full of it, Jimmy. How does that disease or whatever the heck you're talking about have anything to do with why I'm here?"

"This disease has the ability to shorten the victim's fuse. Anger has a way of negating what God is trying to do. For example, we are taught there are nine fruits of the Spirit, right?"

"You're not going to imitate Dad and start preaching to me now, are you, Jimmy? After all, I've been starving for all the good snacks, and with all this preaching going on, I'm beginning to lose my appetite."

"Hear me out. Hatred has the ability to cancel out each of the fruits of goodness. Anger, which is a fruit of hate, cancels them out. Love, joy, peace, patience, goodness, faithfulness, gentleness, kindness, and self-control, which we are to exercise in our lives, are hindered by anger, bitterness, frustrations, and resentments. The attributes of God we are to emulate while on earth could literally be negated by the anger and violence that keep us from being godly while making us worldly. For example, you cannot express love for another while you're angry.

"Let me tell you what I think. I believe that self-control is listed as the ninth and the last, because it is the most difficult to attain." Joey said nothing.

I said, "Love comes easy. While it is the most important, everyone has the ability to love. Even a baby or the most hardened criminals know how to express love. So it's listed as the first of the nine facets mentioned by the apostle Paul, with self-control at the end. This disease consumes all of the goodness you may have to offer, leaving you with the carcass of hatred, thirsting for love."

"Yeah, I've heard it all now. It shortens my fuse, even." Joey became indignant.

"Everyone has a bucket inside, Joey. It's invisible, but surely everyone has one. I call this bucket the *resentment bucket*. We begin to place tiny bubbles of resentment, frustration, bitterness, and disappointment, each time they happen as we live on, into this bucket inside us.

"When you have to give your toys to a younger sibling because he or she is crying and Mom makes you do it, you placed a bubble in the bucket. When a bully takes your milk money from you, that is another bubble inside.

"You break up with your girlfriend because your best friend stole her away from you, then you put two bubbles in the bucket. As a person goes through a severe trauma, the bubble turns into much bigger ones as it enters the bucket." I took a quick drink and continued on before I lost my momentum.

"Then one day, the bucket becomes full. And something makes one upset, and as he or she puts another bubble into the bucket that's full already, it causes his bucket to overflow with all the anguish that had been held inside for so long. Once the bucket becomes full, each time something is upsetting, he or she can no longer hold it in as the bucket has maxed out.

"A guy would be driving down the street, and a person cuts him off. Normally, it would be no big deal. But to a guy whose bucket is full, it could lead to road rage. Even the most minor things become reasons for a guy to go off the handle. A person once so loving and gentle flies off his handle one day and becomes a total jerk all of a sudden."

"So what, once your bucket is full, you are screwed for good? You become a jerk and then you die?"

"Unless you pop away at those bubbles and get rid of some of them or perhaps all of them to keep them from overflowing." Joey didn't respond.

"Everyone needs to empty out their resentment bucket every now and then. It isn't healthy not to. The wisest thing is to pop them as they develop and not put them into the bucket to begin with." I stopped.

"So tell me how you go about popping these bubbles."

"What's the matter, you got some bubble that needs popping or something?"

"Cut the bull and tell me how you go about getting rid of your bubbles."

"Easiest way you may begin is by meditating. That's how I started emptying my *resentment bucket*. I learned how to go to a place I felt safe and comfortable by meditating, and I dealt with the situation that had caused my bubbles.

"But meditation took me only so far. Eventually, I needed to speak with someone who can help me negotiate through the complicated path of recovery. I found counselors I can trust, and I allowed them to help me. A person can benefit from seeking spirituality as well, and many pastors are trained to help those seeking help. I drew strength from knowing I was on the right path, and I never looked back until I felt I was controlling the disease rather than letting it control me." I looked at Joey to see his reaction. He was looking down at his wings without touching them. So I continued, "You could do some reading and learn from various literatures I can send you immediately. When you get out, we'll find you the right person to get you healthy, disease-free."

"It all sounds too easy, and you know what they say about what seems too good to be true ain't true? I kind of believe that's the case here, Jimmy."

"One of these days, I'll share with you what I learned while growing up in your birthplace, O-Jung."

"That's the second time you mentioned it to me. What's with this O-Jung?"

"Just a small town near Daejeon where I witnessed something I wished you had been able to also. You were too young to have the fond memories as I have while growing up there. But what I cherish the most as I look back to these thirty years ago is that in each of us there is the power of forgiveness."

I continued, "This power of forgiveness is greater and mightier than the power of anger and hatred. It has the power to overcome and subdue them. You can find peace in life and be able to focus on what is pertinent, such as raising a family or being a true friend, looking out for the health and safety of everyone you love—those kinds of things.

"You cannot do things on impulse anymore, Joey. People today carry guns and will shoot you for looking at them stupidly. I see the aftereffects of these crimes as well, how it devastates not just the victims but their families and friends. For no reason at all, out of quickness of temper or a short fuse that ignites the bomb in a heartbeat, it ends with someone dead or seriously hurt.

"Over a lane change, people shoot one another while driving, Joey. They cry their eyes out after they come to their senses in a lockup. But it's too late to bring the victims back alive. Shooting at each other while driving, can you believe that?"

"That's pretty crazy. I would never do that."

"But I am afraid your fuse has gotten pretty short, don't you agree?"

"I don't think so."

"What? You can't be serious."

"What are you talking about? I can control myself."

"Yeah right, who was it, Rita or Melissa, you got into a fight over at the Harvest Hotel in Boulder? So this jerk comes on to her, and you figured you had to protect her honor or something? You caved his face in to prove what, that you are an honorable gentleman protecting the reputation of your lady? Is that why we learned tae kwon do? Who was protecting her honor while you were doing two years down at the Canon City prison?

"When you should have been coaching a Little League team or opening your own gym after graduating from school, you spent two years of your precious life in that rathole. And get this. The whole time, your lady had nobody to protect her honor from all the jerks that approached her because you were locked up.

"In the end, Joey, this disease rendered you useless as a coach, as a boyfriend, or even a brother. Sometimes it's the symptoms that will kill you before the disease does. I wonder what Mom thinks as she looks down at us in the middle of this mess."

"I admit, Jimmy, there are some answers I wish I had because it drives me crazy not knowing why I do the things that I do. You struck a chord, and I'm glad you're sharing all these things with me at this moment because I've been doing lot of thinking lately. Having too much time on your hands can be dangerous. I am beginning to agree with you that I am the worst enemy I have, as my actions are detrimental and regretful in the end."

"I believe Confucius said it, when a student is ready to learn, a teacher will appear. If you are ready to deal with this disease, I can begin sending you some books and literatures that will help you understand about the disease and how to overcome it. Maybe you can request to see a shrink or someone who can get you started on getting some counseling or therapy. Don't let the disease take you down further into the darkness of hell."

"How about getting me another soda, *hyung*?" Joey said, as he shook an empty bottle in the air. I noticed he started to call me *hyung* again. I was about to get up, but Uncle Phillip beat me to it.

"Is same kind okay, Joey?" Seeing Joey's nod, Uncle walked toward the vending machines with our coin bucket.

"Let's beat this thing together, Joey, and stop it from continuing to the next generation. You've suffered enough, don't you agree? Now let's try and get you some help to overcome your anger issues."

"Monique didn't come to visit me last weekend. She wrote me a letter saying she was afraid of me when I'm angry. Even during the visits, she said she was afraid to say anything to get me upset because I reacted like a crazy man. I don't even know I am doing it when it happens, let alone the reason why I do."

BOTHER

"Ah, so its back with Monique now, is it?"

"*Was* Monie is more like it. We just found out she was pregnant the day before I got arrested for this beef. But she tells me she's afraid to raise our child with my quick temper and the violent people I'm involved with."

"Did you just say you're pregnant? Whoa, I'm going to be an uncle. Did you hear that, Uncle Phillip? Joey is going to be a daddy. I'll be darned. I can't wait to tell Sarah the good news. She's going to be so excited." Uncle sat down and extended his hand to shake with Joey's, placing the bottle of soda on the table.

"I'm not the one who is pregnant, *hyung*. Man, people will think I'm a weirdo or something," Joey complained, looking around.

"Do you know if it's a boy or girl?" Uncle asked excitedly.

"No. Heck, we just found out Monie was pregnant a month ago. They usually don't know until five or six months into a pregnancy. But I guess it don't matter which because I'll love that child no matter what."

"You are talking about Tricia's little sister, Monique, right?" I asked.

"Uh-huh."

The PA system buzzed with noise and disrupted us.

Each inmate is allowed four hours per visit, unless a visitor is from out of state, in which case eight hours are allowed. It's to accommodate all the visitors in their limited visiting space. The public announcement system called out several inmates' names, indicating their visits were terminated. Joey was one of the first to come out and first to go back in.

Joey gave Uncle and me a hug and grabbed the remaining wings and his soda before walking toward the gate, where other inmates had also started to head for. He looked back and yelled out, "Add some money into my books." I gave him a nod. Then I said, "Congrats on becoming a daddy, Joey. I'll go visit Monique and tell her to come see you."

Joey was allowed to go to the canteen once a month, as each inmate was allowed to buy hygiene products and food items as well as stationeries. Money can be mailed to the inmates, which is deposited into their accounts. An easier way to do so is while visiting, at the reception-cashier desk.

Uncle pulled out three hundred-dollar bills and gave it to the cashier. It would supplement Joey with a monthly supply of zu-zus and wam-wams, the terms prisoners use to describe their treats from the commissary.

The ride home could not have been heavenlier. We decided to get on the State 285 North through the towns of Bailey and Conifer. The autumn Rockies were simply too beautiful for words to describe it. Mother loved autumn leaves more than anyone I know.

My thought turned from Joey to Mother, as I missed her dearly. I asked Uncle, via our communication system, if we could stop by Mom on our way home. My uncle answered back, "A great idea, Jimmy."

CHAPTER 24

1984—Toqui and Jamey

No one saw it coming. One day he was playing a round of golf with his brother, and the next, he dropped to the floor during his evening lecture before a room full of his students. Dad was rushed to the DGH on Valentine's Day 1984 and would never be the same.

While in the hospital, he had the stroke the following day. He lost his faculties, needing diapers and help with each meal.

A week later, Sarah and I brought my dad to our home and converted our living room into his room. Sarah would have killed me if I had lost the argument with Uncle Phillip and Aunt Cindy to care for Dad, as they did put up a good fight.

Judy took a leave of absence from law school to come home to be with Dad. She was in her second-year second semester, which was the most difficult semester among the six she would need to negotiate through. But she was able to arrange with her professors to keep up while visiting Dad after the stroke.

Sarah and I hired an architect to design a home that would accommodate all of us, including Dad and the animals. With Dad living with us, we put up Dad's house for sale. It was the house we had grown up in, but not all the memories were pleasant. It was time to let it go. No one needed it any longer, not even Dad.

We bought a three-acre plot of grassy land between Boulder and Fort Collins near the foot of the Rockies. There is a state park that butts our property line on the west, with a trail leading up to the top of the hill. There's a house about a mile north of our property. Otherwise, it was a ten-minute drive south to reach the city of Boulder, the population of which was ninety thousand.

It was ideal for us as Sarah was spending more time at her Boulder clinic but was still not too far from Fort Collins. She wanted to build a house with easy access and made entries and hallways much larger than the standard. With ten thousand square feet of living space, we were able to take the liberty as designers of our new place and dared to be unconventional.

It took three months and nearly three hundred thousand dollars by the time it was completed. Dad had his own lane pool that pumped water out at him so he could swim in the same spot at his own pace.

We built a sauna room to help him regain his mobility taken from him since his stroke. It had a gym with all the necessary equipment, with a treadmill and a stationary cycle. Finally, in case Dad was interested in seeing a movie, we designed a theater in the basement, with seven La-Z-Boy chairs with armrests and cup holders. There were three chairs in the front row and four in the back.

I took a one-month emergency leave from my job during the move into our new home to help Dad acclimate to his new surroundings. We hired a live-in nurse to care for him around the clock and a maid to help us with the cooking and cleaning.

Dad seemed to enjoy being around Judy as he slowly recovered from the stroke. He reminded me of a helpless baby or a puppy. He only had the use of his left side at first, but by the time Judy was returning to Cambridge a month later, Dad had gradually gained some of the use of his right side as well. Judy returned to her books and the grinds of making up for the lost time. She took comfort in knowing that Dad was improving and getting better each day.

Among the animals we had adopted was a ten-pound female mini pinscher missing her left front leg. She was born with only three legs ten months ago, with her fourth leg being nothing more than an inch-long appendix, limply hanging where her leg should have been. She was mostly black, but her underside had dark-brown areas.

Her owner had given up on her, thinking she was stillborn. Even when she had come to life, the owner had decided to euthanize her rather than to keep her alive. She became a liability to the profit-oriented owner. Sarah decided to keep her rather than to put her down, with the permission from the owner.

BOTHER

When the pup started to get around, she hopped like rabbits on her hind legs, rather than to limp with three legs. So Sarah had named her *To-kee*, which is Korean for "rabbit." The original spelling seemed less fitting for her and took on a French accent and its spelling, ergo *Toqui*.

This little dog had a special gift that far surpassed making up for her physical deficit. She would have brought smiles to the likes of Hitler and Capone, with her amazing display of affections. This tiny little black-and-brown creature was an undercover angel with three wings.

She dazzled my dad with her charming self while Dad needed a standby ready companion. She would not leave his side, awaiting his signal to jump on his lap and begin licking away at his face, from the left to right, top to bottom. She asked for nothing in return and never ran out of affection. Oh, how Dad had benefitted from the release of endorphins her licking had brought on. She was an affection-performing machine. She gave nonstop loving and never tired but seemed to really enjoy giving others her love.

Once on Dad's lap, she would stand on her hind legs and lean in to rub her face on Dad's chest and neck affectionately. At first, one side of her face and then the other, while making a low-pitched whining noise that could melt a heart of steel.

Even those watching her during the affectionate moments smiled without realizing, seeing Dad behave like an ecstatic child enjoying his Christmas presents with each darting of her tongue trying to reach his lips to give him kisses.

Toqui would carefully hop down on her three legs when Dad would tell her to get down and remain quietly lying next to his bed or wheelchair, whichever Dad was in. Only to eat and to relieve herself did she ever leave her new best friend's side.

Dad's improvement in part had to be attributed to this little Godsent creature, whose sole purpose was to bring a smile to the nonparalyzed half of Dad's face. She didn't care why the other half would not smile back. Just the fact that he was happy to be her friend was good enough for Toqui. To love Dad was her pleasure and sole purpose in life.

Dad wanted a digital camcorder so he could record her playful activities. We ordered a camera for southpaws to accommodate his good hand. He went on to record what seemed like gigabytes of footage of her with his new toy.

This little dog had another passion, and that was to take walks and to run freely on three legs, sniffing and leaving scents of her own throughout the two-mile trail behind our home. It was my daily routine at the crack of dawn to spend thirty to forty minutes with our four dogs to walk the trail that is at the base of the state park behind our property to the top of the hill and back.

When I call for her each morning, she would reluctantly walk away from Dad and join us for the walk. It must have stirred something inside Dad, being left behind while everyone went for the walk.

One day, he began asking me if he could go along for the walk on his wheelchair. Each time, my response was "Only if you could walk on your own. It's not possible on your wheelchair." He pouted and threw tantrums at first. One day, I took his camcorder and recorded the entire walk, with Toqui as the focus as she enjoyed being out in the open. Dad sat and watched the entire thirty-minute footage of our walk when we returned.

After the video, he finally stopped sulking and agreed to physical therapy to help restore the use of his right side. Slowly, with the motivation to go for that walk with Toqui, he began improving the use of his right leg. His right arm was showing very little improvement, which concerned me a lot.

Dad got up and joined us one day, much to the delight of Toqui. He started out with us at first for the first five or ten minutes and then sat on a flat rock, waiting for us. Toqui looked back at Dad several times but continued with the animals to join me to the top of the trail. She seemed to be anxious to go back to where Dad was waiting.

Slowly, Dad made it farther and farther each time until he had made it to the top of the trail, four months after he had taken that first walk with us. Coming down the slope was not a problem for him. The fresh air seemed to increase his appetite and strength. The following week, Dad joined the family at the top of the trail to watch the July 4 fireworks taking place in the city of Boulder five miles away. However, the improvement to his right arm was still going slow.

Toqui had motivated the old man to get off his butt and get healthy. If her handicap hadn't stopped her, why should his stop him?

They became an inseparable duo since then, regularly seen taking their walks with the other canine family members through the Rockies.

Dad still needed help with many things. His right hand was never the same, and he had difficulty with buttons or tying his shoes. Sarah and Judy took him shopping during the Easter break and bought clothing with Velcro instead of buttons.

All his shoes were slip-ons or had Velcro laces instead of strings. He became a fan of rip-away training pants the Denver Nuggets players wore during their warm-ups. They ordered each of every color made in his size.

BOTHER

It was one of my fondest memories with Dad to dine with him as I cut his steaks and other tasks that required two hands while eating. It was the only meal I had the chance to share with him since Dad did not eat breakfast. It was becoming my favorite time of the day—to sit and dine with my dad.

At times, we would be engaged in conversations that took us back to the village of O-Jung, where my childhood memories had united with the fondest memories of Dad's first assignment after his military service. Not once did our past of abusive days come up during our conversations. It rarely entered my mind. In times when I thought of the days when he was angry and beating me, it reminded me of how thankful I was that we survived through it. In the end, God's goodness had brought healing and reconciliation to our lives. That is what God does. He restores broken relationships by allowing the healing to take place.

We talked about his days in the Severance Hospital and our commute each day to school and work. As we did, we were becoming more like buddies and not a father and son. Mostly, Dad would talk about all the delightful things Toqui had done throughout the day. That little dog had motivated Dad to live actively, taking part of life. Eventually, the responsibility of feeding the dogs became his, which he did with great care day in and day out.

With his activities, the use of his right hand gradually improved. He slurred less, but some of the damage from the stroke never did go away. It was during our dinner when the phone rang, startling the dogs to bark. Sarah got up to get it.

"Honey, that was Monique on the phone, she is in labor, and her sister Tricia is driving her to the CU Medical Center. I am going to meet her there. Do you want to join me?"

"Yes, I do, if you will give me a minute to grab my jacket." I turned to Dad and said, "Hey, Dad, I think you are about to become a grandfather. Joey's fiancée is about to give birth to your first grandson. Can you hang around for a couple of hours while we go to the hospital? I'll let the nurse and the maid know we will be gone for a few hours. Okay, Dad?" Dad nodded. I thought I saw a smile on his face. I believe the old man was actually excited about finally becoming a grandfather.

It was Sarah's passion to go for long drives. She had even greater reason of late since the purchase of her brand-new Audi Quattro, an all-wheel-drive sedan that handled like a race car. Since trading in her Honda for the Audi a month ago, we've been up to the Estes Park national forest for long afternoon drives each Sunday. She cites Dad's pleasure as the main reason, and he did truly enjoy the rides.

It is heaven to be with your lovely wife, especially when she seems to be bubbling with happiness behind the wheel of her brand-new car. Once we got on Highway 36, I noticed she immediately started to go faster than eighty-five miles per hour. Her new car was powerful and very comfortable to ride in.

"It's not fair," Sarah spoke, catching me off guard.

"What's not fair?"

"We were so prepared for a child and wanted one so badly, yet it doesn't happen. Here's Joey and Monique not even trying, and they already have one. What is she, fifteen years old? It's just not fair at all."

"She is almost nineteen, and sure, life isn't fair. Not to you and me when it comes to becoming parents. To Joey and Monique, it is. For now, we're not in the equation of their joyful moments. Let's be careful not to show any resentment towards their blessing and ruin their happy moments. Don't you agree, sweetie?"

"Yes, I do. It's just that—never mind. You're absolutely right. We'll go and support our little sister as she brings our nephew into the world. What did they decide to name him, Daniel, David? Whatever her dad's name was, I think they decided to name the baby after him."

"Dennis. Dennis Schottenheimer. Monique says she'll kill Joey if he doesn't make an honest woman out of her and marry her when he gets out. I think she is anxious to trade in her fourteen-lettered last name for a three-lettered one. Each time she writes a check, she wishes it was Monique Lee instead of Monique Schottenheimer."

"That's funny. She does love to shop and probably does a lot of check writing. I don't know about Dennis, though. Dennis Lee . . . hmmm. It doesn't sound too bad, I guess. Nothing as boring as my case was when I became Sarah Lee from Sarah Kim. At least 'Nobody doesn't like Sarah Lee' became *my* jingle." She laughed with her snorting sound. I could never grow tired of hearing her laugh. "How did they meet, anyway?" she asked as she negotiated a slow driver ahead of her.

"They used to date off and on but hadn't been dating for several months. She was at a dance club, and Joey was there with his friends, when her ex-boyfriend, whom she had just broken up with, shows up and starts an argument with Monique. This jerk started calling Monie white trailer trash and everything else guys say when they're mad at a woman.

"I guess Joey told the jerk to stop being mean to her, and when the guy told Joey to go *f* off, Joey got up and made the guy sing soprano by kicking him in the groin. For a kick that can break bricks and wooden boards in half, it hurts me just thinking about it. Ouch." Sarah laughed again, driving expertly, getting onto I-25 South from the Boulder turnpike, heading toward Colorado Boulevard.

We were ten minutes away—five, if Sarah decided to play her make-believe game that she was in the middle of Indy 500, racing against Mario Andretti down Interstate 25. Gutsy lady if you ask me, speeding as she does and, as often as she does, right in front of a cop. I loved this crazy animal doctor dearly. I laughed, drawing her look my way.

"What's so funny?"

"You're so funny. You have a funny way of reminding me throughout the day why I fell in love with you. Some corky and crazy things you like doing. How fast are you going, eighty-eight miles per hour? And you are doing all this right in front of a cop sitting right next to you. Those kinds of nutty things you do are the reasons why I am nuts about you."

"If you are trying to get lucky tonight, you are doing a pretty good job there, Sheriff. I was hoping it would be that cute deputy who'd come calling on me tonight, but you'll do."

"Why, madam, you are naughty, and I dare come at all and call upon you this evening." I tried out my best British accent, which was pretty bad.

"Look, there's Holiday Inn, maybe we can pull in for a quickie and try for a baby of our own before going to see Joey and Monie's." My crazy wife looked my way, batting her eyelashes at me in her best Mae West seductive pose.

"Why that's a good idea. For our return trip, that is." I returned her serve with a volley of my own, the best Groucho Marx imitation with my left eyebrow going up and down while motioning with my hand as if to play with a cigar. There it was again. Music to my ears was her snorting laughter as she expertly negotiated the traffic as if it were nothing. Simple and gentle motions to sway in and out a few times, and we were exiting the freeway.

How do you give a birth to a baby weighing eight pounds fifteen ounces when you are merely five feet seven and a buck twenty?

Even when Monique looked as if she was carrying a watermelon in front of her during the last weeks of pregnancy, she weighed no more than a hundred twenty pounds, only ten pounds heavier than her normal "supermodel" weight.

My mom and aunt used to sit and talk when my aunt came for visits. I overheard once about how, when a woman carries a child like a rugby ball cradled in her arms, then it was a girl. If the mother carried the child inside like a watermelon, way below instead, then it's a boy.

I have not been wrong in my predictions with those principles. I knew Monie was carrying a boy and not a girl. It amazed everyone how skinny Monique was able to maintain herself while carrying a child that big inside.

She was holding her son—our nephew—in her arms. My father and belated mother finally had their first grandchild. A healthy boy to carry on our name to the next generation was born to us. Sarah walked over and gave Monique a brief hug and asked if she could hold the baby.

Sarah held Dennis in her arm as if she had done this before. I never saw her beam as she did then. I congratulated Monie and Tricia, her older sister who was in the room when we arrived. Tricia was a brave woman.

Their father, Sergeant Dennis Schottenheimer, who had retired from the USMC, was an abusive man who took out on his two daughters the misery caused by his wife when she left him for another man. He got drunk, and the more he got drunk, the meaner he got. Everyone called him Sarge.

When Joey asked me to find out as much as I could about Monique's father when he had heard from Monique about him, I learned of the man that did not cause me comfort. He abused his wife before she left him, and Tricia had been taken to the hospital on numerous occasions due to the angry attacks from Sarge. She had been molested by her dad since her mom took off, and she would fight back when he would come to her room at night. He would beat her to submission.

When Sarge had started on Monique, Tricia fought against him until she was beaten to the ground, and police were dispatched. In the ambulance, Tricia told the entire story to the social worker who was dispatched to escort minors away from a crime scene.

Sarge was arrested and convicted for sex crimes and various related charges, serving a long-term sentence in Canon City. Sarge knew if he made it to Buena Vista, where Joey was serving time, he was a dead man.

Tricia held her family together by moving into a mobile home park in Broomfield, giving her little sister a homestead while Monie finished with her school.

Tricia was industrious and worked hard as a waitress at the Village Inn Pancake House, making good wages since she was eighteen. For the past six years, she had put her little sister through junior and senior high school. Shortly after graduating, Monique met Joey, and they became lovers, despite the eight-year difference in age.

Tricia was most grateful when she found out our insurance was paying for Monie's medical costs and that the best care was waiting for her and her baby. Sarah had called our insurance agent and added Monie and Joey to our policy when we discovered Monie was pregnant. Now, their baby would be covered by our policy as well.

"Wow, you guys made it here quicker than I expected," said proud Aunt Tricia, sitting by Monique, when we entered the room. Tricia did not have time for a man. She was a beautiful twenty-four-year-old woman who lived each day remembering what her father had done to her. It made her difficult to get close to, especially for a man.

"Had we known Monie was in such a hurry to pop the kid out, I'd have told Sarah to drive even faster. She was already doing ninety, so I didn't want to encourage her any further, ha-ha." Sarah gave me a scolding look, bouncing the baby up and down as she cradled him.

I guess her Indy experiences were meant to be our secrets. She said, "If I had let Jimmy drive, we'd be here sometime in the next hour," then stuck her tongue out at me.

"Well, Jamey was in hurry or something. As soon as we got here and into the delivery room, I heard Jamey crying his lungs out," said Tricia.

"Jamey? I thought you were naming him Dennis?"

"Why would we name the baby after him? We don't want anything to remind us of him. It was your brother and Monie's idea to name him after Joey

"They have been talking about the boy's name ever since that whatchamacallit machine with some kind of echogram or something picked up the baby's tiny little pecker between the legs and called it a boy. Anyway, when they were still deciding, Monique asked what Joe's middle name was. I guess you know it is Jae-min. So that's where Jamey came from."

It was a good thing I didn't make any grateful comment about naming the boy after me. I would have embarrassed myself had I opened my big mouth like I did with Sarah's speeding.

"That is so cool. So it's not shortened from James, but his name is actually Jamey?" I wanted to confirm one more time.

"That's right, Jamey Conner Lee," Monie said, sitting up firmer as she said her son's name. An obvious proud mother she was.

"So you guys have a place for Jamey to stay at your home, Trish?" Sarah asked.

"Yeah, but I was going to ask you and Jimmy if you could help us with the cost of raising Jamey until Joey is out and able."

"Absolutely," Sarah said. "If you want, Monie and Jamey are more than welcome to move in with us. We have plenty of space there, with a live-in nurse around the clock and a cook who can please even a finicky eater like me."

Sarah graciously extended an offer of our home to my brother's family. My bride was a heavenly creature inside and out. She wasn't fond of my dad, yet she didn't speak a negative word about bringing Dad to our home. Now she was offering Monie and Jamey our place to live. I joined in.

"Yes. In fact, no one had ever used the guesthouse next to the pool and Jacuzzi other than to go watch a Broncos game on the giant television in its lounge. It has a king-size bed in the bedroom and a shower that is out of sight, pouring high-pressured water that is so soothing. It's got its own kitchen and a lounge with giant-screen television and hi-fi stereo."

"Are you guys serious? Oh, Tricia, did you hear that?" Monie turned back to face me and Sarah.

"Are you saying I can move in with Jamey and stay at your pool house for as long as we want to?"

"Yes," Sarah and I said it at the exact same time, causing everyone to laugh. Sarah continued, "I am hoping, until Joey comes home and you guys decide to live elsewhere, you are welcome to stay with us forever. Besides, what I hear from Mr. West, as soon as the one-year parole violation is up next week, Joey is eligible for bail hearing. We hope he can come home to his wife and son next week."

"Hey, I like the sound of that—wife and son. I would love to make it legal. I'm his wife already, but I wish we could have a wedding ceremony."

"We will take it one thing at a time. Just focus on being a mom for now. When Joey gets home, then we'll think about the being-the-bride part. A little backward if you ask me, but one thing at a time nonetheless," I added, with chuckles.

I turned to see Tricia shedding tears. She was relieved, as her concern for her sister's baby caused quite a burden on her during the last few weeks. The recent development to Monie's situation was too much for her to hold in as the joy flooded her soul.

CHAPTER 25

1998—Oktoberfest

Everyone was busy with planning for Dad's seventieth birthday. With our family, Oktoberfest had a different meaning from the rest of the world. It meant the celebration time of our father's birthday. It had been a long recovery for Dad since the heart attack and the stroke fourteen years ago. Dad was able to regain most of the use of his body, including his right hand.

The US Census Bureau's estimated population of America was 268,921,733 in January of 1998, as Nagano, Japan, began hosting the Eighteenth Winter Olympics. Tom Clancy paid over $200 million to purchase the Minnesota Vikings. Mercedes-Benz paid $40 billion to purchase Chrysler. Elton John was knighted by the queen of England. The Unabomber, Theodore Kaczynski, received four life sentences plus thirty years in a plea to avoid the death penalty.

Pope John Paul II visited Cuba on January 21 and, on my birthday two days later, condemned the US embargo against Cuba. Later in the year, the pope asked God for forgiveness for some of the Roman Catholics who had remained inactive and silent during the Holocaust. It was a slow year for our pope.

President Bill Clinton had been exposed of his extra activities while in the White House. First with Monica Lewinsky, who signed an affidavit denying she did the unthinkable to the president under the desk in the oval office. Clinton denied that oral sex was real sex; therefore, he did not have sex with Monica Lewinsky. Later, he would go on to defend himself against the sexual harassment charge from Paula Jones. It was a busy year in the office for our president.

The Broncos beat the Steelers in the AFC Championship, 24-21, and went on to beat Brett Favre and the defending champion the Green Bay Packers, 31-24, in the Super Bowl XXXII. John Elway's passing and Terrell Davis's three rushing touchdowns rocked the fans in the Qualcomm Stadium, attended by almost sixty-nine thousand fans standing on their feet, cheering.

Uncle Phillip had purchased four tickets for his family and made the trip to San Diego, California. Uncle called it their family's first honeymoon. The old man was getting sentimental with age. After the game, they drove across the border to Tijuana on a rented Dodge Caravan and traveled south into the Baja peninsula.

His family swam in clear-water waves and dined on lobsters in fine restaurants. The next day, they enjoyed the authentic food with the live mariachi bands. Uncle danced with Aunt, joining the jovial diners who had started to dance the minute the band had started to play. He came back to the hotel, nicely toasted. Lisa had to drive back to the hotel, according to Aunt Cindy's account with snickers.

Uncle Phillip would become a big fan of the Super Bowl in addition to being a Broncos die-hard fan. Each year, whichever city was hosting the game became their location for the family vacation. It made Sarah and me to begin thinking about our own version, with Dad and the animals. A crazy notion, to imagine you can travel with an old man and four dogs.

Since coming to America and working for Safeway, Uncle had done very well for himself during the past twenty-eight years. For his older brother's seventieth birthday bash, he was dropping thirty thousand dollars for the event activities that included live musicians and entertainments. Since opening his seventh location, which he called the Lucky Last, he stopped opening any more.

He was approached by many entrepreneurs who wished to buy out the rights to use his name for the packaging and franchise. He simply did not wish to go public or open any more locations since he felt he was unable to handle any more. He had many friends and family to help him, but he felt he was stretched to the max with his ability to run high-quality restaurants.

In the end, he knew when he was at his limit. No more, no less. At an age of sixty-three, he still worked forty hours per week—ten to six, Monday through Friday, week in and week out. Weekends belonged to the family, but he was clockwork when it came to work habits. People came to appreciate that about him, and it exemplified well to his employees.

He went on to pay off his million-dollar mortgage in just a handful of years. Eventually, the six out of the seven location buildings were bought and owned by the holding company Lisa had created, reducing the liability to their locations from the previous landlords who owned the property. The seventh location was inside the mall, and the property was not available for individual purchase.

Cousin Lisa was a shrewd businesswoman. I was so glad she was my cousin and on my side. The City of Boulder tried to eminent-domain Uncle's business that was in the way of their upcoming road-widening project. Other business owners had begun to succumb to the pressure from the City, but Lisa stood.

With a team of relatively young and inexperienced attorneys but with ambitions nonetheless, Lisa fought the City and made them pay Uncle Phillip nearly $300,000 for the damage to their business and moved the business into a newly developing Crossroad shopping mall in 1987.

Brand-new facility, brand-new decor, furniture, and fixtures for the kitchen that was as large as the dining area. The place was a heaven for the chefs. Everyone claimed that the food actually improved, if that was possible, when they moved into the new location.

Whatever was the reason, this branch that they relocated—which did pretty good business even before the relocation—became the highest-yielding location out of the seven. The second wasn't even close. It just ran away from any other locations, outdoing them by three to five times the business. Cousin Lisa was a tough lady with brains to go with. She made her parents very wealthy by investing their earnings well in properties and blue-chip stocks, protecting them safely. Her stock portfolio was impressive.

Someone else had noticed that about her. During the battle with the City of Boulder, their attorney, Uncle's opposing attorney, took fancy to Lisa. This sly man had devised a plan for a win-win situation while doing his job.

Scott Romney, whose uncle was an incumbent Republican state senator, was following his uncle's steps as an attorney. He was working for his father's law firm that represented the City of Boulder in the eminent-domain process. Scott met Lisa when she was representing her father in the court as an agent.

Much to the relief of Uncle and Aunt, as they were concerned over their aging daughter who did not seem to ever date, Lisa finally married at the age of thirty. Scott Romney proposed to her after the case was over, stunning the unsuspecting cousin Lisa, who had despised Scott until that moment. She did not have any other feelings for Scott until she had to think about it, so she said as a matter of fact.

The governor of Colorado wrote Scott a letter of congratulations, handwritten and personally delivered by the lieutenant governor, who read the letter before the wedding crowd gathered in the chapel. The letter was later framed to be displayed. It was a gesture more for the senator in the audience rather than the groom, but it was impressive.

Nearly nine years had gone by since Lisa and Scott Romney started to raise their family. Scott was thirty-two years old himself. The window of opportunity to raise a family was running out on them quickly. How Lisa was able to manage her position with the business while going through all the pregnancies and raising the little ones as she kept on adding more was remarkable.

They went on to give birth to a total of two girls and three boys in a span of six years. Becky was born on Christmas Day of 1991, two years after the wedding. The twins, Bob and Brent, came a year later—a day after Thanksgiving. She didn't have any room in her stomach with twins occupying yet overate and ended up inducing her labor. It was truly one of the most thankful Thanksgivings I can remember. Something about holidays and birth of children ran in the Romney family.

You would've thought they had enough with Becky and the twins, but apparently not, as Burt came along two years later in 1994, not on any particular holiday, but he did miss being born on Labor Day, a week too late. Brenda was an accident, so Lisa claims, but a blessed one. She shared her first birthday celebration with her great-uncle, who was born on the same day, seventy years ago.

Scott and Lisa had been waiting for a property near her father's mansion even before the wedding and bought a home three blocks away from Uncle Phillip's place in 1991, just before the birth of Becky. An eight-bedroom estate, just in case they had more children after Becky, was what they said during the housewarming party. There were two empty rooms remaining. I am not giving up on Scott and Lisa yet. They might fill those rooms just yet.

With Lisa out of the way, it did not take long for Sharon to get on with her matrimony a year later in 1990. After becoming a police dispatcher, she started to attend the University of Colorado, Denver. Graduating from UCD with a degree in criminal justice in 1988, she was recruited by the FBI.

It got the attention of Chief Dysart who has been in charge of the DPD since 1987. If she was good enough for the FBI, she was good enough for DPD. She began her training to join the force, and upon graduation, she was assigned to detectives working on felonies. With the time served as the dispatcher, she was given a top-seniority pay grade even as a rookie officer. She was a good addition to the DPD.

During her first year, she was investigating a burglary that took place in the residence of a physician who stood next to Scott as his best man during her sister Lisa's wedding. Sharon and the doctor had walked down the aisle together, following the bride and the groom, as best man and matron of honor.

Sharon had no romantic interest in the doctor, nor did she know he was a prominent physicist before attending the Johns Hopkins Medical School to become a physician and incorporating laser surgeries on human organs, saving lives. He was well compensated for what he did. Dr. Levi, on the other hand, took fancy to Sharon the first moment he had laid his eyes on her. His name was Solomon Levi, but everyone called him Jed. When King David and Bathsheba had lost their first child, God comforted them with another, which was Solomon. When God saw Solomon, God was pleased with him and sent the prophet Nathan to name the child Jedidiah. In the Jewish community little Sol had grown up in, he was known as Jed, Dr. Levi's only son, who became a physician himself.

When his house was broken into, Sharon was assigned to the case. That is when she realized how the seriously rich folks lived. The stuff that was taken by the burglars alone was a million dollars' worth of artworks. One thing led to another, and for the second time, they walked down the aisle together, as a bride and her groom.

Neither seemed to mind having no children of their own. They were the best uncle and aunt Lisa's children could ever have. They seem to be content with being an occasional parent whenever their careers allowed them to break away.

Ever since Becky turned five, she joined Sharon and Jed in various musicals and plays performed at the Denver Center for the Performing Arts capping off each season with *The Nutcracker* production by the Denver Symphony, accompanied by the Denver Metro Dance Company.

Bob and Brent did not care for that kind of stuff. But they were impressed with Uncle Jed's VIP suite at the Mile High Stadium, as they joined their uncle during the Rockies major league baseball games. They could scream and yell, jump around, and drop food on the floor, and no one yelled at them. Their enthusiasms for baseball seemed to increase with each trip, and their T-ball game activities became much more enjoyable for them as well as their parents.

My Aunt Cindy was the most proud grandmother, attending each and every T-ball, soccer, and swimming event the twins were involved in. Aunt

Cindy became their permanent escort and their nanny, never leaving their side.

Judy became an attorney in 1986. After graduating from Harvard Law, she took the bar exam and received a letter from the ABA, congratulating her. In 1984, Dwight had proposed to Judy, but Judy said no. Judy changed her mind a day later, prior to Dwight returning to Denver to join his father's law firm. Judy began serving pro bono as the in-house advocate and legal counsel for the Denver Child Care Agency since returning home in 1986.

The West and West Law Firm represented Harvard Law School very well and most happy to add the third alum as their partner, when Judy married Dwight in the summer of 1990.

Judy refused to change her last name. She insisted that when she became a judge, it was going to be Judge Judith J. Lee. Father and son would do well with Judy on their side. The firm outdueled opponents, and it did not matter whichever court the battle was on. The Lee, West, and West Law Firm was continuing the legacy the elder West had established. Now they were three times the strength.

The ability of Judy to formulate her plan of attacks on the district attorneys became the talk of the legal community, where ridiculed DAs joined the ranks of those who had fallen victim to Judy's masterminded plans. It even dazzled the elder West and stunned her husband with the brilliant battle plans that utilized both science and deduction.

Judy, in short, won the hearts of the peers sitting in the jury box. District attorneys didn't have a chance against her charm and charismatic brilliance.

Dwight and Judy celebrated this New Year's Day by giving birth to Katie, a little girl who looked just like Judy, with auburn hair. I am not sure if this world was ready for a red-haired Judy. They named her after Dwight's mother, Katherine.

Dwight was forty-four and Judy thirty-eight years old when Katie was born, much to the relief of the whole clan. Judy was four months into her second pregnancy. The second child was due on April Fools' Day of the coming year. I was hoping the child would hang on and show up on Easter Sunday instead.

Judy and Dwight bought a home inside the Cherry Creek Country Club in south Denver shortly after their wedding. The West family had been a member for three generations, going back to Dwight's grandfather, a retired commander and a US Navy fighter pilot. This golf course was designed by the great Jack Nicklaus, offering the best experience golf has to offer.

Uncle drove past numerous championship golf courses each Sunday the Broncos were not playing at home, to play a round at CCCC, an hour away from his home in Boulder.

He was joined by Dwight and his father, along with Dr. Jed, Uncle's son-in-law. This foursome was known for their par handicaps, as each was a scratch golfer. Their rounds did not include mulligan, and they walked the entire course rather than use the cart, as would the pros. They were serious amateur golfers. They played each round, and the loser would pick up the dinner tab. The bill could run to over hundreds of dollars if they dined at the clubhouse famous for their fine dining.

Joey benefitted from the success of Mr. West in 1984 for the second time. He beat the weapons charge against him. He was released upon completion of his one-year parole violation term. He came home to a newly born son, Jamey, and a soon-to-be-wedded bride, Monique Ann Schottenheimer.

Joey and Monie married each other at Uncle's house, with over two hundred people attending. His parole officer was there too. It was quite the mixed gathering. There were dignitaries in tuxedos, mingling with the bikers and people with pierced body parts and tattoos.

Everyone had a wonderful time at the party, which was entertained by a banjo band. This band had a bass that was made out of a bathtub made of tin, turned upside down, with a pole and a string. Other instruments were limited to a kazoo, a clarinet, and a plastic-bottle drum set with a washboard that produced awesome hip-swinging tunes. And banjo, of course. Their tunes made everyone feel like dancing. Champagne and caviar, to beer and cheesy nachos, and everything in between had continued to flow until the wee hours of the morning.

The bride and groom were satisfied, and Tricia couldn't stop crying. Even while eating her shrimp cocktail, she choked up, thinking of her sister's beautiful wedding. She was very happy for her sister's family.

Joey took Monie to Vail for three days of honeymoon while we cared for Jamey. It took three months before the honeymoon phase was over. Joey's behavior returned back to being violent and short of patience. He had an argument with Dad and took off without saying a word to anyone.

Three weeks later, I received a collect call from the Orange County Jail, in Santa Ana, California. It was Joey. He was arrested for possession of an armed weapon by a felon. He was caught with three AK-47s with over a thousand rounds of ammos.

Mr. West flew to John Wayne Airport in Orange County, California, to represent Joey for the third time. It was very hard to fight for a cookie thief caught with his hands in the jar. Joey pleaded to the mandatory ten-year sentence for possessing an automatic weapon. He was extremely lucky, as the law in California was about to change. For each bullet, Joey could have gotten a year. Theoretically, Joey could have been sentenced to over a thousand years.

In addition to ten years, he received a five-year consecutive sentence for the assault on the peace officers during the arrest. He was not eligible for good-time discounts. He was required to serve 85 percent of the fifteen years.

Monie had moved out to California when Joey was sentenced in 1986 after two years of trial. Joey was sent to Wasco Reception Center and transferred four times during the past twelve years. Since Wasco, she moved with Joey each time he did. Currently, she lives in Represa, California, where Folsom prison is located. She worked as a live-in nanny for a doctor couple's three-year-old girl and visited Joey during Saturdays and Sundays when visiting was allowed. Joey was granted conjugal visits every two to three months, depending on the schedule.

She had stuck by Joey for the past fourteen years and two prison terms. She was no longer a teenager infatuated with a knight in shining armor who had rescued her from the abusive ex. She was a thirty-three-year-old woman who stood by her man through thick and thin. Monie had long ago earned my respect, and I took care of her as if she were my own sister.

Joey should have been out by now had it not for the loss of good time for various infractions. He ended up having to serve the entire fifteen, plus change. Monie had another year to go before her husband could walk out a free man.

Monie flew in last night to attend Dad's seventieth. She had a two-day leave, which meant she had to fly back the day after the party. She's a trooper when it came to being a family member.

She had come to love Dad dearly and became quite close to him while she stayed at the pool house for two years. Jamey has lived with Sarah and me since he came home from the hospital in 1984. Monie felt she could only focus on being a full-time wife and couldn't provide for Jamey as well.

Sarah and I went through the guardianship process to become Jamey's legal parents. He gets visits from Monie several times throughout the year. He would fly out to California to be with his parents during the conjugal visits where he spends two days with his parents in a trailer just inside the prison grounds.

They'd talk, barbecue steaks and chicken, and watch videos as they would on normal weekends, as any other family. Then he would fly back home to Colorado and resume his life in school. Through it all, he kept a good head on his shoulders, receiving great marks from all his classes.

Jamey learned to play chess at an early age of four. While Dad had to humor him and take it easy on the kid for the first few years, by the time Jamey was in second grade, Dad had to fight for each victory.

Jamey's game was tennis. His backhand volleys were so powerful it was hard for me to deal with. Jamey was already approaching six feet at age fourteen. He had both of his parents to thank for the perfect physique a tennis player could want—long and lean.

His school basketball coach had been pulling his hair out, since Jamey wasn't interested in the hoops and refused to join the team. Jamey's sole dream was to have his father be free to witness him become a pro tennis player and travel with him throughout the circuit, making up for the lost times. He had a year to look forward to, when his dad would be released.

Jamey is currently ranked top five in the intramural circuit in Colorado in his age-group. He had set his sights on playing for the Stanford University in four years, if he didn't turn pro beforehand. For now, as a freshman in high school, tennis to him was fun and a game that he was good at.

Jamey was the apple of my dad's eyes. Since the death of Toqui three years ago, Jamey was the sole buddy Dad had. When Toqui had turned twelve and was ailing from various conditions, it became too much for such a delicate creature. She came to fulfill her purpose in life and did it well.

She was the benefactor to Dad's mobility. Without her, who knows if Dad would've been motivated to get through the physical therapies and strength training he was up against?

After eleven years of companionship, it was very hard for Dad in his grieving. Jamey, since he was old enough to reach his grandpa's hand, had tagged along for the daily walks with the dogs until he started going to preschool. Then, it was just the weekend rituals, as Jamey had become fond of Toqui as anyone close to Dad had.

Jamey orchestrated a most loving funeral for Toqui, inviting several dozens of people to the site at the very northeast corner of our property for her burial.

It was the most touching gesture an eleven-year-old child could have engineered. He printed invitations from his computer, made copies, and stuffed those in the hand-addressed envelopes.

It took Jamey and me until 10:00 p.m. on a school night, driving around town, hand-delivering the invitations for the funeral the following day. Jamey had told his music teacher, Mr. O'Sullivan, about the funeral he was planning. This fine Irish gent brought his well-used bagpipe and played the purest rendition of "Amazing Grace" one had ever heard.

For a tiny little dog, whose original owner had discarded her upon birth a dozen years ago, nearly two dozen folks stood silently as Mr. O'Sullivan played on in his windpipe.

For the love which had transcended beyond helping an old man to regain his life, we paid tribute to this tiny dog. It touched me deeply that my Jamey was learning from such a talented man with a heart. Every child needs a mentor like him.

Jamey's touching eulogy made everyone cry their eyeballs out, including me. Sarah sat next to me and held my hand tightly, telling me through her teary eyes that she understood my pain for Dad. She put her arms around me and just held me, like Mom used to. It made me think of Mom, and that caused me to cry even harder. It had been over thirty years since Mom had left us. I still miss her dearly. I felt the pain Dad must have been going through, burying Toqui.

Since then, Dad had learned to get out of the house, joining Jamey in his tennis matches throughout the Boulder county school district, as he ranked number one, and was excited to watch his matches.

Where Toqui had brought Dad through his recovery, Jamey took Dad to another level of recovery. Jamey got Dad out of the house to actively enjoy being away from home. When the nurse retired, we did not replace her with another. Dad was no longer in need of a live-in nurse.

Dad and Jamey were still the movie buddies down at the basement during the snowstorms. They loved watching Clint Eastwood movies over and over again. They had gone through Clint's war movies, the Westerns, and the Inspector "Dirty Harry" Callahan series, watching them repeatedly all night, eating their popcorn and drinking hot chocolate.

When the movie came to their favorite parts, they knew the lines by heart and became excited and loud. It was their ritual for quite some time when Jamey was younger, but eventually, Jamey started noticing the girls noticing him.

Dr. Bill retired in 1991, true to his promise that he would retire at the age of seventy. Sarah and Bill had opened their second hospital in Boulder before his retirement. They had worked together for twelve years, as he took on a student and helped Sarah become a top-notch veterinarian surgeon in the nation. He would be missed by many animals and their owners who had received his service for over forty years. He had sold his interest of the hospitals to his son, Bill Junior, who had served at the Fort Collins hospital as the resident radiologist since 1988. Junior and Sarah worked well as the coadministrators of the hospital.

Junior had been running the Fort Collins location since his father's retirement. Sarah concentrated on the Boulder location. In just two years, the new hospital became a stable entity filling the void that had been there for quite some time. Wealthy equestrians in Boulder had to travel to Denver for the treatment Sarah provided in her hospital. Demands for her service were overwhelming. She had doubled the staff by hiring two more full-time veterinarians and opening a second internship position to meet the demand. Eventually, she needed a team of eight veterinarians to man the hospital. She was able to work less hours now that the hospital was running on its own.

I had been a law-enforcement officer for a quarter of a century—the first three years aboard USS *Dixon*, eight years with DPD, and fourteen years with FCPD. I became a lieutenant in 1987, six years after becoming a sergeant. The days of cow-tipping pranks by the CSU students being the highlight of the department were long gone. As the city began to grow and expand, the agricultural industry along with the ranches began yielding to the developers anxious to build shopping centers and apartment buildings. The population had doubled from sixty thousand when I joined the force back in 1984.

The whole time, our department was trying hard to keep up with the growing pains the Fort Collins area was going through, without increase in the budget. Whether I was going through my second puberty or job pressure was getting to me, I wasn't enjoying my job anymore. I was dealing with the budgets and was buried in paperwork all day, leaving me very little time to be a lawman solving crimes.

I was taking as many vacations from work as I could but didn't really go anywhere. My dad was no longer willing to fly with the commercial airlines since the previous trip had turned disastrous when his baggage came up missing. It never turned up, along with the personal items that meant a lot to him. My dad never flew with the commercial airlines since.

Uncle Phillip began his vacation about that time and planned to go up to Yellowstone Park on a forty-foot bus with some of his employees who had never been to the national park.

Mostly, they worked six days a week, sending money back home to Guatemala, Argentina, or Chile, as six of his employees had been for some time. Last year, right before the Valentines weekend, one of his restaurants went through a three-week renovation due to minor fire damage that started in the kitchen.

It was a big weekend businesswise, but instead of complaining, Uncle Phillip gave each and every employee and their family a choice of a paid vacation from the menu. The choice was between a week in Hawaii or in New Orleans, where the Mardi Gras was about to start. Included were plane tickets and hotel reservations for their spouses and children as well.

When he found out there were four dedicated employees, two couples to be exact, who did not have the necessary identification, he researched and discovered the service that rents buses out to average Joes like us. He took two sets of families—one family with just one child and the other couple with three young children—to the Yellowstone Park on that bus.

He took the time explaining the life of America as it had been told to him by his nephew when he took the trip for the first time as a fresh immigrant twenty-five years ago. The children feasted from the menus of McDonald's, Burger King, Kentucky Fried Chicken, and Denny's restaurants, which did not seem to bother their parents any. They were ready for something different than Chinese, no matter how delicious it may be.

One night, he got six large pizzas from a well-known Chicago restaurant as they drove through the windy city and a dozen full racks of baby back ribs from a restaurant that was St. Louis's pride while stopping to show the famous arch to the four younger travelers. He went up the arch on a tram, much to the delight of the children as their parents were getting dizzy from being inside the arch, looking down at the river.

They spent overnight at a camp by the Missouri Lake. As the chill brought everyone closer to each other and to the fire in the middle, they sang songs in Spanish and drank the night away.

Uncle Phillip hummed away, not knowing a single word in Spanish, yet having a blast nonetheless. He paid for the week's trip out of his pocket, as he stopped each night at the luxurious hotel available and booked suites for each family while he slept on the bus. He was feeling the pain his employees felt. He was a good Samaritan and a neighbor willing to love his fellow brothers and sisters. He had won the hearts of four employees and their children.

Uncle solved the problem of these folks who could not travel on planes by using a "Madden coach." When Raiders coach, John Madden, had retired and became a broadcaster, he had the occasion to borrow a private bus from Dolly Parton to make a trip to his next game, broadcasting.

Coach Madden was very impressed with the comfort as he traveled to his next location while being prepared by the team for the next telecast. He went and ordered a forty-five-foot bus customized with a queen-size bed and a bathroom big enough for a giant like him. He travelled from city to city in luxury while being prepped by his team aboard the bus.

It was Sarah's idea to get a "Madden coach" to fit the needs of Dad and hire a driver to take him on trips to all the wonderful places near or far. It accommodated seven adults comfortably. When parked, the kitchenette moved outward on the driver side of the bus by two feet, while the bedroom compartment slid outward by two feet on the passenger side of the bus.

It was truly amazing how conveniently these vehicles were built, with wireless fiber-optic Internet connections and cable televisions. Children could play video games while parents were talking to people from all over the world via Skype while the bus was rolling. It had a powerful motor to pass slow vehicles with ease.

By the time Dad's party had arrived, the bus had been finished to order, and the newly hired driver was instructed to drive the bus to our home where the party was being held. When the driver received a call on his mobile phone, he was to drive the bus right up to the house parking lot. The party was everything we had anticipated.

Over a hundred people came to wish Dad blessings on his birthday. The music had everyone swaying, and there was plenty of food for everyone. What was to be a three-hour event had turned into an all-day bash. It would have gone on longer, but then the bus arrived.

Theoretically, the party was over for Dad, and it was now time for his vacations. Dad didn't come out of the bus until all the guests had left. He was still mumbling about the amenities the bus came with when we finally escorted him off the bus. It came with a microwave oven over the regular gas range and a full-size oven beneath the range, with two compartment sinks.

It had large water capacity to accommodate showers and dish washing aboard the bus. Dad would never have to leave the bus. He was ready to go on the road.

I had accumulated almost a month of sick days and some unused vacation time. I put in for my vacation time to go on a trip to California. I was going to take Dad to see Joey in Folsom. With Uncle Phillip and Jamey, I figured the four of us would have a trip just for the guys on the bus to California.

Skipper, our driver, took Dad and whomever was able to join him, on many short trips to various spots within several hundred miles from our home. Our plan was to leave the day after Jamey was out of school on winter break to go visit Joey in California. Dad had counted down the fifty-three days since his birthday and the day of our departure.

On the bus were Dad, Uncle, Jamey, Skipper, and me, along with my two old dogs and a year-old Beagle that belonged to Jamey. Eight males—five humans and three canines—headed west on I-70. We spent the night at Reno right before heading into Represa, a city that is located east of Sacramento. We took a dinner and show package deal at the casino that was worth every penny. Feasting on steaks and lobsters while rows of ladies danced topless was a new twist to the fine-dining experience for all of us, especially for Jamey.

I wished Joey was with us. I had failed him as a "bother." I should have been firm in getting him to the therapist and counseling sessions, but I procrastinated, and it was too late to save him from doing fifteen years in prison.

But I was glad he was only a year away from coming home. I told myself I would not make the same mistake next time. I won't let this disease continue with us any longer. This new generation, Jamey and Katie and the little one yet to be born, must not experience what Dad, Joey, and I had gone through.

CHAPTER 26

Monie

Everyone tells me God does not give us more than we can handle, so shut up and get over it—deal with life. I'd sure like to talk to God when I see him. Just what was he thinking when he let me go on and deal with all that I had experienced in my thirty-four years? Don't get me wrong; I'm plenty grateful to God for giving me the nerve to face what I had to and to come out alive.

Mama told me that men are no good and they will always break my heart if I give them the chance. To Tricia, Mama said to take good care of me, and she took off. The old man told everyone she had run off with a younger man, but he was nothing but a liar. Mama got the heck away from him because the old man was beating her. Each time he took the beating to Mama, he could easily have killed her if he didn't stop there and then. Mama flew back to Frankfurt, Germany, her hometown.

I was eleven and Tricia was fifteen when Mama ran back to Germany. No one has heard from her since. The old man ended up going to prison three years after Mama was gone, for raping Tricia and attempting to rape me. I moved into a trailer apartment with Tricia, and she had taken care of me ever since. She made pretty good money as a waitress, and we didn't need to beg for anything.

Just prior to hooking up with Joey, I was in an abusive relationship with a guy who was beating me. I broke up with him, but he had a problem letting me go and followed me around wherever I went. One day, I was at a club in

Boulder with my friends, dancing, when Greg, my ex, showed up. He started to make a scene, calling me names. That's when Joey kicked the hell out of Greg and rescued me from what could have been a beating of my own that night.

No man ever stood up for me before. Like Mama said, they all wanted one thing from me, and it wasn't love. Joey was different. He was a perfect gentleman and treated me like a lady. For the first time in my life, I was loved by a gentleman. I fell in love with Joey. Even though we were careful, I got pregnant with Jamey.

Joey was on parole when I first met him. When he got out, he started selling guns. He told me he doesn't need guns but that the world needs them to equalize powers. Otherwise, the bigger and stronger ones take it all, leaving nothing for the little ones. It becomes wrong only when the gun is used to wrong someone.

It was wrong all right, because he got arrested for conspiracy to sell automatic weapons. He only had a clip with a round of ammos, not the rifle. It was enough to violate his parole and make him serve a year. I started seeing a different side of Joey as he became easily agitated and lost his cool. When I told him I was pregnant and that his violent behavior scared me, he cried, apologizing.

Shortly after that, Sarah and Jimmy came to see me. Sarah asked me if I was willing to let their health insurance care for me during my pregnancy. They already had an insurance card with my name on it. Joey had told Jimmy I was pregnant with his child. Jimmy and Sarah were very thoughtful people. How could I say no?

Jimmy asked me if I would see a psychiatrist friend of his, who could help me prepare myself as a parent. Jimmy and Sarah had gone to this doctor to help him overcome his trauma during the beatings his father gave Jimmy. Jimmy felt he needed to be sure he could raise a child in a safe environment. At first, I was offended they didn't think I was capable of parenting a child. Then I thought these people were only trying to help me and my baby. I went along with their suggestion, even though I didn't think I needed help to become a mother.

Dr. Carol was amazing. She knew how to unleash the emotions that I had bottled up inside. By the time Jamey was born, I was feeling wonderful about myself and was much better prepared to bring a child into this world. I had gone through the layers of emotions that had been neglected. I had the chance to heal from the layers of suppressed painful emotions.

I shared with Tricia how I was learning to forgive the old man, and it was liberating me from the prison that had imprisoned my spirit all these years. She laughed it off as a crazy notion.

When I asked her if she would go see Dr. Carol as well, she thought I was fooling myself. Tricia vowed to never forget what the old man had done to her. Tricia said she certainly didn't need anyone to help her forgive the old bastard.

I understood her feelings. I hoped she would eventually let the past go and live in the present, let the healing take place. As long as she harbored her anger for the old man, she was unable to forgive him. Instead, she had become an angry, bitter woman. I began praying for her to find peace somehow.

I moved into Jimmy's pool house with Jamey when he was born. When Joey got out, we got married in front of all our friends and family. He even took me on a honeymoon to Vail, Colorado. My life seemed to be finally at peace. But something was bothering Joey. He was twenty-seven and living off his brother—no income and no savings—with a wife and a boy almost a year old.

Joey would admit he doesn't handle pressure well. It would make him edgy and short-tempered. Rather than thinking through, he always rushed into things.

He got back with his old hookups and started dealing guns again. It was easy money when a man needed some. I didn't know about it, but Jimmy did. He warned me that Joey was seeing his old buddies and that I should talk some sense into him.

When Joey came home, I was in a middle of a chess game with Doc, Joey's dad. I started calling him Doc when I found out he was a doctor of philosophy. I learned so much from talking to him about life in general. We were in the back patio when Joey started yelling at me from the pool house across the yard, "Hey, are you going to fix me some to eat or what?"

It woke Jamey from his sleep. Doc told me to go fix Joey something to eat while he calmed Jamey down and stayed with him. When I went to Joey, he raised his hand to hit me, but I told him if he did, he would never see Jamey and me again. That's when Doc came over and told Joey to leave until he had the chance to cool down. Joey stormed out after that.

Jimmy looked for Joey for three weeks nonstop. He had vanished, and no one knew where he had gone to. That's when he got busted trying to unload some automatic rifles and ammos to a group in Huntington Beach,

California. He was facing some serious time. I was done with him. I was sad for Jamey, but I was done with Joey. That's when Jimmy came to me with an offer I had to think twice about. His offer was simple. Stay with Joey until the trial was over. Jimmy offered to hire a full-time nanny to care for Jamey so I could stay in California during the trial. A man with his wife standing by him looked better to the jury during the trial.

Sarah had a cousin on her mother's side, Toni, who was married and with children and lived in Garden Grove, California, just three miles from the Orange County Superior Courthouse. Garden Grove had a density of Koreans there, where they had gathered to build a community of their own, with markets and restaurants. Toni's husband, who was into motorcycles, decided to take Joey's bike in exchange for renting their spare bedroom out during the eighteen months the trial had taken.

I visited Joey for three weekend visiting days at the OC Jail. I sat in every court appearance. I was with Joey every step of the way during his trial. When the trial started, the case didn't go well at all. The prosecution seemed to gain ground each time their witnesses got up to the stand to testify against Joey. The codefendants had made the deals with the DA to testify in exchange for a lighter sentence. If Joey was found guilty, he was looking at some serious time.

Joey pleaded to fifteen years in prison just before the trial ended. He was facing over a thousand years had he not taken the plea deal. It was a bargain compared to what he could have gotten. DAs did not care to plea with the rifle dealers. But in the end, their knowledge of the reputation Bill West had brought to the table made them take the deal and go for a sure thing.

I was ready to quit on him for the second time when Jimmy came to the rescue again. We talked for a long time about how precious life was. To give up on one was hard for him and asked me to think about what it meant to walk out on Joey and what that would do to Jamey and to all the family.

He offered to find me a place to live and give me a thousand dollars each month for expenses in addition to rent. Then, he gave me a credit card with my name on it. He said it was dangerous to carry cash and that the card was good for five grand.

I would charge air fares to visit Jamey in Colorado and buy gas for my car and food with the card he gave me. Jimmy was a big brother to me when I needed one the most. I had no one else giving me any hint as to what I should be doing. Jimmy always stood by me and Joey, giving us the firm foundation we needed.

He wanted me to concentrate on supporting his brother, Joey, to stand by him as his wife. Sarah and Jimmy offered to take care of Jamey, giving him the best of care he deserved. Sarah promised to send plane tickets for me to travel to visit with Jamey, whenever my time permitted.

I was overwhelmed with their generosity. It was the first time I began to think I would be able to keep my family together after all. After some soul searching, I decided to accept the offer and go on supporting my husband through the good times and bad. He needed me now more than ever, when I was about to run out on him. I agreed to give Jimmy and Sarah guardianship of Jamey while I was in California.

Three weeks after he was sentenced from the OC Superior Court in July of 1986, Joey caught the chain. That's the term he used anyway. Catching a chain means going to the state pen after the sentence. The bus does not leave on a regular basis. When the reception center has open beds, each of the counties in California gets permission to send up x amount of inmates.

The transferring inmates are chained up to prevent any attempt of running off during the transportation. That's what "catching the chain" means. He was sent to Wasco Reception Center, an hour north on I-5, just over the Grapevine from the city of Los Angeles.

Normally, an inmate would stay at the reception center for two to three months while the classification committee determined what kind of individual you are.

It is the committee's job to try and determine which of thirty-three California Department of Corrections prisons here was best suited for you. After nine weeks at Wasco, Joey was sent to Corcoran Level 4, B yard. It seemed as if Corcoran was on lockdown all the time. This high-security prison held infamous inmates, such as Charles Manson and Sirhan Sirhan, who had killed Robert Kennedy.

All I remember is the many times my visit was cancelled due to the riots and lockdowns. Joey was allowed conjugal visits every two to three months. We had to order food through a vendor who prepared the food and delivered it to the trailer where the visitation takes place.

Long ago, inmates' wives were allowed to bring their own groceries to cook and eat, but too much contraband was being brought in and caused problems for the prison. The trailers had two to three bedrooms, so children could visit their father while he served time in prison. For forty-eight hours, inmates were granted leaves of absence from their work and housing assignments and be with their family. It was an incentive program to keep married inmates behaving to keep the privilege.

Two years went by when Joey was told to pack up and get ready for transfer. A new prison was built way out in the middle of a desert, just west of Blythe. Chuckawalla Valley State Prison, also known as the Chuckey's house.

It wasn't a place I would have wanted to live had it not been for Joey. It got up to 130 degrees at times, to a point it was like I couldn't breathe. I had to stay inside where it was cool with an AC during the hot days. I was glad to work inside a hotel where it was nice and cool all the time. A lady I met at a church happened to be the manager at the Ramada Inn hotel restaurant. She gave me a full-time job just like that.

I waited on lonely travelers from two to closing, which was 10:00 p.m. on weekdays. I went to see my husband on Saturdays and Sundays from nine to five. During the weekdays, I started to take an art class at the community college. It relaxed me, and I enjoyed creating art. I was told I was good at it, and I continued on with another class when the semester was over.

Chuckawalla prison was jumping off too. The heat was getting to the inmates, who wanted more ice for their beverages and less work hours under the blazing sun. It all made sense to me. Give them more ice. And for crying out loud, how could any man work under a 130-degree sun?

But this riot continued on for two weeks before it finally ended with lots of inmates getting hurt, but with everything else remaining just the same. They were still allowed only one cup of ice per inmate, and it was still a six-hour workday.

Joey worked at a furniture-manufacturing shop as a clerk, operated by the Prison Industry Authority, which hired inmates to do their work under a contract with the CDC. It kept inmates working, making some money while at it. Joey earned nine dollars per day at a buck fifty an hour.

The paychecks from PIA went directly into the inmates' accounts. It was a great concept for the CDC, who got the remainder of the fifteen dollars per hour after the inmates got their 10 percent. It was keeping the inmates busy and happy as well. Too much time on their hands would give them time to design stupid ideas.

In 1994, Ironwood State Prison was finally completed right next to Chuckey's house and needed to fill in the empty beds. ISP had several yards, level 1 and level 3 housings. Joey had gone through several classification committees at the Chuckawalla during the past six years and finally lowered his status from level 4 to 3. He was one of three hundred inmates selected from thirty other locations to fill the brand-new cells. It was the second time for Joey to break in a new prison.

It was actually good for Joey to have some change in life after six years of Chuckawalla. He had the choice of jobs and housing at ISP as everything was vacant, and he was one of the first few inmates brought to ISP. I didn't have to move since Ironwood prison was only half an hour away from my apartment. It allowed me to continue with my art classes during the week while working at the hotel restaurant during the evenings.

I missed Jamey in between my visits to Colorado or when he flew out to join us during the conjugal visits. He was the exact opposite of Joey in his behavior. Jamey was a confident young man with a calm and gentle way about doing things. He was never out of control or lost his cool, even when he was down a set or facing a match point against him. His positive attitude did wonders in helping him to get out of a jam without getting worked up like his daddy.

There aren't enough Skype or phone conversations to replace hugging your son to tell him you're proud of his achievements in person or planting kisses on his forehead. I swallowed many tears while talking to him, praying this would be over and we could all be together in one place, not three.

During the visits, Joey and I rarely talk about the past. It didn't serve a purpose. I could see Joey change as the years passed. At first, Joey was all about getting respect from others. That's all he talked about. He would tell me about the politics that was going on inside the walls. When you do a long stretch of time, it's hard to not be involved in prison politics. Joey tried to keep to himself, but eventually, he was calling the shots for the Asians.

Joey didn't appreciate the way some of the weaker brothers were treated by a previous shot caller and stepped in to correct things as it should have been. Everyone appreciated what Joey stood for, and since then, they turned to him for leadership.

In 1997, Joey became a level 2 security, but Ironwood did not have level 2 yards. Joey was sent up north to Old Folsom's level 2 yard. It was in Represa, California, near Sacramento. I moved with Joey. I was fortunate enough to get a job as a live-in nanny for a veterinarian couple's three-year-old girl. Watching Jamey's nanny over the years had given me a pretty good idea of what a nanny's duties were.

Sarah had come through for me once again, introducing me to her alum Dr. Beth and her husband, who was also a vet, living in Sacramento. With Sarah vouching for me, I became little Sue's nanny.

I spent the weekdays with this precious little girl, drawing pictures and going to the parks or museums, according to the schedule Dr. Beth and I had created for the week. On weekends, I drove forty-five minutes to Represa, where Joey was waiting for me.

Our conversation began shifting from all the prison talks to planning for the future as Joey's parole date neared. Level 2 yards could be stressful at times, but it was much easier on Joey's nerve. The population consisted of short termers doing a handful of years or those who had gone through the large chunk of their sentence with a small portion remaining.

There were minimum-yard gangsters flexing their muscles on the yard among the small-timers, which made Joey laugh with pity. All in all, Joey was finally able to relax and retire from his prison political career.

There was an *uso* running the Asians in Folsom when Joey got there. Joey said *uso* is Samoan for "brother." James was his name, but he didn't care for that name. So everyone just called him Uso. Joey said he was a nice guy but had to hustle a lot because he had no family outside to look out for him, to send him packages and spending money. He was sentenced to do 80 percent of a twenty-year sentence. He had done fourteen of the sixteen and was now doing the final stretch at Folsom's 2 yard.

Since Joey met Uso, I had sent a quarterly package to Uso, as directed by Joey. I had a few twenties added to Uso's account, also as instructed by Joey. It was that kind of sensitivity Joey had for others that made me fall in love with him. But Joey played it off by saying, "It doesn't look good for an Asian homey to have to hustle when other homeys can look out for him." It made Joey and other Asians look bad, he said.

Joey stayed out of harm's way and kept to himself, trying not to delay getting home with infractions or violations that added to your time. He had aged a lot, as I did. He spoke of doing things right this time, not getting involved with his past life.

Folsom offered their residents various classes, such as communication skills, anger management, and mediation techniques. The prison staffed counselors and therapists to work on issues that may have brought the inmates there in the first place. Joey took advantage of everything there was. He had nothing but time. Joey said he could do two remaining years sitting on a toilet—whatever that meant.

He actually talked about how good the food was compared to Chuckey's or Ironwood. There was a prison dairy industry ran by the level 1 inmate population living on the farm. Having your own dairy farm could certainly improve your menu. Folsom's prison bakery produced some great aroma even for the visitors, as they baked bear claws on weekends for all the inmates in different level yards at Folsom.

Jamey seemed to enjoy the conjugal visits with his dad in Folsom much better than when Joey was in the desert. The temperatures got so high in the desert all the activities took place inside. The temperatures at Represa were something Jamey was more familiar with, living in Colorado. Since the move, the relationship between Joey and Jamey seemed to blossom even more.

When I flew to Denver for Doc's seventieth, Doc told me that Jimmy and Jamey were going to bring Doc to Folsom on a custom-made bus when Jamey got out of school for the holidays.

Doc was always interested in how Joey was doing but was unable to visit him due to his decision to not fly with the commercial airlines. Even traveling on car would have been difficult as he needed to use the bathroom every half an hour or so.

I was so excited, as I had prayed for the opportunity to have them start talking to each other and getting along once again. Unexpectedly, the prayer was answered. Doc was going to visit Joey. I knew Joey would be excited to hear the news. It was going to be one heck of a Christmas present.

Much to my amazement, Joey got mad when he found out Doc was coming to see him. He was so upset he wouldn't eat or talk during the remainder of the visit.

He just sat there drinking his soda until the visiting hour was over. I told him, as I left, not to expect any visits from me if he refused his dad's visit.

"Imagine Jamey as he wonders why you wouldn't see your own father, when Doc wants to travel all this way to see you," I asked my husband.

"Why now, after all these years he never came to see me once, and now that I am ready to come home, he wants to come see me. Why is that?"

"Who cares why, Joey? Doesn't the fact that he is coming to you says it loud enough that he's sorry, that he wants to make things right between you two? Perhaps in his aging days he needs to close some chapters, make amends and that kind of thing. I can see that."

". . ."

"It isn't about you coming home that prompted the visit, I don't think. I think it's something else. The fact is, he couldn't come to visit you in California, not that he didn't. You know that."

". . ."

"You should've seen Doc when you went missing. Because he freaked out, thinking he may have caused you to harm yourself somehow. When I was living in the pool house, he shared with me that he used to want to tell you and Jimmy how terrible he felt inside because of the past relationships you all had. He used to choke up when he talked about how badly he felt about his past.

"I would have forgiven my old man if he would have asked me to. Even after what he tried to do. Because when someone is sincerely sorry and trying to make things right, you must accept their apology and give them a chance to amend, to atone. Give them parole and release them from their burden of carrying all their guilt, for crying out loud."

". . ."

"Jimmy got it from Doc just as badly as you did, if not more. Am I right? Yet he has learned to forgive Doc and let the past go. Jimmy exemplifies as he tells me to live the present and look forward to the future. But first, we have to let the past be the past. Not allowing the past to destroy the present as well as the future. That should be your goal too, Joey." I looked at him before continuing.

"Let go of the past and dwell on the present. Jimmy lives in peace with the man who had beaten on him when he was a child. You're living in misery while Doc is nowhere near you. I don't get it."

"I don't want you to get it. It's my misery, and I'll deal with it the way I want to."

"Wah, poor me, call me a wah-mbulance 'cuz I've fallen and can't get up, wah. Don't expect me to keep your misery company. And don't worry about your little pretty head over your son's misery either. What are you going to tell Jamey, huh? What are you going to tell him when he asks you why you won't allow Doc's visit? I mean, what kind of example is that for you to set for your son?

". . ."

"Say something. How are you going to expect Jamey to forgive you for abandoning him for the past fourteen years from the time when he was a baby, while not forgiving your own father?"

"It's not the same. Look, I need to think about it, can I do that? I am not saying one way or another. Just give me some time to think about it, gee."

"Just remember it's not just Jamey but everyone who's been praying for you and supporting you while you're here. You'll be forty-three when you come home, not the twenty-six-year-old youngster I met, who had his life ahead of him.

"You think I would've stuck by you all these years if I hadn't learned to forgive and forget? I couldn't dwell in the past because it sickened me. So I moved on living each day, one day at a time, in the present. I don't go back to what I am trying to forget. I moved on from all that. But you, for some reason, really want to hold on to the memory that seems to bother you so much. What's with you?"

"..."

"All the guys making passes at me, but I tell them to get lost, thinking you're my man and daddy to Jamey. I was hoping to raise him together with a sensible man, while Jamey went through his puberty and all that hormone stuff. Don't make me regret passing up on the opportunity to replace you when I had the chance. Jamey is looking forward to this trip with his grandpa like you wouldn't believe. You need to stop thinking about yourself and grow up."

"All right already. It's still five weeks away, so why you tripping?"

"Because they have been planning it for a month already, going through all the reservations and getting things lined up. They hired a driver to drive the bus, Uncle Phillip and Jimmy had scheduled time off to make the trip. Don't go making this Christmas a big bummer for everyone. Sarah and Judy won't be coming. Did I tell you Judy was pregnant again?"

"Yeah, like five times. Does Jamey ever talk about wanting a younger brother or sister?"

"What's the use, it would have been too much for me to handle. I was too lonely and awfully sad too many times being away from Jamey. If I had two or more, I would have lived with them and raised them, not chased you around the desert as I did." I took a breather before continuing.

"You wouldn't believe how many times I felt like I was falling for your smooth talking about *this* and *that* when you get out. I trusted you anyway, and now, I want you to live up to all the fancy promises about how you are a changed man and all that."

"I am changed, honey. I'm just having a little difficulty dealing with my old man, if you can understand that. I want to do what's right. Not for you, Jamey, or for my father, but for me. So let me think through it and prepare for the visit in five weeks. How is that?"

"More like a man with some sense. It's difficult letting your past go, you know. It's like saying good-bye to a longtime friend. Same as kicking a habit of smoking or drinking or even gambling, it isn't something that just happens by itself. You know what happened to my sis Tricia."

"Yeah, how is she doing anyway?"

"All those times I asked her to go see Dr. Carol and get help, she just laughed at me, and now look at her. After she pleaded not guilty due to the reason of insanity, the judge sentenced her to the mental institution for an indeterminate period of time, until I guess she gets well, if ever."

"Sarge was crazy to show up at her work like that, unannounced, and causing Tricia to freak out like that. I can't believe she stabbed him two dozen times and killed him. After he was transferred to Centennial Correctional Facility, it was hard to get to him. Otherwise, I would have taken him out myself before Tricia had the chance. I swear he's lucky he checked himself into the hole and stayed there while I was doing time in Colorado."

"There you go again, from the sweet old man I adore, to that angry avenger ready to kill, in three seconds flat. Is that one of the first things you're going to teach your son? How to take out the enemy at the first opportunity you get?

"I buried my old man, and I'm dealing with it just fine, so why are you tripping and unable to let him be dead? The guy is dead, for crying out loud. But your father isn't, and he's trying to make it right with you. If Tricia had accepted my old man's apology when he showed up at her work, he'd be alive so you could kill him and go back to jail after you got out while my sister would be living a life as a free woman. Too bad for you it looks like that isn't going to happen since he's already dead. But you have a chance to make things right. Haven't you seen enough of what hate can do to you? Give your father a chance to come and see you. Listen to what he has to say. Let the man die in peace."

"I guess there is a reason why I married you, because you make up for the brain I was born without. Thanks for your patience and never giving up on me and opening my eyes to make me see things." Joey came to his senses finally. He was speaking like Joey who had his head screwed on correctly.

CHAPTER 27

Summer 1999

God gives and takes. On the Easter Sunday, fourth of April, God gave us Jake William West. He was six pounds eleven ounces when he arrived, two pounds four ounces lighter than his cousin Jamey when he was born. He was a healthy boy with a full set of hair that looked like he needed a haircut; it was so bushy.

Shortly after the birth of Jake, God took Dad from us. He went to join Mom in heaven. On the morning of April 20, Dad did not wake up. He died in his sleep, peacefully. Before he left, he had the chance to meet his second grandson. He held Jake in his arms and cooed at him, telling Judy just how proud he was of Dwight and Judy for giving him such a fine grandson.

Dad was spared from witnessing the terrible event that shook the nation. It took place just a few hours after he had passed away. Eric Harris and Dylan Klebold killed thirteen people and injured twenty-four others before committing suicide at Columbine High School in Lakewood, an hour away from our home.
Instead, he was in heaven, telling Mom about all their grandchildren—Jamey, Katie, and Jake. I was sure Mom was celebrating both the birth of Jake and the death of Dad, as they were united again in heaven as the children of God.

My dad did the best he could without his helpmate, overcoming such sad tragedy and continuing on. In the end, Dad was free of the disease that had once leashed its fury on him. He died in peace. He tried hard to reconcile and make amends with everyone. He did it in his own way, in his own time, but he did it in time.

He wanted to properly send off his past in order that he could begin his preparation to meet his Maker. He did well with what was dealt to him. He may have been carrying something far more than anyone could imagine. The baggage that reminded him of what he used to be could've been quite burdensome.

Had I known he would be taken from us so soon, I would have started our vacations sooner. I thanked God that before he passed on, he was able to take the trip with his brother, son, and grandson to go see Joey after all these years. For fifteen years, he had regretted, every single day, for fighting with Joey on the day Joey took off. He had been blaming himself for what happened to Joey.

Arriving into Represa and approaching old Folsom, my dad actually hyperventilated, becoming too anxious about facing Joey. He had waited fifteen years to have the chance to make it right. And it was finally happening for him. It was too much excitement for the old guy.

There was a limitation of three visitors per inmate per visit. So Monie used her knowledge to have me and Uncle Phillip approved to visit Uso a month ago, while Dad was added to Joey's visitation list at the same time. Monie and Jamey had been on Joey's approved visitors list for many years.

Uso, whose name was James, did not have a family in the mainland. He hadn't received a single visit in over a decade he had been doing time. He had a sister in Samoa but didn't know if she was still alive or not. He had lost contact with her.

Once inside the visiting room, we grabbed two tables next to each other. Dad sat between Joey and Jamey along with Monie, while Uso joined me and Uncle Phillip. The guard gave us the permission to join the two tables together. Uso reminded me of my old partner, Pat Lalua. He was just as kind and friendly as you would expect from Santa Claus. His presence was helpful during our visit, as Joey seemed to benefit from having his best buddy around during the awkward moment.

Watching Uso put away sandwich after another, gulping down soda bottles after another, was the most amazing thing to watch. I felt like I had the front-row seat in a food-eating contest. Dad made me buy photo ducats. The ducat was a raffle-ticket-looking thing that you purchased from a cashier and gave to an inmate photographer roaming the visiting room. He took Polaroid pictures of inmates with families visiting in exchange for the ducats.

It was nice to have photos of your loved ones, even though they may be locked up. We took a total of eleven photos. Dad wanted to make sure he would walk away with plenty of Joey's photos.

The conversation never got too serious, and no one was interested in saying too much. But everyone had fun during the visit. Dad must have hugged Joey a dozen times. Looking back, it seemed as if Dad knew it was going to be their last visit. The next day, we did everything over again. Uso ate lots of food, Dad took some photos with Joey, and everyone laughed a lot.

Dad insisted we add plenty of money into both Joey's and Uso's accounts. He pulled out ten crisp hundred-dollar bills, adding five hundred into each of their accounts. When Uso learned of Dad's gesture, this gigantic man stopped eating and cried like a baby, not knowing how to show his appreciation. Uso received occasional funds from us along with birthday cards and letters since the visit.

We buried Dad next to Mom. Little did anyone know that Dad had bought two plots when we buried Mom thirty-two years ago. He planned on being buried next to his bride all along. It sure made it convenient for us to visit them together.

He was survived by a brother and his wife, three children and their spouses, two nieces and their husbands, three grandchildren, and five grandnieces and grandnephews.

Joey was six months away from parole when he was granted to be released to a halfway house in Sacramento. He needed permission from the CDC to travel to Colorado for his father's funeral. He was given a seventy-two-hour pass to attend the funeral. He flew in with Monie on Wednesday morning before the funeral.

It was the first reunion between the three siblings in fifteen years. Joey would meet his niece and nephew for the first time. By the time the funeral had started in the early afternoon, it started to drizzle. It was a gentle April shower coming down upon those gathered to say good-bye to Dad.

After the funeral, everyone was gathered at our house with lots of food and drinks. Due to the Columbine incident that took place a few days before, the mood in the Denver area was just as dampened and dreary as the weather.

When all the well-wishers had left, only the Lee clans had remained. When Dad came to Denver to study in 1964, I'm certain he had no idea his family would grow to be twenty members strong thirty-five years later.

I had been carefully asking questions regarding the legality of my funds that had been collecting compound interests for the past twenty-six years since I came home from the navy. The original balance of $700,000 each in two accounts had turned into $1,486,220 each. There was almost three million dollars at my disposal. I was expecting to pay a chunk of tax in order to make the fund usable. I learned that if I was to donate the fund into a nonprofit organization, the tax owed would be exempt. I was excited with the news and was looking forward to this moment to share the information with the family.

Uncle Phillip stood before the gathered family near the fireplace. Children held by their parents or uncles and aunts, some standing, some sitting, drew closer to each other as asked by my uncle. He was visibly hurt by the loss of his brother. He seemed to have aged quite a bit in the last three days.

"I don't think anyone truly knew my brother. He was not an easy man to read. I guess I knew him better than anyone else. With a seven-year difference in our ages, I didn't get to know him much at all, growing up. With war and the evacuation from the north, we didn't get to spend too much time with each other. When we finally settled in Busan and were about to live together, he joined the army and moved away from home. Then he got married and came to America, as we all know. He never stopped looking to improve the quality of living for his family. It is due to his ambition that I'm able to enjoy the wonderful life I have with my loved ones." Uncle looked around the room before he continued.

"I was drinking my life away as a functioning alcoholic, living an aimless life in South Korea. Even when I first arrived in America, I complained about losing my dignity and pride, unable to communicate in English and becoming so frustrated. I thank God I had Jimmy to be my friend, lending me his shoulder to cry on. And my dear wife, who never complained even when things were going tough. Having her next to me made it easy to endure through those dark moments.

"In the end, God blessed me with two wonderful sons-in-law—an attorney and a surgeon and, most of all, a couple of great human beings. God gave me five grandchildren that are out of this world." Uncle got too emotional to continue. He took a moment to compose himself.

"I've decided to retire. I realize just how precious time is. At the beginning of this year, I decided to go public with my company and entered into an agreement with a venture capital banker to franchise my restaurants throughout the globe. I realized I could no longer singly handle the business. However, my limitations should not lead to forfeiture of good fortune in front of us. It has become too big for me to handle alone. I'm getting old, and I believe the decision to go public was the right one."

"The Peking Palace Food Incorporated and its packaging facility, the warehouses, fleet of trucks and semis, the seven restaurant locations and six of its properties owned by the company have come to a total of just over $22 million in assets with zero account payables. I have instructed my attorney to divide the stocks into following portions. My five children, Jimmy, Joey, Lisa, Judy, and Sharon, will each receive 10 percent of the company stocks. Each of the eight grandchildren will receive 5 percent of the company each, leaving 10 percent for my wife's brothers and their family members." Uncle called Joey, Judy, and me his children, not nephews and niece. Indeed, he was my father, and I, his son. Uncle Phillip reached for Aunt Cindy, who stood and came to him, as he continued.

"Cindy's two brothers will each have 5 percent interest in the business. Their presence was instrumental in becoming who we are, and they would be necessary ingredients in maintaining the excellence they have brought to the company.

"You may do what you wish with your stocks. Keep them and receive dividends as the company is making profit, or you may liquidate it as you wish. I ask only that you give family members the first opportunity to buy your stocks. Otherwise, I ask that the majority stockholders must accept or approve the purchase by an outsider.

"I will step down immediately, giving Lisa total control of the business. She's been aware of the plan since the onset of this year. She's quite capable of handling the business and overseeing the franchise end of the business. We're bringing in some experts to help her as well. We're hoping Joey and Monie will join the company. We could use some fresh energy, and you'll be well compensated for your efforts, of course.

"My advisors believe the stock could skyrocket and double itself if all goes well, according to our plan. When that happens, Lisa deserves a raise. I believe she is making barely $5,000 a month now. I didn't realize I was such a slave driver because Lisa has never said a word that she never got a raise in eighteen years. Some patience she has. Her salary will be doubled. A CEO of such a fine company should make at least a six-figure annual salary, what do you think?" He looked around the room to see everyone nodding and smiling.

"I have saved more money than I could possibly spend in one lifetime. So from now on, my bride and I will begin enjoying each other while traveling. Upon completion of my mourning, my wife and I will take some time to travel around the globe, starting with South America. Brazil is where my bride's baby brother lives, and she wants to go see him and his family. I'm afraid she had been quite concerned for them and wishes to visit them as soon as possible. Her concern is my concern, so I will plan for the trip in the next month or so. If you don't mind, I'm a little tired. I'll leave you young ones to continue enjoying each other's presence, but I'm going to go home and get some rest. I didn't realize burying your brother can take such a toll on you."

Everyone stood as Uncle and Aunt Cindy made their exit, hugging everyone on their way out of the room. When they had left, Judy asked everyone quietly to gather around once again, handing sleeping Jake to Dwight.

"I am going to make this very quick and short. Dad came to me several years ago and asked me to draw up his will. I had referred him to a capable attorney friend of mine. She helped him finalize it and holds the original copy.

"I have in my possession a copy of my father's will. It basically outlines his properties, his retirement savings, and trust accounts in the total sum of just over $695,000. Of course, the attorney's fee was deducted from the original sum already. We, the vultures, got to get our portions first. It helps us to offset our expensive tuitions.

"Dad made the instructions very clear that everything he owned would be left for my brother Joey. I hope no one is offended by his decision, as our dad knew Joey *oppa* could benefit from his life savings the most. That was until Uncle Phillip practically made everyone in this room a millionaire.

"Once you arrive at Dad's attorney's office, *oppa*, she is ready to cut you a check for the lump sum of $695,000 in a certified check. I am sure you and Monie could use it as you begin your new start. Everyone here has been pulling for you, *oppa*. We are so proud of you and Monie. You guys fought through it all and never gave up. Here's a toast to you two." She raised her glass as everyone else did. Even the kids lifted their hot chocolates up to toast Joey and Monie.

"If no one has any questions regarding Daddy's will, I just want to thank you all for all you have done with such short notice to host nearly a thousand guests that came to pay our dad their respect." I stood as Judy sat down, taking her baby son from her husband.

"I have something I need to share with everyone here also. First of all, I echo Judy in thanking everyone for doing such a fine job of hosting such a large amount of people who braved the bad weather to pay tribute to our dear father. It pleases me that so many had come to honor my dad.

"Sarah and I have been discussing a matter for some time, and recently I've been seeking advice from the attorneys regarding this matter." Everyone looked concerned. I continued.

"In 1973, I had to make a decision that was a very difficult one to make. I had a choice to arrest my best friend after he tried to smuggle two pure gold bars from PI. I was going to arrest him. Had I done that, he would have been deported to the Philippines along with his aging mother.

"I believe some of you may have met Mama Tessi on my wedding day, as she flew in from San Diego to attend the wedding. Mama Tessi was very dear to me, and I couldn't do anything that would devastate her well-being. So I gave my buddy a onetime pass and didn't arrest him, along with his two accomplices.

"They went on with their operations without my knowledge for three years, yielding some impressive profits. With the proceeds, they have invested well on my behalf as well, to show their appreciation. I received two bankbooks from them on the last evening I spent in San Diego before heading back home. Much to my amazement, there was over $700,000 in each of the account. For the past twenty-three years, it had been collecting compounded interests accrued to $1,486,220 in each of the account, a total of $2,972,440, or $27,560 shy of three million bucks." I stopped to look around the room full of family members, wooing and expressing smiles in surprise at the enormous amount of money I had mentioned.

"Long ago, I envisioned building shelters for abused women and children. I asked God to open doors and create opportunities so that my dream would one day become realized. Each paycheck I received since my first job with Safeway Grocers as a teenager, I gave my tithe to God, and the second tenth went into my savings account for the purpose of building shelters. I believe I have little over a hundred grand saved up from my paychecks since that first.

"At the time I opened these offshore accounts, I guess my duty to Joey and Judy as their brother made me open the accounts in their names. Judy and I have already discussed over this matter as I needed Dwight and her legal advices.

"You Joey, and of course Judy as well, may claim the money by using your SSN and DOB in correct sequence and have the money transferred to anywhere in the world. You can use the money for your family, to invest, or to help the needy.

"Once the money is transferred into a bank in American soil, the money becomes taxable. Believe me when I tell you that IRS will come knocking if you don't ante up. They will take a chunk of it, 40 percent to be exact."

I took a deep breath before continuing. "If the fund is given to a nonprofit organization, however, the tax becomes exempt." I stopped to see if anyone had something to say. Everyone seemed to be in deep thought. I believe they were able to imagine an organization that could benefit from such an endowment.

"Until my dear old dad passed away, it would have been difficult for me to build shelters for the victims of domestic violence. As some of you may know already, our dad was suffering from manic depression, also known as bipolar II. He had, in the past, expressed his anger in a less than ideal manner, which he had to live with for many years. He had these mood swings that took him from being the nicest man to a mean and angry one. No one understood the manic side of the depression, simply thinking Dad was an angry old man.

"When we discovered his bipolar II condition, it was a matter of simply taking a prescribed medication to control his mood swings. He slept better, ate better, and became happier in life. The wonder of modern medicine doing its magic on Dad was enjoyable to watch.

"In his own simple and quiet way, my dad went through repentance and worked hard to seek everyone's forgiveness. Now that our dear dad is no longer with us, I do not fear offending him by building shelters for the abused folks." I looked around the room. Then I turned to Joey.

"I will give you time to make your decision, Joey. Judy has given me her answer already in what to do with her portion. I hope you will use the money to join me in my plan to build shelters. If you do, I could borrow against the $2.2 mil my uncle just gave me and turn yours and Judy's funds into five million dollars in usable funds for the foundation to educate the public in battle against domestic violence." I sat down, having said all I needed to. Joey spoke up.

"I can't believe what is happening to me. First, Uncle Phillip gives me two million dollars and then my old man left me a chunk of money, so I found out."

Joey continued, "I am still in shock when *hyung* gives me a bankbook with another one and a half million. Am I still dreaming? Because if I am, please, don't wake me. A broke bloke to a multimillionaire in a matter of minutes, is this for real?" Everyone laughed. Joey continued, "I am throwing in my $2.2 mil with *hyung* along with this bankbook. You do what you need to with it and build your shelters, *hyung*." That's when my longtime best friend and my brother-in-law Dwight spoke up, still sitting next to his wife, looking down at his newborn son.

"My father, Judge West, had to leave immediately following the funeral service to return to his courtroom. He's in the middle of a big trial. For some time, he had been discussing with Judy and me regarding Jimmy's offshore accounts. He has given me and Judy advice on how to best utilize the fund Jimmy spoke of. In addition to the advice, he has extended me the liberty to match the total sum that would be raised for the foundation Jimmy discussed with my father. My father would be quite surprised he is going to match a total of $7.4 million. But he wouldn't have sent me on this mission if he wasn't prepared to back up his claim."

"I hope your father is prepared for my $2.2 million as well," said Lisa, hugging her husband, Scott, who had responded warmly by rubbing her back.

"If $2.2 million is all it takes to play this game, don't count us out," said Dr. Jed. To him, it was a chump change. My cousin Sharon snuggled with him, leaning her head against his shoulder in contentment.

"If my math is correct, I think that's $11.8 million Judge West needs to match. Is that something he had in mind, you think?" I asked Dwight with a chuckle.

"We will see. When my grandfather passed away, I know he left Dad well over eight figures in estate and cash. Now that he is at the end of his long, lustrous career, he is looking for other ways to contribute. Perhaps we could name the foundation in his honor or something, to keep him from changing his mind, ha-ha."

"That's a great idea, the name of a foundation is very important, and to name it after a judge who is also the chief benefactor is not a bad idea. Not that your father will change his mind if we don't name the foundation after him."

"If he wasn't my father-in-law, I would throw in my portion of the stock as well, but it would deem inappropriate against Bill if I did that, causing further burden upon what is already a large sum for him to have to match, so you all understand I will hold on to my portion for now for the rainy day, which I hope will never come," Judy offered.

"In addition to my father's contribution," Dwight continued, "the firm has decided to allow Judy to take a leave of absence from the firm and chair the foundation, overseeing its operations. She is already on maternity leave as it stands, so it won't be a total shock to the firm to be without her. I'm going to assign an accountant to man the trust account down to every cent's accuracy and transparency. The foundation should begin its search for a potential board of trustees to oversee the foundation," Dwight said, as he bounced Jake as he started to cry. He handed Jake over to Judy. Judy exited the room to breastfeed her son. Dwight stood, slowly turned to look at everyone around the room, and then turned to me.

"I'll speak with my father this evening and let you know what he has to say, okay, Jimmy?" I nodded. Lisa spoke up.

"I believe I can help with the board of trustee issues, as my father's—excuse me—our company had gone through the process only months ago. In addition, we may be able to let this foundation piggyback with my father's corporate credit rating. That would allow everyone, including Judge West, to keep their portion of the $23.6 million while borrowing against it and use the money that belongs to the bank. Some lending institutions are looking for just the kind of opportunity to offset their corporate taxable liabilities.

"I think I know just the creditor who would be interested. This bank will gladly lend 80 percent of the trust amount on my dad's signature alone. Not to brag, but my dad can get hold of $500 million on his signature alone.

"I saw it happen only months ago, as his venture capitalist partners handed him half a billion dollars with simply signing his signature. Of course, it is yours truly who now has the total use of all that money. Not bad for a hick chick from Korea, huh?" to which everyone laughed.

Lisa continued, "Anyway, it will give the foundation nearly $20 million in start-up funds, guaranteed by the bank, while our own money will earn interest remaining in our possession and control. The beauty of it is, once the foundation shows stability and success over the certain amount of period, it could easily become eligible for the federal grants to mandate the foundation's operational costs. We could pay off any creditors and sustain operation in black while saving the foundation's trust fund to invest or generate revenue for the future use.

"If everyone agrees, I will have my legal department draw up contracts to surrender your assets and add it into the trust. Once everyone signs it, I can initiate the negotiation with the bank to replace our fund with theirs." Lisa sat. She was impressive. She knew her stuff.

"What about me, could I put in my $1.1 million into it?" It was Jamey who spoke.

"No can do, young man," said Lisa. "This may be a good time for me to get to the fine prints I didn't get to earlier about the 5 percent interest of the company given to all eight of you children by my father. It states that, you are forbidden to make any transactions or forfeit your ownership by giving it to anyone until you turn twenty-five years old. The dividends will go directly into your trust accounts until then. Don't ask me why the age of twenty-five, but that's what my father came up with. So you may not put your portion of the stock into the foundation until you turn twenty-five. Your gesture is well noted and appreciated, young man. You make us proud," said Lisa. I finished my drink and stood.

"When the foundation is formed, its primary goal is to acquire some properties that are either already utilized as shelters or could easily be converted into one. The foundation will focus on victims with children.

"We cannot help everyone who needs help. No single organization could. We must be efficient and effective, knowing who to help and how before we start. The goal is to keep the family intact against all their odds. We hope to educate the abusers so they see what they are doing, repent, and rejoin their family. Our goal isn't to destroy families by separating them forever.

"We must hire teachers to operate homeschooling from K to 12. The children attending school outside the shelter would simply lead their stalking fathers to where their mothers are hiding, rendering the shelter useless once the location becomes known to the abusers. Meantime, the foundation will fund educations for the mothers to earn trades such as being an x-ray technician, a dental hygienist, a pharmacy tech, or a beautician, just to name a few. If individuals have the training from the past, we will do everything we can to get their career going, helping them to stand on their own, giving them continuous guidance and support.

"Remember, we must bring as much awareness as possible without attracting any attention to us, the foundation, and to the shelters. We must remain in low profile. You see the anti-abortion demonstrators attacking abortion clinics and blowing them up and killing the doctors nowadays. An angry man in desperation may do something terrible to get his family back. We must remember, our actions must be done quietly. So quietly so that our left hand won't know what our right hand is doing. Your response here today was very encouraging and hopeful. Thank you, everyone."

There was the feeling of celebration in the air as everyone turned to each other in discussions over what had taken place before us in the past hour. Joey walked over to me, opening his arms to invite my hug. We hugged. We held each other in our arms as we spoke.

"*Hyung*, I never knew. Why didn't you tell me sooner? Forget I just said that. I've learned enough about me to know I would have blown it one way or another in some stupid stuff. What can I say, *hyung*? You looked out for me when I deserved none of it." Joey broke the hug and looked into my face.

"I know what you did. I heard about your deals with Monie, to keep her from walking away from me for good. Twice is what I was told. You kept me from doing some crazy stuff, *hyung*. If I didn't have Monie and Jamey to stand by me and support me for the past fifteen years, I would have killed at least a couple of those crazy fools and never gotten home. But she was there, thick and thin, thanks to you. I found out you bribed her with money. But it worked, huh, bro?"

"I was desperate but didn't have to bribe her, Joey. It was her decision to stay with you. I didn't know what else to do but everything possible to keep you and the family together. I'm glad you understand."

"Understand? *Hyung*, you saved my life, man. My family is intact because of you. I owe you big time." Joey's eyes got shiny with moisture. He quickly changed his face into a smile as he said, "Wow, with Dad's money, I could give my family a real-deal home for us to live in." As Joey spoke, I could see Judy returning from Dad's room where she had been nursing Jake.

Sarah stood and walked over to Judy and took Jake from her. My wife had the biggest smile on her face as she cuddled our nephew.

Joey continued, "I was hoping you could help me find a home in Huntington Beach for me to purchase, some place near a high school that has a good tennis program for Jamey. Now that he's going to be a junior, we need to think about which college he's going to apply to, and he's pretty adamant about trying for Stanford."

"I will, Joey. You make sure you get through the remainder of your time at the halfway house and your parole. Let everyone else worry about themselves, including Jamey. When you get back California, I will have a realtor from OC contact you, and you can tell him directly just what you are looking for in a home. If you ask me, I'd say Newport Beach over HB, if you are looking for a senior high school with better tennis programs. I can't say the same for its football or basket programs. Mater Dei High School in Santa Ana is pretty strong with their athletics department, including its tennis program. Looks like we got ourselves a tennis pro in our family, huh?" I stuck my hand out for a shake. Joey gave me a handshake as our hands met in front of our faces saying, "I heard that, *hyung*." Jamey walked over to his father just then.

"Hey, old man, I hear you just became a millionaire since I spoke with you last. You don't mind if I join your club, do you? Hoo-hoo. Did you ever dream there would be a day like this? Now you can travel with me and watch me kick ass as I become the US Open champ." Jamey gave his father a huge hug as he spoke.

"You bet your ass-kicking butt, champ," said my brother, beaming brightly as he hugged his son ever so tightly, lifting him off the ground.

I was happy to witness such a beautiful act of love between my brother and his son for the first time as free people. Dad was gone, but his death seemed to have brought something good for everyone. For me, I felt like a child running freely back in the village of O-Jung with the big boys. I felt like a soaring eagle free to go anywhere I wished.

Monie and Joey flew back to Sacramento on Friday, while Jamey remained to finish his semester. As soon as the school's out in a few weeks, he was joining his parents in their new California home. Knowing Joey was no longer locked up was a comforting thought. Another six months in the halfway house, and he would be moving in to his new home in Newport Beach, California, where his wife and son would be waiting for him.

For now, he had to maintain a job to satisfy parole condition and stay cool until then.

CHAPTER 28

January 2012

Instead of celebrating my fifty-eighth birthday, we were sadly burying Uncle Phillip. We bought two plots and buried him in one, about thirty yards or so away from where my parents were buried. He was seventy-six years old as he went on to join my mom and dad, leaving Aunt Cindy and so many of us to mourn him. For the past dozen years, he had travelled the world and enjoyed life as one should at his age.

Each time they had returned home to renew their passports, Uncle Phillip and Aunt Cindy seemed younger and younger. But when they returned from their trip to China in 2009, he did not feel well. That's when we discovered his stage IV pancreatic cancer. It is the most painful cancer of them all.

When Patrick Swayze, the actor of fame from the movies *Dirty Dancing* and *Ghost*, discovered his pancreatic cancer in 2008, he spoke of the amazing pain that was overwhelming to bear. This cancer seemed to suck the life out of Patrick as he started to lose weight drastically.

The following year on September 14, Patrick Swayze left us and went to a much better place. On the same day, everyone would learn that Uncle Phillip had the same cancer that just took Patrick away from us. It wasn't a good day for the family of Patrick and neither was it for all of us, shocked with the news, concerned with Uncle Phillip's health.

Bless his heart, as Uncle Phillip fought through it like a true champ. He tried so hard not to disrupt the lives of his loved ones. He endured as much pain as possible but eventually had to be sedated more and more. During the last few weeks before he left us, it became painful for me to watch him suffer. I'm certain I wasn't the only one praying that God would take him sooner than later.

Uncle Phillip left strict final instruction to celebrate his death and not to mourn. He said he knows where he is headed, and the place he is going required a celebratory send-off and certainly not grieving on his behalf. I understood exactly what he was saying. He said it ought to be something that resembled a Mardi Gras—like atmosphere rather than a miserable funeral.

Lisa contacted the Columbine High School music director, inviting their marching band to join the funeral. The campus was only a few minutes away from where my uncle's burial service was to take place in Littleton. The Columbine band gladly accepted the invitation to play at my uncle's funeral.

I wondered if they woke any of the dead, as the sixty musicians played their instruments very loudly while enthusiastically marching in their places. They played "When the Saints Go Marching In" and jumped right into the song "La Bamba," then back to "When the Saints," before finishing with "Free Bird" by Lynyrd Skynyrd in their liveliest rendition. I liked Uncle Phillip's style. He had class. I missed him dearly already.

For their efforts, the Columbine High School Music Department would receive a large contribution to its program from Lisa and the PPF International. Never before had anyone contributed such a large amount to their school in its history.

Uncle Phillip's will was read before us, as we comforted one another after we put the dirt over him. He left every one of us, including his wife's family all the way to the youngest Jake, plenty to remember him by. In addition, he left the William West Foundation five million dollars in addition to his previous five-million-dollar contribution. Aunt Cindy was not forgotten by my uncle, making certain she would not be without.

Lisa had turned a local business into an international business conglomerate holding company. Each time she opened a branch office or warehouse, the company began by acquiring the property they needed before the operation was instituted into place. The principle, which was practiced by her father and continued on by Lisa, had done well for the company. Now, PPF International owned properties throughout the globe. Her new headquarters was no longer Denver but New York as it became necessary. But she lived in Washington, DC, with her husband, Scott, who had been successful in his second bidding to become a politician. As the state representative of our district, they spent most of their time in their DC home.

Their Boulder property had been occupied by the twins attending CU and perhaps some extra curriculums for the twins after the school hours. I heard from a friend of mine serving in the Boulder Police Department there was a new party mansion in Boulder that I should know about. I never confronted Bob and Brent about it. I was young once, and I wanted them to enjoy their youth.

PPF International had an office in Long Beach that oversaw all the packaging and shipping to locations in Hawaii, Alaska, Australia, and New Zealand that left LAX in frozen-cargo planes. Monie was currently in charge of the West Coast office and its staff of two dozen.

Lisa's children are grown now, with Becky twenty-one and ready to finish her degree in biology from Cal Berkeley. She hopes to follow Aunt Sarah's footstep and become an animal doctor. Bob was completing first year of CU Pharmacy School, while his twin brother, Brent, was majoring in English literature at CU. Burt was a freshman at Texas A&M as he swam his way into a scholarship. The youngest, Brenda, was a freshman at Calvin Christian High in Boulder until she moved to DC with her parents.

Sharon and Dr. Jed went on to adopt a boy and a girl from Korea in 2003. Two unrelated one-year-old toddlers arrived with Dr. Jed and Sharon, who flew to Inchon Airport to pick their children up once the papers were completed for their adoptions.

Sharon quit the police force immediately to be a full-time mother. Andy and Audrey are ten now. Andy Levi is a musically gifted child who has been playing piano in the concert halls since he was seven years old. He has taken the spotlight away from his famous father. He seems to know nothing about the fame he has brought to himself. All the television interviews and magazine articles did not seem to have any effect on him.

While Audrey's violin skills did not receive the kind of recognition her sibling had, she was nonetheless a vibrant and intelligent kid doing well in life. They are well loved and have an army of extended family that dote on them.

In 1999, Joey and Monie had bought a three-bedroom townhome in a privately gated community just across the PCH from the Fashion Island shopping center. It was about thirty minutes of commute to Monie's office in LB. The place was rather small, but it had a wonderful view of the Newport Harbor. Their $350,000 investment had turned into over a million in equity since.

When Jamey graduated from NB High in 2001, he was able to fulfill his dream of playing tennis for the Stanford University. He was able to see the sacrifice his family would've had to make if he chose to go pro. He didn't want that. After waiting fifteen years so all three of them could live a normal life together under one roof, he didn't want to start living on the road and burdening his parents.

He had thought of becoming a lawyer since he was a child. He thought highly of Dwight and Judy since he was just a child and wanted to be a lawyer like them. He played tennis for Stanford, which was fun and not stressful as it would have been if he had turned pro. He thought it was great he could still enjoy his favorite game while studying to become an attorney someday.

In 2005 when he graduated with a degree in economics, he was accepted by the Stanford Law and remained a resident of Palo Alto for three more years. He was asked by the Stanford tennis coach to join the coaching staff, working with the undergrads.

Jamey thought it would be a great opportunity to continue with the game that he loved while earning some tuition money. He couldn't believe his good fortune. I thought God was opening doors for Jamey, as things were lining up in his favor.

Imagine him saving his parents from paying the Stanford Law School tuition by working for their tennis team. He had learned that he enjoyed coaching and seemed to be good at it.

I had been concerned as to how he would turn out growing up without his father by his side. I prayed that God would be kind to Jamey and bless his path. God was kind to my Jamey.

Jamey was a fun-loving, life-enjoying, happy kid. He could just as easily have gotten a scholarship for golf instead of tennis, as he was a three-handy golfer and could have gone pro had he put his heart into it. Instead, he just wanted to enjoy the moment and play for fun instead. He was seen often joining a young lady golf protégé from Hawaii, who was his classmate for rounds of golf, giving her a run for her money.

Upon graduation, he passed the bar and began working for the Orange County DA's office as an assistant district attorney prosecuting felony crimes in 2009. Two years later, Jamey joined the Lee, West, and West Law Firm in Denver. Jamey hooked up with his first girlfriend from Fairview High School in Boulder, who became Miss Colorado in 2002. They were talking marriage in the coming year.

He still played tennis, but his serves no longer caused fear in his opponents. While he no longer served aces, his backhand was still quite fierce. Jamey's tennis game reminded me of what life was like in general. While he may have lost a step or two, he played smarter. While he had fewer winning shots, his errors had been reduced as well. As we age, we rely less on our physical strength and more on our knowledge that comes from previous experiences. While passing shots become less, so does the double faults, as we age.

Jamey made some right decisions in his life. I don't mean in making the correct shots during his tennis matches. He had decided against becoming a pro, and I was glad when he made that choice. He had come to me and Sarah about the decision to turn pro.

Sarah came right out and said the fact that Jamey needed to ask us seemed to indicate that going pro may not be the best of his choice. I was always admiring other people's answers that seemed so much smarter than mine.

Jamey weighed things out and decided to accept the Stanford's offer to become a Cardinal. Jamey did not resent or regret his decision against the life of fame but truly enjoyed the high energy and the intelligent surroundings of Stanford.

When he started working for the OC DA's office, it was an eye-opening experience for him. He discovered the views and the attitudes of the majority of his peers that looked at the defendants as guilty before the trial had even begun. Most of the associates he worked with considered people like his father worthless individuals.

He was unable to enjoy his career as a prosecutor. He sought after Judy and Dwight's advice regarding his dilemma. He wanted to fight for the defendants rather than the prosecution. With that kind of attitude, it was easy for Dwight to offer his nephew a position in his ever-so-busy firm.

I believe average individuals in Jamey's position would have foregone what they stood for, for the sake of their careers. Jamey did not want to turn a blind eye to justice for the sake of his career. He wanted to do what was right according to the law, unlike his associates who did not care one way or the other. Jamey is a kid after my own heart.

Jamey tells me he is much happier now. He missed Colorado, where he grew up, but he was glad to be back. I think he is happier because he is about to marry Vicky in a few months. Not every man can say they are marrying an ex-Miss America contestant. His fiancée was Victoria Kendall, the Miss Colorado of 2002. The two made a handsome couple, and Denver area media were all over them.

Monie was in charge of the West Coast office in LB. She joined the company in 1999 as an office manager and moved up the rank all the way to the top. Lisa is always going on about how she would not be able to manage the business without Monie running the West Coast office.

Monie was a natural businesswoman, and she enjoyed being one. She began taking evening classes at Orange Coast Community College and transferred to UC Irvine, where she finished a degree in business. She went on to complete her MBA from UCI in 2010. As a chief executive, she ran a tight outfit, managing her staff of twenty with high efficiency.

Monie reported only to Lisa. Everyone who worked for her loved Monie dearly, as her people skills were quite admirable. She was the main reason the employees didn't move on but stayed with the company for years.

Joey struggled at first when he was released to the halfway house in Sacramento. Fifteen years of living inside the walls with its own set of social skills was over. Now he had to face the real world with a totally different set of rules. It had to be quite a shock to anyone in such a situation, as the transition took about ninety minutes altogether.

After Dad's funeral, Joey's edginess had eased a little. Joey was in a much better financial position, and it may have given him the confidence so he could better handle whatever the situation he may be facing. In July of 1999, when Monie and Joey purchased their home in NB, he was allowed to transfer to a halfway house near his home in NB for the remaining three months. But even before he was finished packing his bag, the CDC gave him three months' early parole instead. The prison-overcrowding situation had brought about the decision, I believe.

Rather than Joey hassling with the parole department for the travel permit to Colorado, everyone hopped on the next flight to OC instead. Uncle Phillip and Aunt Cindy were travelling abroad but celebrated with us in spirit, while visiting her brother in São Paulo, Brazil. Dad had missed Joey's homecoming by three months.

Lisa's family was unable to join us. If she didn't have her hands full with running a multibillion-dollar business while raising five children, Scott's campaign to unseat the incumbent state senator who had unseated his uncle a few years back was in full swing.

Sharon and Jed flew with me and Sarah, along with Dwight, Judy, Katie, who was eighteen months old, and a three-month-old Jake. And Jamey was with us of course, who would not be returning with us as he would start his junior year at Newport High in September.

While Jamey grieved for the friends left behind, he was finally living with both of his parents in their own house. It wouldn't take him long to forget about Colorado, with beaches full of bikinis so close to his house.

We gathered at Joe's Crab Shack on PCH, about a mile from Joey's new home, to celebrate his homecoming. My ex-boss from the USS *Dixon* had retired and became a realtor. He helped Joey with finding and purchasing his home in NB. He was kind enough to make the time to join us.

The weather was perfect, and we were offered their largest table by the window that gave us the most beautiful view of the sun settling into the Pacific Ocean. It had painted the sky in the most radiant orange and lavender shades that seemed to accentuate the bright and cheery mood of the group.

Twelve of us were ready for some fun and dining, celebrating Joey's freedom. Though it was Wednesday, the place was packed. In Southern California, every summer day was a Friday. Much to everyone's delight, especially to Katie, all the staff serving the packed house stopped every thirty minutes and danced to the music while disco lights flashed for the duration of the song.

Katie bounced up and down in her baby seat, banging on the table with glee, while Jake slept through it all. Lucky parents, that Jake could sleep through an earthquake. He must have been tired from the first flight of his life.

When the music stopped, the Shack employees went back to serving their customers and making their drinks behind the bar as if nothing had happened. Everyone had a good time. It had been a long time coming for Joey to join the family in such wholesome fun. Two days later, we left Joey and his family and flew back to Colorado.

Joey's parole officer insisted that he hold down a full-time job, no matter how well his financial situation might have been. It was part of his parole condition. He went to work for a company called BTIS (Blake and Tanner Investigative Services) as a professional bodyguard escorting very important people around Southern California.

His expertise in tae kwon do had truly impressed Tanner, who was a black belt himself. Tanner was humbled by Joey's outrageous abilities that made his techniques seem like child's play as they worked out together in an Irvine dojo (gym). Tanner offered Joey a well-paid position to fill the high-demand position in his firm.

Joey made good income while enjoying the high-profile scenes of Southern California. Hollywood and their glitzy people needed to be protected from the harms of the world as they pampered themselves. Joey provided protections for A1-list clientele.

As a felon, he had to get a special permit to handle any weapons, though he needed none. He carried one because it was required by his boss. Eventually, the fun wore off, and he got bored with his job.

He was about to look for another line of work when something caught his attention. He had discovered that his boss was cheating his deceased partner's widow out of business.

Blake and Tanner, two police detectives, quit the force and formed a partnership in 1990. Each had put in $200,000 to purchase the equipment necessary for dispatchers, to lease a fleet of vehicles and to arm their security personnel. A large developer in the city of Irvine began developing massively in OC about the same time they started their security firm.

BTIS landed the Irvine developer as their client, immediately creating massive revenues. Then suddenly, Blake had a cardiac arrest and died unexpectedly, just as they were about to celebrate their first ten years of business.

Blake's widow received handsomely amounted checks from BTIS on a regular basis for about six months, but it stopped coming without any explanations. When several months had gone by, Mrs. Blake was told by Tanner that the firm was having financial difficulties. Tanner had forced Mrs. Blake to sign a loan document to borrow a half-million dollars against her equity to save the firm from going under. The memories of loving husband made her sign the document against her better judgment.

At the beginning of his position with BTIS, Joey was assigned to drive Mrs. Blake from her home in Dana Point to the John Wayne Airport customs office. Since then, she had asked specifically for Joey for the service each time she travelled. She was a woman in her midseventies when Joey first met her.

After several trips of thirty-minute rides each way, Mrs. Blake felt comfortable enough with Joey to begin confiding in him her concerns regarding the firm. Contrary to his promise when she signed for the loan, Tanner had never made the payments on her loan. Mrs. Blake was receiving letters from the bank threatening to liquidate her home to recoup their money.

Joey knew something wasn't right. The firm was doing very well, generating excellent revenues even during the struggling economy when the competitors were closing shops. BTIS has assets worth well over a million. Tanner did not need Mrs. Blake to take a loan out on her house. And if the firm was having such financial woes that it could not make the widow's loan payments, there was no sign of it.

Joey began looking into the matter. It didn't take a whole lot of investigation to discover that Tanner had just closed a deal to sell the security patrol portion of the business to a competitor for a cool million. BTIS would no longer have dispatchers and the guards in their fleet of vehicles. It was sold and about to be someone else's. In addition, Tanner was waiting for the escrow to close on the sale of his house in Costa Mesa. He had reduced the price to sell it quick. He was about to take a trip to Barbados with his girlfriend who was half his age.

Joey contacted Mrs. Blake with the findings, and she called her good friend the OC police commissioner. Tanner was arrested just in time, and his funds were frozen. He was facing serious time for embezzlement and felony fraud. The luxurious life he had come to know was over. Joey thought that Tanner better pray he wouldn't end up in a joint full of people he had arrested and convicted.

Mrs. Blake's bank got the full amount of the loan returned to her bank account from the Tanner's personal bank account that was seized. And the million-dollar proceeds from selling the security service portion of the firm was seized as well and returned to the firm. Tanner's portion of the stocks became his partner's, or his surviving widow's in this case, as mandated by their corporate clause. If one of the partners is convicted of a crime, it would result in the forfeiture of the stock to his remaining partner.

You could only imagine how relieved Mrs. Blake must have been. Not only did she save herself from serious embarrassment by recovering her money and saving her home but discovered the firm which she now owned entirely was worth millions and thriving rather than going under. She was ecstatic to learn that the million dollars Tanner had embezzled from the firm had been returned to the firm's account for now.

The security patrol company was sold without proper signatures from the widow as Tanner had used forgery. The federal judge in OC Federal Courthouse ordered the sale to be reversed. The million would be returned to the buyer, and the security patrol company would belong to BTIS, negating the sale.

Joey told the widow she was entitled to the money, but recommended she use the fund to stabilize the firm to survive the competitor's bid to take over the business. Joey told her he felt the firm had a good reputation and she should reap from it. The investigative works for the corporate community and the denizens of old and serious money holders wished to keep the police out of their lives. It was a lucrative portion of her business, and Joey hoped she would keep it, cashing in on the goodwill of the company they had worked hard to build on.

Joey and Monie invited Mrs. Blake to join us for our Thanksgiving Day dinner in Colorado. Mrs. Blake, a childless woman who was now in her early eighties, was still as beautiful as when she was making movies five decades ago. Joey told Mrs. Blake he was going to have all the travel arrangement taken care of.

That's when they learned that Mrs. Blake had a private plane in John Wayne Airport. Her 2006 Learjet 60SE seated seven comfortably. Some people, as my dad had, refused to travel with the commercial airlines. The whole time when Joey had dropped her and her luggage off at the customs office, it was because she was entering a private plane, not as Joey had originally thought that rich folks had an easy way through the airport security. Jamey was ecstatic to learn he was about to travel in Mrs. Blake's private jet.

The private plane certainly made their travel schedule flexible. The four of them entered her Lear with two pilot/attendants and left John Wayne Airport the balmy eve of Thanksgiving Day, around 6:00 p.m. Monie had phoned ahead and picked up four steak dinners from Ruth's Chris Steak House in Irvine on their way to the John Wayne Airport. Two hours later and fully sated from the hefty meal, they landed in DIA about 9:00 p.m. They lost an hour traveling in an easterly direction. I was waiting for them in an SUV, awaiting their phone call, as the snow began falling. It was cotton ball-shaped thick snow that stuck to the windshield.

It was Sarah's latest notion to buy this V-8 4×4 Land Rover SUV, trading in her well-driven 1985 Audi. She had put over 325,000 miles on the Audi but refused to take less than the blue book value as her trade-in and got what she wanted. She was a penny-pinching millionaire, my kind of woman.

She finally forced me to stop driving my 1968 Chevy truck that I had been driving for twenty-seven years since 1972, when my dad passed away in 1999. The truck sits in a garage, still runs, but now I don't use it on a regular basis.

One afternoon, as I was working on our tomato garden, an unfamiliar car drove up our long driveway. It was Sarah, driving a brand-new charcoal-colored 1999 Toyota Land Cruiser. I figured her Audi was sixteen years old, so she got herself a new ride. I thought she would have chosen a brighter-colored vehicle for herself. Charcoal was my favorite color, but she wouldn't buy one for my sake.

But she did. She bought a car for me to cheer me up after Dad had passed away. She said it looked more like a policeman's vehicle than my truck, which made me look like a high school math teacher. I told her I would take that as a compliment. Sarah called me a cuckoo bird while motioning her finger in circles around over her right ear. She tossed me the key and told me to take her to the dealership where her Audi remained parked.

That day, I took a Saturday-afternoon ride with my bride of twenty-three years in my brand-new SUV with leather seats, power everything, and a sunroof. I opened up the sunroof even though it was a sweater-and-jacket weather.

I cranked up my sixteen-speaker sound system when the Rolling Stones' "Start Me Up" came on the radio, singing along. Sarah did the air guitar solo that was very well done. I forgot all about the death of my father a week earlier. That was over twelve years ago, almost thirteen. What a nice present it had been. But it was nothing like Sarah's new Rover that I drove to pick up my brother's family and Mrs. Blake. My four passengers from Southern California nearly froze between the customs office to where I was parked, half of a football field length away.

They were unprepared for the unexpected snowfall. The ride to our home from the DIA took about an hour and half, twice the trip there, due to the snow that had started to fall. It was a nightmare for holiday travelers. Mrs. Blake was very articulate and an animated lady full of life. Her conversation made the traffic seem very pleasant. She was tired from the flight, but full of energy as she shared one story of herself after another.

We had turned Dad's room into a nice guest quarter equal to a fancy hotel suite, but Mrs. Blake preferred our pool house instead. It had been a long time since Jamey and Monie used to stay there. Since then, it had been used for football game days on occasion, and that's about it.

The next morning, I heard a sound of someone swimming in the pool. It was Mrs. Blake, swimming in our lap pool amid snowfall at six in the morning.

Though the pool was maintained well, cleaned on regular basis, and heated to seventy-two degrees at all times, I would have never gotten into it when it was snowing, at six o'clock in the morning.

Mrs. Blake turned out to be quite agile for her age, as she swam daily as part of her exercise regimen. Much to her delight, she learned we had a pool, and she was able to maintain her daily routine. That was the reason for choosing the pool house over the plushy guest room.

Sarah and the maid had done us proud with all the fixings and trimmings, sides, and the baked goods around a twenty-pound bird roasted to perfection. Snow continued to fall during our early afternoon Thanksgiving meal, as Mrs. Blake shared with us the colorful story of her life.

She was the only child of a Rhode Island senator. The senator and his wife were on a business trip to Southwest Asia when the plane exploded just as it left an airfield in Cambodia. The senator's aid, a photojournalist, and two pilots along with Mrs. Blake's parents died in that explosion when she was nine years old. She went to live with her maternal grandparents living in Carmel, California, until she was eighteen.

She was well loved and did well in school, but it was her beauty that brought her to Hollywood and a movie career in 1938 when she was just an eighteen-year-old child. She was a multimillionaire even before she went on to make several major movies as a lead actress. When she turned eighteen, she came into the estate her parents had left behind.

Each movie was a smash, making Hollywood producers lots of money. She had fancy memoirs, giving her the billings and some fond memories, but didn't make all the money the public had believed.

She hadn't been in front of a camera since 1948, when she was nominated for best actress along with Olivia de Havilland for her role in *The Snake Pit* and Ingrid Bergman for her role in *Joan of Arc*, along with Jane Wyman, who had won with her role in *Johnny Belinda*, getting more votes than did our Mrs. Blake.

She married Blake in 1960. Blake grew up in an orphanage until he was eighteen, when he joined the army. He became a police officer and worked for the Santa Ana Police Department when he met his first wife.

It turned out that Mr. Blake's number one wife was our widow's best friend. When Blake's first wife died of cervical cancer, her best friend came to console him. She had been secretly envying her friend's marriage, as Blake was a loving man, not to mention quite handsome. Blake was a giant of a man at six four, but a teddy bear, tender and caring. It was easy for her to fall in love with Blake. They were married three years after the death of his first wife.

It was a good marriage, and Blake worked hard to provide well for her. Slowly as the generation that recognized her had died away, she became just another senior citizen in the crowd. She blended in well with the tanned senior citizens of Southern California. She was happy with living in the present and letting her past be her fond memories.

Then her husband of forty years passed away, just as his business seemed to start doing well. She had only one relative left in the world, a distant cousin living in Germany whom she had not seen in twenty years. Blake was an orphan, leaving her truly alone.

When she was done sharing her stories with us, Mrs. Blake gave me the opportunity to share with her about the William West Foundation. She was fascinated that there was a group of people that actually cared about these unfortunate folks enough to spend their money building shelters.

She learned of the abused families throughout the major cities in the United States. She asked lots of questions, which was delightful for me to answer.

On Sunday afternoon, her plane carried the four of them into a sunny sky, heading west. They were about to enjoy a long sunset all the way to OC. The next morning, Joey learned he had a new office. He was the firm's new boss. Mrs. Blake had phoned her attorney before leaving for Denver to draw legal papers to transfer 49 percent of the business to Joey, making him the operating partner of the firm. It came with a handsome salary as well.

When Joey insisted that he pay for the stock in fair market value, she flat-out rejected the idea. She told him she sincerely believed that without Joey's active involvement, she would have lost everything. The business would have been gone for sure and possibly her home as well. In her opinion, Joey well deserved what he received.

That was the beginning of the Blake and Lee Investigations Service Ltd. Mrs. Blake took Joey's advice and went on to recruit shining stars from the FBI and NCIS, as well as the local agencies. She in actuality went on to build a dream team of investigators.

Joey added to the firm some of the finest forensics scientists available, forming a formidable team to be reckoned with. Mrs. Blake's active role in the business had rejuvenated her both physically and spiritually.

Many high-profiled defendants throughout the world sought to employ B&L to either clear their names or undermine the prosecution for acquittal.

While their fancy attorney clients claimed victories in the courtroom, it was the work of Joey and his men behind the scene that made their clients look good. That's why their clients paid them the big bucks.

Mrs. Blake became involved with the WW Foundation, and eventually, she sat on their board of trustees. She went on to invest into the foundation as well, in the sum of seven million dollars. She shared with us half of her entire savings. She wanted to see her money doing good deeds rather than sitting in the bank.

Her donation had allowed the city of Detroit to get their shelter, as it was next on the list of projects for WW Foundation. In addition, the cities of Cincinnati, Cleveland, Pittsburgh, and Philadelphia became recipients of her generosity, making it a total of seventeen shelters throughout the Midwest and eastern part of the nation the foundation had built shelters in.

My bride of thirty-six years was still going strong, taking care of her patients with the latest techniques with the least painful methods possible.

She developed a network for the Fort Collins and Boulder area vets to use her hospitals to do the surgeries on their patients, making them associates and partners of the hospital. It was the kindest gesture she could have extended to her colleagues, who would otherwise be helpless competitors watching what the hospital was doing with the equipments that were out of the price range for the average vet clinics to handle.

Sarah was no longer the hands-on operator of her hospitals but wisely placed around herself capable administrators to handle the daily operations. Her parents—first her father and then her mother—passed away within two weeks of each other last year, devastating Sarah. You see, her parents and Sarah had buried Ken, Sarah's only sibling due to bone cancer, just prior to her parents' passing. In a matter of eighteen months, she had lost her parents and her brother.

Gradually, she became more involved with the WW Foundation, traveling with Mrs. Blake in her jet, accompanying her to New York for the board of trustees gathered there semiannually. Talk about Sarah being spoiled by her adoptive mother.

Judy kept a friendly relationship with her mentor, President Bush Senior, who had joined the foundation at the onset of the William West Foundation. He believed it was a wonderful program to be involved with and glad he was still able to serve.

The Democratic Party would not be denied, as President Jimmy Carter joined a couple years after President Bush had joined, making the WW Foundation the rare organization that had two surviving ex-presidents sitting on their board of trustees. Not bad for an old-fashioned cop serving a community of ranchers and farmers.

I was looking forward to my retirement in two more years. I had been with the Fort Collins Police Department for the past twenty-eight years. I was going to hang it up when I turned sixty. The fact my thirtieth year with the department would coincide with my sixtieth birthday seemed like a good sign to retire.

I saw the benefit Uncle Phillip and Aunt Cindy had reaped from quitting while they were still healthy and able to enjoy active lives for years after the retirement. I was going to talk Sarah into retiring with me and traveling the world. It was going to be a task I did not look forward to, as she had told me many times she was not going to retire until she was buried six feet deep.

Mama Tessi had passed away at the good old age of ninety-two. I flew to San Diego with Sarah to attend her funeral. Kino had aged since I last saw him. He had black bags under his eyes. He had been selling insurance to the sailors since he retired from the US Navy in 1989.

Kino did well with his insurance business. He had been contributing to the West Foundation on a regular basis since the onset of the foundation for the last twelve years.

A movie producer from Hollywood had coveted our property and offered five million. He was flying over our property one day as he was preparing to make his movie in a nearby location and realized he could build a runway in this property.

Three acres of plot at twenty-five thousand per acre, we had paid seventy-five thousand dollars for the land and spent about three hundred thousand dollars to build onto it in 1984. It was worth about four—four and a half million at best—so the five million offer was generous, but we were not interested. When we turned the offer down, he went ballistic. His agent went ballistic.

"He doubled the offer, Lieutenant Lee." It was the Red Carpet Realtor Randy Butler on the phone two days after we rejected his client's offer. He is a tall and skinny Texan in a leisure suit with skinny strings for a tie, with cowboy boots, who showed potential buyers around in his helicopter, from Boulder to Vail and Aspen.

"Let me get this straight. Your client is offering ten million for my property, the same one he had offered only five million two days ago? Well, that seems like something I should discuss with my wife about. But I wouldn't get your hopes up," I said, trying hard to contain my excitement.

Sarah quietly came to hug me gently after I told her the news and then grabbed a chunk of my gluteus maximus with both hands and said, "I vote to sell."

"Are you sure? Because we will not be able to top this one. If we accept, we must start looking right away."

"Accept the offer before he changes his mind. He must be out of his mind, but if he is willing to pay, sold! I am sure something just right for us will show up when the time is right. Heck, with ten million, we can do like the rock and roll stars and live in penthouses of five-star hotels, knocking walls down between suites."

Sarah hopped on one leg, playing her air-guitar mimicking like she was singing. She was still the same wild and crazy woman I had fallen in love with during our senior prom at South High. She stopped her prancing and said, "I was beginning to think that living on three acres of land and ten thousand square feet of living spaces was a tad bit too much for just the two of us. But to have an offer of ten million dollars has to be something close to winning a lottery. So let's sell it and buy something closer to town, something smaller." In thirty-seven days, the escrow was closed, and we held a $10 million check in our possession. The new owner immediately built a landing strip for his plane and a helicopter pad on the property. We moved into Uncle Phillip's mansion.

Lisa lived in Washington, DC, most of the time with her husband. She was happy to relinquish much of her duties to her executives, to stand by her husband as he vied for the Republican senator candidacy.

Dr. Jed was offered a position to head the neurosurgery department in Cedars-Sinai Hospital in West Hollywood. When Sharon moved to Bel Air behind the campus of UCLA, Aunt Cindy moved with them. Andy and Audrey Levi refused to live in a place where their *haal-muh-nee* (grandma) would not be around after their school to walk home with them, doting on them as she had for the past four years.

Aunt Cindy no longer needed the mansion they purchased back in 1982, where she had lived for the past thirty years. Aunt Cindy was about to put her house on the market when we got the offer from the movie producer.

We offered Aunt Cindy the market price of three million in cash, and she gladly accepted it. We were able to eliminate a broker, as no agent knew more or better about this property than me. Aunt Cindy had no idea it would remain in the family when she contacted me, asking me to refer her to a realtor. The timing was so perfect it was as if God had designed it just for us so that it all worked out perfectly.

That is how we came to live in the mansion that had the best view in the city of Boulder. This acre of property looked down at every property in the city, halfway up the Flatiron, the protruding rock that plays as the backdrop of the city of Boulder.

From the front patio, you could look down at the engineering tower of the University of Colorado way down below. It was a steal at three million dollars to me because it came with the memories my family had made there during the past thirty years.

During the move, I came across a box that held my early childhood memories. As I went through it, I came across an algebra exam I had aced, back in 1967. Mom never got to see it. I didn't realize I had saved it all these years. Just a piece of paper with twenty questions and twenty correct answers on it, but it had triggered a flood of memories.

Mr. Evans had put a smiling face next to 100 A+ mark at the top of the front page of the test. He used purple Magic Marker. It was Mom's favorite color.

I guess I was never able to forget about Mom. I honored her for the past fifty-eight years—forty-five years of it since her passing. In my heart, I knew that no matter what my mom and dad did or didn't do, however long or short they lived, didn't matter. It was simply my job to honor them, dead or alive.

Until I die and join them in heaven. There, we would all join together to honor and glorify God as his children. I took my algebra test and went to visit my parents. Neither had the chance to see their eldest son's aced test paper before.

As a child, I saw my grandmother honoring God with her life when I lived with her before coming to America. She would begin preparing for Sunday worships on Mondays and throughout the week. She would do all the mending of her clothes, of which she did not own too many, before she washed and pressed them to be worn on Sunday mornings.

She would carefully calculate the amount of gifts she received if there were any, then add that to her salary and determine the tithe. She would not receive a knitted sweater from a parishioner without tithing on it. Then, she would go through and find the newest and the cleanest bills and place the amount in the envelope before she fell asleep on the eve of the worship.

When none of the bills were satisfactory to her standard, she would iron the bills to make them crease-free before she placed them into the tithe and offering envelopes. I was so fortunate to have such a wonderful ancestor's examples to follow. I had followed her examples since, and I believe God had found pleasure with my humble efforts.

I have discovered long ago that God heard each and every prayer I had lifted up to him. At times, it took a while for his answers to reach me, but he heard every word I cried out to him, every vow I made before him or spoke to him in confidence.

God had heard each and every utterance I made to him in prayers, including my childhood prayers to become his agent. I wanted to be an *am-heng-uh-sah* (a secret agent for the king). He heard my prayers and gave me the opportunity to become one. God is the King of Kings, and he would give an opportunity to a simple man like me, as he looks at our heart and not the qualifications or outer appearances. God neither needs help with our qualifications nor impressive looks. He simply requires our hearts.

While I did not fully understand what I was praying for, God allowed me to see his children suffering firsthand and created in me the desire to do something about it. I saw what God's enemy was doing to us, and I wanted to fight against him. With only a high school diploma and no college education, I did not have any qualifications to design or build shelters. I simply dreamt a dream as my hero Reverend MLK had, desiring to fight for God's children.

My boyhood dream must have touched God's heart. Why else would I have the chance to bat for him? I am ever so grateful and feel honored for that, because I got on base. Not quite a home run but ready to score anytime soon.

The activities that took place between my dad and me were not some kind of punishment from God but the necessary training to become his agent, *am-heng-uh-sah*. It gives me goose bumps all over again just thinking about it. God used me. To me, the suffering was an opportunity to experience the humility of Christ. He had first set the example for us, as he had gone through the suffering in order to understand our pains and sufferings firsthand. Without experiencing the humility and the love of God, it's difficult, if not impossible, to truly feel the sufferings of others.

It was training for Dad as well, as he had discovered that no amount of training could replace God's help. No one could heal and restore relationships like God could.

Throughout my life, God created opportunities and opened doors for me. But he did not allow me to skip the training part, no matter how painful or difficult it got at times. After all, I did pray for such training to become his agent.

By the time we went through our impromptu meeting after my dad's funeral, there was nearly thirty million dollars pledged toward the foundation.
Uncle Phillip learned of our meeting the next day and added five million dollars to the kitty, bringing the total to thirty-five million. My lovely bride had secretly added five million dollars through her accountant anonymously, nearly all the profit from our real-estate transactions. In the end, God had provided nearly forty million dollars in start-up fund for the William West Foundation.

A childhood dream became a reality. Imagine two former presidents of the United States of America and a legendary movie star as the members of the board of directors in an organization that was but a childhood fantasy. God honored it, as he had heard my prayers that were lifted up to him from my heart.

I don't know how many families benefited from these shelters. I am not interested in keeping a tally or any kind of statistics. I leave all that stuff to Judy and Lisa. If one child, one family was helped by it, all the millions of dollars and all the efforts of the staff would have been worth it.

Whether as a "bother" to Joey and Judy or as an *am-heng-uh-sah* to the King of Kings, I was content with the life I had lived. I fought hard as a "bother" to keep Joey from simply becoming another victim to the disease. I had feared losing him for good. In the end, he came through it all, unscathed, other than some gray hairs and wrinkles. It was all due to the grace of God, and I believe Joey finally saw that.

I think it is safe to say that the chain of violence was finally broken for the Lees. I look back and realize it was a blessing that I became a "bother" to Joey and Judy as it had given me the purpose in life when I needed one.

It was a warm and sunny winter day in the Rockies. I opened up my sunroof. It was a perfect afternoon, and I didn't have a care in the world. It was a pleasant drive as I headed for my parents' resting place.

Edwards Brothers Malloy
Thorofare, NJ USA
November 7, 2013